Sweet Little Lies

AN L.A. CANDY NOVEL

BOOKS BY LAUREN CONRAD

L.A. Candy

Sweet Little Lies
AN L.A. CANDY NOVEL

HARPER
An Imprint of HarperCollins*Publishers*

References to real people, events, establishments, organizations, or locales are intended only to provide a sense of authenticity, and are used fictitiously. All other characters and all incidents and dialogue are drawn from the author's imagination and are not to be construed as "real."

Sweet Little Lies

 For information address HarperCollins Children's Books, a division of HarperCollins Publishers, 10 East 53rd Street, New York, NY 10022.

www.harperteen.com

Library of Congress Cataloging-in-Publication Data is available.

ISBN 978-0-06-176760-9 (trade bdg.)

ISBN 978-0-06-198572-0 (int. edition)

Typography by Andrea Vandergrift

10 11 12 13 14 CG/BV 10 9 8 7 6 5 4 3 2 1

❖

First Edition

To my dear friend Sophia.
Your friendship and support have meant
so much to me. I love you, big sister.

GOSSIP

YOUR #1 SOURCE FOR ALL THE HOLLYWOOD DIRT THAT'S FIT TO SLING

PopTV's newest hit series is all about good friends living the good life in L.A.—right? Last we checked, friends don't lie to each other—or stab each other in the well-dressed back. On famed reality TV producer Trevor Lord's sugarcoated confection, it's hard to tell who's really friends and who's just making nice for more airtime. But one thing's for sure: This candy isn't as sweet as it appears to be. In fact, it just might be toxic.

1

YOU NEVER KNOW WHEN THERE MIGHT BE A PHOTOGRAPHER AROUND

Jane Roberts sat up on her white chaise longue and gazed at the horizon between the vast blue ocean and the vast blue sky. She could hear the distant cries of seagulls and the roar of the surf as it curled in, approaching high tide. The breeze, dry and warm for December, stirred her long, wavy blond hair. She reached for the cactus-pear margarita on top of the small hand-painted table next to her and took a long sip.

It was a perfect day on a perfect beach in Cabo San Lucas, Mexico. But not for Jane, who felt perfectly awful.

"Another margarita, sweetie?"

Jane glanced over her shoulder and saw her friend Madison Parker walking toward her. Despite her mood, Jane had to smile. Madison was wearing a bronze bikini that barely covered her size-zero figure, along with five-inch wedges and full makeup, including bright coral lipstick. But that was Madison. She never went anywhere, not even to the beach, without spending an hour and a half getting ready.

"I'm good, thanks. Where's your Gucci purse? And your gold jewelry?" Jane teased.

Madison slid onto the chaise longue next to Jane's. "Hey, a girl's gotta look her best, right? You never know when there might be a photographer around. Or a hot guy." She lowered her massive Dolce & Gabbana sunglasses to stare at a nearby lifeguard with an impressive six-pack. "Like him. Hmm, I call dibs!"

"He's all yours," Jane said. After the boy drama she'd been through lately, she really wasn't interested. She was in Mexico to get away from her disastrous love life and the media circus, not to scope out guys. "Anyway, I thought you said this was a private resort and that photographers couldn't get in."

"Yeah, I meant like other guests with cameras," Madison replied, still staring at the lifeguard. "I'll see if he has a friend for you. Back in a sec." She rose to her feet, fluffed her long platinum-blond hair, and struggled through the sand in her heels.

Jane had to laugh. *Poor guy has no idea what's coming.*

Jane and Madison had been at Madison's parents' condo for the last five days, doing not much besides swimming, tanning, drinking, and checking out guys. Well, Madison had been checking out guys. Jane couldn't stop thinking about what she had done to her boyfriend (now ex-boyfriend), Jesse, back in L.A., and how she had run away when everything had gone so wrong. A guy was the last thing she needed right now. Unless he had a PhD in psychology, he was of little use.

Jane leaned back and tried to relax. The sun felt so nice, and the sound of the waves in the background *should* have been calming. But her mind still raced with worries. Her life used to be so normal. A little boring, but wonderfully normal. When she and her best friend, Scarlett Harp, had moved to L.A. from Santa Barbara after high school, it was so Jane could pursue an internship with Fiona Chen, one of the top event planners in the business, and Scarlett could attend USC. They'd hoped to add a little excitement to their lives by meeting new people and experiencing L.A. nightlife. But they'd never planned on meeting Trevor Lord at Les Deux.

Jane still couldn't believe that out of a roomful of pretty girls Trevor had asked her and Scar to audition for *L.A. Candy*, the new reality show he was producing for PopTV. And that he'd actually cast them.

As Jane sat there on that beach so far away from everything, she wished she could go back in time to that night in August and say, *Thanks, but no, thanks.* Although it's not like she could've predicted what was about to happen to her. She and Scar had figured the show would flop but they'd get some fun nights from it. Of course, the show ended up being a hit, and soon after the series premiere in October, Jane found herself unable to walk into a restaurant or down the street without someone recognizing her.

Magazines called her "America's sweetheart." Blogs called her . . . well, other things. Her face was everywhere.

At first, her sudden fame was exciting and flattering. Now *she* was one of the beautiful, glamorous people. She got all the best tables at all the best clubs. Designers sent her clothes to wear, for free. She was invited to a different Hollywood party almost every night, rubbing shoulders with A-list insiders she used to only read about or see on TV.

But all the attention was also confusing. What had she done to deserve it? The *L.A. Candy* cameras merely filmed her living her life: cooking dinner, doing the laundry, going out with her friends, working as Fiona's slave-slash-assistant. Everyday stuff. How, exactly, did that make her worthy of celebrity status?

More important, why had it turned her into a tabloid target? That was the reason she was here, attempting to relax on this beach with Madison. Five days ago—was it only five days ago?—*Gossip* magazine published a story about Jane hooking up with her boyfriend Jesse's best friend and housemate, Braden. The story didn't mention that Jane and Jesse had been fighting. No one who read it knew how trashed he'd gotten at Goa or knew about the girl he'd been all over that night. They didn't know how vulnerable Jane was when Braden, who had been her friend before she met Jesse, came over, and they definitely didn't know about her long-standing, unspoken crush on him. All they knew was that there were photos of Jane and

Braden in little more than their underwear, in her bedroom. A photographer had somehow gotten those shots of them through her window—why, *why* had she left the curtains open? And what kind of sick person shoots into a girl's bedroom? Talk about invasion of privacy . . . and that was coming from someone on a reality show. The photos ended up all over the internet for everyone in the world to see, including Jane's parents . . . her little sisters, Lacie and Nora . . . Trevor . . . Fiona . . . and, of course, Jesse.

Jane couldn't bring herself to face Jesse when the story broke. Actually, she didn't have the guts to face anyone. So she didn't. That same day, she let Madison whisk her away to the Parkers' gorgeous, exclusive condo in Cabo to escape the photographers (who were camped out at Jane's apartment building) and her phone (which was ringing nonstop). Jane made only one call before departing: to her parents, leaving them a message that she was okay and that she was going away for a few days. Luckily there was no cell reception at the Parkers' condo. Jane knew there must be hundreds of messages waiting for her: from her parents, Scar, Trevor, Fiona, random reporters, and who knew who else. She also knew there was a very real chance that she would never check her voice mail again.

She squeezed her eyes shut, but it wasn't to block out the sun. Had Braden been trying to contact her since she left L.A.? Jane wondered, not for the first time. Had Jesse? She opened her eyes and seriously considered staying in Mexico forever.

It wasn't like she had a job to go back to. Jane figured that the boss lady would likely fire her for taking off without a word and for generating headlines like *L.A.* CANDY STAR NOT SO SWEET (probably not good for the company image). And as for Trevor . . . would he fire her, too? She had been scheduled to film each of the last five days she had been in Cabo with Madison. The idea of leaving the show was definitely tempting, but Jane knew there would be consequences. Back in September, she had signed a contract with PopTV to do ten episodes, and they still had several episodes to go until the season finale. Would Trevor sue her for breaking the contract? Would he kick Jane and Scarlett out of their amazing apartment, which the show was paying for? Scarlett would be homeless, all because of Jane. Well, maybe not homeless, but they would have to return to their apartment with the gross walls and nonstop traffic noise. She couldn't go back there. She liked their nice, quiet apartment with the pretty white walls.

Scarlett. On top of everything else, Jane felt really guilty about leaving L.A. without talking to her best friend. She knew Scarlett must be so worried about her. They had been practically inseparable since kindergarten, and Scarlett had always been so protective of Jane. Lately, things had been kind of strained between them. For one thing, Jane liked their *L.A. Candy* costars—Madison and another girl named Gaby Garcia—and Scar didn't. Scar often made bitchy remarks about them, on- and off-camera, which was so uncalled-for. Also, Scar didn't approve of

Jane's relationship (now ex-relationship) with Jesse because of his history with girls . . . and drinking . . . and drugs . . . and girls. But "history" was exactly what it was. Jesse didn't do stuff like that anymore (except for that little slipup at Goa). He had changed, and he had practically been a perfect boyfriend. It was Jane who had screwed up and cheated on him with Braden.

Jane stirred her mostly melted drink and swallowed the watery remains in one gulp. She wished that she had never heard of Trevor Lord—or *L.A. Candy*. Yes, the incident with Braden was 100 percent on her. But back when she was just plain old Jane Roberts from Santa Barbara, the press wouldn't have taken pictures and splashed them all over the place, humiliating her and destroying her relationship with Jesse. It was bad enough that she'd made a mistake—now she had to share her mistakes with the whole country. No amount of free designer clothes would make that okay. She wanted to rewind time to when she and Scar were nobodies, when they had first moved to L.A., full of hopes and dreams for their fabulous new life in a fabulous new city. Instead, she was living a nightmare.

Madison returned, teetering on her heels. "Gay," she said, shrugging. She sat down and stretched out her long tanned legs. "He invited us to a party, though. Hey, you okay? What's wrong?"

"Two words. 'Jane Ho.'"

"What?" Madison said, confused.

"That's the last headline I read before we left the

apartment," Jane said with a sigh. "I was just thinking that if I'd never signed on to do the show, then none of this would have happened."

Madison leaned over and placed her hand (decked out in long acrylic fingernails) on Jane's arm. "Relax. It's gonna be okay. I promise. You know someone's gonna do something way sluttier this week, so by the time we get back, your little slip will be old news."

"I hope so," Jane said, although she wasn't sure of this at all. And she was a bit stung by Madison's implying that she was slutty. Still, Madison had been such a good friend to her these last few days—bringing her to Cabo, taking care of her, ordering her frilly drinks, distracting her with funny stories about her Swiss boarding school, her parents, her crazy aunt Letitia. "You've been so sweet. Seriously. But we can't stay here forever. Christmas is the day after tomorrow, and I've gotta go home. My mom and dad'll be expecting me."

"No, *stay*!" Madison begged. "We could have a Cabo Christmas together! We'll get a little palm tree for the condo and decorate it with pretty lights!"

"You know I would love to stay here, but I can't," Jane said. "Besides, your mom and dad'll be expecting you, too." Madison didn't respond, which made Jane wonder what her family life was like. Come to think of it, Madison rarely talked about her family. Jane hoped she hadn't stuck her foot in her mouth, and decided to change the subject. "Hey, do you know if *anyone* has internet in this resort?

I wanna check out flights to LAX. And I wanna send an email to Scar, to let her know I'm okay and stuff."

"Nah, this place is completely backward. No cell reception, no internet, nothing. They do that deliberately, so super-rich, super-busy people like my parents can get away from it all or whatever." Madison hesitated. "Actually, about Scarlett? I've kinda been meaning to talk to you about her."

Jane frowned. "What about?"

"The day the *Gossip* story came out? When the three of us were in your apartment together? She was acting kinda weird," Madison said.

"What do you mean, 'kinda weird'?"

"Haven't you wondered? You know, like, who tipped off the photographer about you and Braden being together in your apartment that night?" Madison said. "I'm sorry to bring that up, but . . . well, you know I'm just looking out for you, sweetie."

"What are you saying?"

"I'm just saying . . . I know she's your friend. But . . ." Madison's voice trailed off. "Oh, I just got it." She grinned. "Jane Ho, like Jane Doe. Funny."

Jane turned to gaze out at the water. Was Madison hinting that Scar could have been behind the photos? There was no way. There was no way *anyone* Jane knew could have been behind them. No one in her universe was *that* mean or vengeful or manipulative. Much less her very best friend.

As far as Jane was concerned, there was only one logical explanation. That photographer must have been hanging around her apartment building, waiting for a scoop. Or he must have followed Braden there because he knew Braden was a friend of Jane's. Whatever. Really, she didn't want to think about it anymore. The whole thing was too horrible.

"I mean, there was that rumor I heard about Jesse shopping those photos around to the tabs," Madison persisted. "But I've been thinking. Maybe it's someone else. So . . . who knew Braden was at your place that night?"

Jane shrugged. "Well, Scar. And my goldfish, Penny," she said with a straight face.

"Oh, well, then, it was obviously the fish who tipped off the photographer!" Madison said, giggling. "Maybe Penny has a thing for Jesse and wanted to break you guys up?"

"Penny would never," Jane replied, thinking how nice it felt to joke around after so many days of wallowing in misery. "Penny prefers tall, dark, and . . ."

But Jane didn't finish her sentence. She was distracted by a strange movement behind a palm tree about thirty feet to the right of her. She shifted in her chair, trying to see.

Click, click, click. A middle-aged guy in aviator shades stepped out from behind the tree, angling his super-long telephoto lens—*at her.*

"Oh my God!" Jane cried out, instinctively shielding her face with her hand. She grabbed her towel and beach bag and jumped to her feet. "Madison, there's a paparazzo over there."

"Really?" Madison plastered on a smile and glanced around. "Where?"

"Never mind. God, I hate this. I can't even get away from them in another country!" Jane said, her voice trembling. She began wrapping the towel around her waist, ready to head back to the condo.

Madison's smile vanished. She got her stuff and rose to her feet. "I'm sorry. You're so right," she said quickly. "Come on, let's go inside and get away from that jerk. You wanna rent some DVDs from the clubhouse? And later we could go to that party my new lifeguard friend invited us to."

Jane shook her head. "The photographer's a sign, Madison. I can't run away from it anymore. I *have* to go home," she declared, heading back inside.

"Whatever you say, Jane Ho," Madison joked.

Not funny, Jane thought.

2

JUST ANOTHER GUY

Scarlett Harp tried not to swear too much as she stuffed her clothes into a suitcase. Christmas in Aspen? Who celebrated Christmas in Aspen? *Well, probably a lot of people,* she thought, but she wasn't the Christmas-in-Aspen type. It had been her parents' idea to rent some posh condo there and spend the holiday on the slopes. Mr. and Mrs. Harp—actually, Dr. and Dr. Harp (he was a plastic surgeon; she was a shrink) didn't believe in "sentimental" traditions like decorating a tree or hanging stockings on the mantel. Every year they spent the holidays in a different vacation spot. Last year had been the Bahamas. The year before, Paris. And Hawaii before that.

It was bad enough that Scarlett had to pack for a trip she didn't want to go on. The worst part was, she wasn't alone. There were people in her bedroom watching her. *Lots* of people, in fact. A director, two cameramen, a sound guy, and a producer. And Gaby, her annoying costar, who had been sent over by Trevor to be Scarlett's stand-in friend and keep her company while she packed. Translation: Jane and Madison were MIA, and the show was desperate for footage, so Trevor and another producer, Dana, were setting up scenes that were totally bogus. So much for *L.A. Candy* being a *reality* show. Scarlett would never hang out with Gaby unless she was forced to. Which she currently was.

Gaby was sitting on the bed, trying to make conversation and commenting on Scarlett's clothes—90 percent of which were jeans and T-shirts.

"Ooooh, that top is so cute!" Gaby pointed to a purple tee that Scar was rumpling into a ball and shoving into her suitcase. "What do you call that color? Eggplant? Violet? Magenta?"

"Purple," Scarlett grumbled. "Don't you have somewhere you need to be today?"

"Nope, all yours. Hey, what time's your flight? I could use a mani-pedi, couldn't you? You wanna see if we can get in somewhere after lunch?"

Gaby glanced over at Dana, no doubt to see if her mani-pedi comment had registered. Scarlett knew that the panic on Dana's face meant she'd caught it and was thinking that if they wanted to find a salon to film in, they would have to call and set that up now.

Scarlett held up her nails, two of which were broken. "No, I'm good. You go without me."

"Well, *that's* no fun!" Gaby complained.

Scarlett's cell phone buzzed in her back pocket and she grabbed it quickly, thinking it might be Jane—finally! She had been trying to reach her best friend for the last five days, leaving dozens of frantic messages: *Call me! Where are you? I'm so worried about you! Call me!* There were other messages, too—along the lines of *Get away from that crazy bitch Madison ASAP!* Scarlett couldn't remember the exact wording.

Her face fell when she saw the name on the screen. It was yet another text message from Dana. CD U SLOW DOWN W/ THE PACKING? AND BE NICE 2 GABY PLZ.

Scarlett sighed. Dana was fond of texting Scarlett directions in the middle of a shoot, telling her to do this or say that. Not that Scarlett ever actually did what Dana asked. Scarlett didn't do *nice.* She believed in saying whatever was on her mind, and if it came out a little harsh—well, the truth hurts, people.

The thing was, with each episode of *L.A. Candy* she watched, Scarlett was growing increasingly frustrated by the disconnect between her TV self and her real self. The way Trevor edited the footage made Scarlett seem like a shy, quiet bookworm. Every time she was in a scene with Jane or the other girls, Scarlett ended up with almost no lines—just stuff like *yeah* and *no, thanks* and *bye, gotta get to class!* Sure, she *looked* good, with her long, wavy black hair, emerald green eyes, and five-foot-nine, gym-toned bod. But she *sounded* like she had nothing to say. Which was the exact opposite of who she was.

"Okay, guys, we have to break for lunch, and then we'll head over to LAX," Dana called out. *Hmm, why doesn't she just text everyone?* Scarlett thought as the crew slowly started removing their equipment from her room.

Gaby pouted. "Why is this taking so long? I'm starving."

"There're some leftovers in the fridge, I think. Help yourself," Scarlett offered. The show usually had chips and pretzels as part of their craft service, which was hardly "lunch."

"'Kay." Gaby jumped to her feet and disappeared in the direction of the kitchen.

Scarlett sighed again. This was such bullshit. If only Jane were here, things would be different. They'd be watching lame Christmas specials they had TiVo'd or doing last-minute shopping together at the Grove while fake snow fell around them. Scarlett could spend Christmas at the Robertses' house instead of jetting off to Aspen; Jane's family was actually *normal* (in a good way) and nicer than her own family. Mr. and Mrs. Roberts didn't sit in total, icy silence at the dinner table, CNN in the background, cutting quietly into their forty-dollar rib-eye steaks. They didn't spend more time on the phone with their patients than with each other. They didn't psychoanalyze their children with comments like, *So, Scarlett—do you think your choice to go to USC rather than Harvard or Columbia has to do with your unconscious fear of success?*

Where *was* Jane, anyway? The note Jane had left for

Scarlett in the apartment five days ago said that Madison had taken her to Mexico to get away, and that she'd be back soon. The problem was, Madison was the person who had orchestrated the whole *Gossip* scandal in the first place, and Jane had no idea.

Before disappearing with Jane, Madison had whispered in Scarlett's ear that Jesse Edwards was the one who had leaked those photos to *Gossip*. So Scarlett had gone to Jesse's house to deliver a few choice words she had for him, personally. When she got there, Jesse told her that *Madison* was the guilty one, that Madison had tried to convince him to leak the photos to *Gossip*, and he'd refused (despite being beyond furious about his girlfriend hooking up with his best friend). And Scarlett had believed him. He was a drunk, ungrateful, publicity-hungry man-whore. But on this one crucial occasion, he had been telling the truth. She was sure of it.

Desperate to track Jane down, Scarlett had asked Gaby if she knew the location of Madison's parents' condo . . . or had any contact info for the Parkers. But Gaby had been clueless, as usual. Although it was surprising that she wasn't more informed, since she and Madison always seemed to be hanging out. Scarlett had also Googled the Parkers but had turned up nothing. Which was kinda strange, given the fact that they were supposedly zillionaire real-estate developers or whatever. Maybe they preferred to keep a lower profile than their daughter, who would happily attend the opening of an envelope if there were cameras there.

Whatever. As soon as Jane returned, the two of them were going to straighten out this whole stupid mess about Madison and the pictures. And they would work on getting their friendship back on track. So many things (and people) had come between them in the last few months: the show, Madison, Gaby, Jesse. Their lowest moment was probably when Scarlett had to find out about Jane hooking up with Braden from a damned website. She and Jane *never* used to keep secrets from each other.

Alone in the room, finally—the crew members seemed to have spread out into the hallway—Scarlett walked over to her desk, in search of her passport. She would need it if she ended up having to go to Mexico herself and drag Jane home. As she was rifling through the topmost drawer, she heard a voice behind her.

"Hey, you doing okay?"

Scarlett turned around. It was Liam, one of the cameramen. Well, not just one of the cameramen. Scarlett had had a secret crush on him for the last few weeks (speaking of secrets). It was secret because, according to the PopTV rules, the "talent" wasn't allowed to get involved with the crew (not that a crush was the same as getting involved, but the former could always lead to the latter). It was a secret, too, because Scarlett didn't really have crushes. She had a long and perfectly happy history of hooking up with guys once, maybe twice, and then never seeing them again. It had always worked for her. It was certainly better than relationships, like Jane's disasters with Jesse and her high school boyfriend, Caleb Hunt, who had (in Scarlett's humble opinion) strung her along long-distance when he started college and then broken up with her with some very original excuse like "I love you, but you deserve better." (Scarlett's theory was that Caleb had been cheating on Jane at Yale, but that was all it was—a theory. She'd never found any proof.)

Liam, her noncrush, was standing there watching her with a friendly, concerned expression. Wow, his eyes were *so* blue. The same shade of blue as the bandanna that held back his long, light brown wavy hair, and the same color as the soft, faded tee that accentuated his slender but well-sculpted torso. Scarlett had tried to ignore him all morning during filming. But now, alone with him in her bedroom, she found it was not so easy.

"Hey," Scarlett said, turning back to her desk. "I'm great, thanks. I'll be even better when this shoot's over."

"No, I meant because . . . Jane. I'm sure you're worried about her."

Scarlett hesitated. Liam was the only person on the crew who had been thoughtful enough to realize this. And she hardly knew him. In fact, they had barely said more than "hi" to each other since he joined the show in September. "Um, well, yeah."

"I'm sure she's fine. And this whole stupid media circus—it'll blow over as soon as the next national emergency happens, like some It Girl gaining five pounds or

Leda Phillips wearing something ugly to the *Wuthering Heights* premiere."

Scarlett cracked a smile. He was funny . . . and nice . . . and cute. *Great.* "They remade *Wuthering Heights*?" she said lightly. "Why?"

"Dunno. Leda Phillips is Catherine, and Gus O'Dell is Heathcliff. So lame compared to Merle Oberon and Laurence Olivier, right? And even lamer compared to Emily Brontë's novel."

"*Charlotte* Brontë," Scarlett corrected him.

"No, *Emily*. Wanna bet?" Liam held out his hand, grinning.

Scarlett frowned. Then she picked up her BlackBerry (courtesy of PopTV, so they could always reach her . . . *gag*) and looked up *Wuthering Heights* on the internet. *Hmm.* Emily Brontë. *Damn!*

So Liam was funny, nice, cute, *and* knew his Brontë sisters. It was a dangerous—and irresistible—combination, especially for a voracious reader like her. (She plowed through novels in their original Spanish or French or Italian, just for fun.) Actually, she had seen Liam reading some of her favorite books during breaks: *One Hundred Years of Solitude* by Gabriel García Marquez one time, and *Middlemarch* by George Eliot another. It was one of the reasons she'd noticed him.

"Yeah, okay, it's Emily," Scarlett admitted. "What, you a SparkNotes fan?"

Liam laughed and pretended to look hurt. "You don't think I can read a whole novel?"

"Well, maybe a short one. Like a novella."

"Oh, that's—"

Their conversation was interrupted by footsteps: Gaby wandered in and sank onto the bed, chomping down on what looked like cold pepperoni pizza. "Whatcha talking about?"

"Nothing, just grabbing the rest of the stuff in here." Liam picked up a rolled-up electrical cord.

Scarlett smiled and gave a little wave as she watched Liam walk out of her room. *He's just another guy,* Scarlett told herself. So why did she feel a warm, nervous, giddy feeling in the pit of her stomach? What the hell *was* that feeling, anyway? Maybe she ate something bad? She eyed the pizza in Gaby's hand and couldn't recall when exactly she had ordered it. She watched Gaby take another bite . . . and said nothing. As long as Gaby was eating, Gaby wasn't talking. And that was a good thing.

Later that day, Scarlett was sitting on the airplane just before takeoff when her cell rang. She looked at the screen but didn't recognize the number.

GOT UR NUMBER FROM CALLSHEET, HOPE ITS OK. SHH DONT TELL DANA. MY ROOMMATES AND I R HAVING A NEW YEARS EVE PARTY. IF UR BACK FROM ASPEN AND WANT 2 COME TEXT ME AND ILL GIVE U THE ADDRESS. MERRY XMAS. LIAM.

Scarlett felt her heart race and her palms get hot. Flying always did that to her—didn't it? She scrolled up and down, rereading the message. Why was Liam inviting her to his party? Was he just being polite? She reread the message again, trying to translate it, until the flight attendant announced that everyone had to turn off their portable electronic devices in preparation for takeoff. By then, it didn't matter, though. Scarlett had the message memorized.

3

IS THAT THE GIRL FROM THAT SHOW?

Jane hurried toward baggage claim, eager to get out of LAX as quickly as possible. With Christmas only two days away, the place was packed. Good—she would be able to slip in and out without anyone bothering her. Her baseball cap and oversize Chanel sunglasses would keep her anonymous. Or scream, "I'm a celebrity in hiding." Jane never thought she would actually *crave* anonymity, but she did. Now more than ever.

She felt her bikini bottoms chafing against her hips. In her rush to leave the Parkers' condo, she had slipped her jeans on over her bathing suit, practically running out the door with her hastily packed suitcase into the waiting cab. She glanced at the clock on the departures-and-arrivals board: 4:15. If she had stayed in Cabo, she and Madison would be catching the sunset on the beach . . . or mixing margaritas in the kitchen . . . or making plans for the evening. Jane had grown accustomed to the slow, lazy rhythm of their days, their carefree routine. The way Madison made Jane breakfast every morning (coffee, yogurt, and fresh fruit arranged in the shape of a smiley face), talked her down whenever she was in one of her funks, entertained her, distracted her, comforted her. Madison had been a perfect friend.

Jane passed an airport newsstand and turned her head to avoid catching a glimpse of the tabloids. She prayed her face was no longer plastered on any of them, but she didn't want to risk looking. For a brief second, she had the impulse to turn around and get on the next flight back to Cabo. But she knew she couldn't, and besides, Madison had probably taken off herself to meet her parents for the holidays in . . . Where exactly did Madison say she was going? Jane had asked her several times, and Madison had been vague about it. New York? Boston? London? Some island somewhere? But that was Madison: always full of fun, fabulous, half-formed plans.

As for Jane, it was time to face the music. Hopefully not all at once. Her immediate goal was to get to the apartment, unpack, repack, grab the Christmas presents she'd bought for her family, then jump into her car and drive up the coast to Santa Barbara. And at some point she might have to listen to the thirty-one messages that were waiting for her on her phone. She assumed it hadn't taken long for her voice mailbox to fill up.

If she was lucky, maybe Scar would still be in their apartment, and they could talk in person. She knew that the Harps were headed to Aspen at some point, but she wasn't sure exactly when.

Rounding the corner, Jane passed another magazine stand—and stopped in her tracks. There was her face, up and down one of the racks, on the cover of *Talk* magazine. It featured a photo of her with the cover line, *L.A. CANDY* STAR CAUGHT IN LOVE TRIANGLE.

Jane bit her lip, trying not to freak out.

Just days ago, she had been a rising star, "America's sweetheart," a normal girl with normal problems whom everyone could relate to and wanted to see on TV week after week. A few issues ago, *Talk* had dubbed her "Hollywood's Newest It Girl." And *now* what was she? A slut who cheated on her boyfriend with his best friend? It didn't get much worse.

How had her image gone from good to terrible in such a short time?

Jane had to get out of LAX, ASAP. She saw the sign that said, BAGGAGE CLAIM, and hurried toward it. Once there, she scanned the crowded carousels, trying to figure out which one would have her bag. Within a few minutes, she spotted her baby blue rolling suitcase rounding the nearest carousel. She picked it up and turned to go. *That was easy,* she thought.

She heard them before she saw them.

"Jane!"

"Over here, Jane!"

Jane whirled around, knocking her suitcase over. There

were four in all: three photographers and a fourth guy with a handheld camcorder. They must not have noticed her at first.

"Jane, have you talked to Jesse?"

"How do you feel about the photos being released?"

"Is it true that you leaked your own photos?"

"Jane, why did you cheat on Jesse?"

They were shouting at her, their voices so much louder than the background noise of flight announcements and crying toddlers. Everyone around them turned to stare at her. She heard nearby murmurs—"Who is she?" "Ohmigod, is that the girl from that show?" "Jane! Isn't she that actress?"—and saw people pulling out their cells and snapping pictures of her. Jane felt frozen in place—trapped.

Then she took a deep breath and remembered what to do. She picked up her suitcase, walked briskly past the shouting photographers and ogling crowd, and headed through the sliding glass doors in the direction of the taxi stand. With her hat over her eyes, her sunglasses in place, and her head held high . . . *-ish.*

"Jane, just one smile!"

"Come on, Jane . . . don't you like taking pictures with your clothes on?"

They followed her all the way to the taxi stand, seemingly frustrated by the way she kept turning her face away from them. At one point they began holding their cameras only a few feet from her eyes and flashing. She could barely see where she was going.

It wasn't until she got inside a cab, and they had pulled away from LAX and away from the photographers, that she allowed herself to slump down in her seat—and cry.

"Scar?"

No reply. Jane closed the door behind her and threw her keys on the hall table. The apartment was totally quiet: no TV, no music, no Scar conjugating Spanish verbs out loud. On the counter, Jane noticed an empty to-go cup from 7-Eleven. *Ah, so the crew has been here filming,* she thought. She was really, really glad she'd missed them. She didn't need the cameras spontaneously documenting her "homecoming," especially with her feeling so crappy and her face streaked with tears.

Jane thought about the ambush at the airport and felt a fresh wave of distress—and anger, too. She decided to hide out in her apartment until late, at least midnight, before hitting the road for Santa Barbara. It was the only way she could be sure not to be followed by more of them.

She walked into the kitchen and saw a big note plastered on the marble counter:

> Janie, it's 2 p.m., and I'm off to catch my flight to Aspen. I have my cell, so call me!!!!!!!! Love, Scar, 12/23

Jane realized that she had just missed Scar. In fact, maybe they were at LAX at the same time?

There was another note next to the first one:

To the person from Angelo's Pet-sitting Service: Penny is in the last bedroom on the right. Plz feed her the fish food that's next to her bowl.

Scar had added her cell phone number in case of an emergency.

Aw, Jane thought. That was so sweet of Scar to remember Penny. Especially since Jane had taken off for Cabo without remembering to ask Scar to take care of her (yet another thing she felt incredibly guilty about).

The kitchen was really clean: no dirty dishes in the sink, no empty pizza boxes piling up next to the trash can. In general, Scar tended to be much neater and more organized than Jane. (Except in the grooming and fashion departments, although Scar was so naturally stunning that she always got away with not brushing her hair, putting on makeup, or wearing anything other than jeans and a wrinkled tee. Jane, while pretty, required a little more effort.) Although, speaking of the trash can . . . Jane noticed dozens of Post-it notes and scraps of paper spilling out of it. She fished them out.

They were all messages from Scar to her, dated between five days ago and today:

Janie, call me!

I'm off to the library to return books. Back by 9 a.m.

I have to talk to you about Madison ASAP!

Your mom called.

Call me!

Trevor called like fifty times—can u call him back?

Fiona Chen's office called.

At the gym (new personal trainer!), back noon. If you're home wait for me!!!

Call me!

Starbucks, back in an hour.

Trevor called again.

Last exam for the semester, back by dinner.

Fiona Chen's office called again.

Your dad called.

Filming at some stupid club, back by midnight.

Janie, call me!!!!!

And more of the same.

Jane's chest tightened. Scar had obviously been worried about her and trying to connect with her at every opportunity. And Jane had completely blown her off. Okay, so she didn't have cell reception or internet at Madison's parents' condo. She should have called or texted Scar from the Cabo airport or LAX or wherever.

She scanned the messages again, pausing on the one about Madison. What did Scar mean, she had to talk to her about Madison ASAP? That seemed so random. Jane knew that Scar thought Madison was a shallow, pretentious bitch who only looked out for herself. No emergency there. Like all of Scarlett's opinions, she wasn't shy about voicing it. But as far as Jane could tell, Madison had always been friendly to Scar, inviting her to parties, spa outings, and more. Scar was the one who turned her nose up at stuff like that. She prided herself on being different, apart, an outsider.

But that was Scar. She could sometimes be too intense and critical when it came to people, especially people in Jane's universe. Jane knew Scar was just looking out for her, but still. Scar had been this way with a couple of Jane's friends in high school, and with some of her boyfriends, too, including Caleb (Scar was totally against their long-distance relationship when he started college) and Jesse (whom she rarely referred to by his name, preferring "man-whore" and similarly flattering nicknames).

Scar was Jane's best friend, though. And Jane was *way* overdue in reaching out to her. Her friendship with Scar wasn't going so well these days. Like everything else in her life.

Jane pulled her cell out of her bag and quickly typed:

SCAR, IM SO SORRY IVE BEEN OUT OF TOUCH BUT IM BACK AT APT NOW AND ON MY WAY TO SANTA BARBARA. IM OKAY. LUV U, JANE

Jane hit Send and smiled to herself. That was that. She had made first contact after her self-imposed exile.

That wasn't so hard, was it?

Now she just had to do the same thing with her mom and dad and Trevor and Fiona and whoever else had left messages for her. *Yeah, piece of cake,* she thought.

4

YOU'RE DOING THIS FOR A GOOD REASON

Considering that it was Christmas Eve, the Blue Dolphin was surprisingly crowded. The blinking neon Santa Claus and the Christmas lights and fishing net that decorated the walls were more depressing than festive and did nothing to disguise its cheap vinyl booths, dingy pool tables, and lame jukebox. (Jimmy Buffett? Seriously?) It was the kind of place where a mostly older crowd could drink a lot of cheap beer, play darts, and yell at whatever game happened to be on the minuscule TV set above the bar.

It was also perfect for twenty-year-old Madison Parker's purposes tonight. These people were not PopTV fans; no one would know who she was. And while she usually loved to be seen, she didn't want to be recognized this evening. As much as she would have preferred meeting her contact at her office—or better yet, over martinis at Bar Marmont—she didn't dare take the chance, not so soon after the story had broken. Maybe she was being overly paranoid, but better safe than sorry.

She sat in one of the booths in the corner, her body angled so that she had a view of the room but no one could see her face.

When her phone buzzed, Madison expected to see a text making excuses about traffic or whatever. She reached into her quilted Chanel bag and pulled out her cell.

It was from Jane:

THANK U FOR CABO! U SAVED MY LIFE! IM SO LUCKY TO HAVE YOU AS A FRIEND. MERRY XMAS! LUV U, JANE

Madison's fingers trembled slightly as she clutched the phone. Her reaction should have been annoyance. She should be scoffing at this sweet little message from sweet little Jane, whose sweetness generally made her want to puke, but for a moment she felt a pang of . . . what? Guilt? Regret? Jane thought of her as a friend. A *good* friend. And for those few days in Cabo, Madison had been just that. It had been fun hanging out on the beach and talking about clothes and boys. Being away from L.A. and from the twenty-four/seven pressure of being "on," Madison had almost relaxed into normalcy with Jane. Madison had never had a best friend growing up. In some ways, ironically, Jane was the closest thing to a best friend she'd ever had.

Madison shook her head sharply. *Stop it,* she told herself. *You have to focus. You're doing this for a good reason.*

After all, it wasn't like she was *hurting* Jane. Sure, Jane was upset now, but she would get over it. Any publicity was good publicity, right? If no one knew who Jane Roberts was before, they sure did now. And if Jane ended up with really minor story lines because of this—or off *L.A. Candy* altogether—then it was for the best. Hadn't she told Madison the entire time they were in Cabo that she wished she'd never signed on to do the show? Madison was just helping Jane get what she wanted.

Besides, Jane was not meant to be the star of *L.A. Candy.* She didn't even want it. Madison, on the other hand, *needed* this, and would never take it for granted. Paparazzi were part of the job. Madison would never have run away from a scandal. In fact, she would have made sure to get a *Maxim* or *FHM* cover out of those photos. And loved every second of it.

"Traffic was a joke, and what bar doesn't have valet?"

Madison glanced up, startled. She hadn't noticed Veronica Bliss standing there. She was holding a glass of what looked like scotch on the rocks, which she set down on the table next to Madison's untouched glass of white wine.

"Hi, how are you?" Madison said brightly.

"Fine, fine."

Madison watched Veronica as she slid into the seat

across from her. The forty-something woman was tiny—five feet tall and petite—with short red hair and piercing light blue eyes behind stylish black Chanel frames. Her simple black suit with pearls was at odds with the tacky decor in the Blue Dolphin.

Even though Veronica was physically diminutive, most people in Hollywood were terrified of her. And for good reason. As the editor in chief of *Gossip* magazine, Veronica could make or break a person's reputation and career with just one well-timed, well-placed story or photo.

A person like, say, Jane Roberts.

"Enjoy yourself in Cabo?" Veronica asked.

"The weather was to die for."

"Anything you want to share?" Veronica gazed squarely at Madison.

Madison stirred uncomfortably. Veronica had the weirdest way of staring at a person and not breaking eye contact, even for a second. It was creepy.

"You know, it was all baking on the beach and downing margaritas," Madison said, shrugging.

Veronica took a sip of her drink. "Well, I certainly appreciate your emailing me from Cabo with your location. My photographer flew in and got some great shots of Jane."

"Did he get any of me?" Madison said, remembering the guy with the aviators. At Veronica's silence, she continued, "I had to sneak into town to send you that email, 'cause our resort has no internet access, and—"

"Yes, yes, I'm grateful," Veronica cut in, not sounding appreciative at all.

Madison flinched. The woman owed her, big-time. Why wasn't she being nicer? Maybe she needed reminding.

"So. How are the newsstand sales of the big Jane/Braden/Jesse issue?" Madison asked, taking a sip of her wine.

Veronica's blue eyes lit up. "Excellent. The numbers are incredible. You really came through with those photos."

Madison smiled smugly.

"I'm curious, though. How, exactly, did you obtain them?"

"I know a photographer. He's not afraid of heights, if you know what I mean." Veronica just stared at her, so Madison continued to explain. "There's a big tree near Jane's bedroom window, and she never closes her curtains, and . . . well, you can guess the rest."

"Impressive."

"So, will those pictures from Cabo be part of a follow-up story?" Madison asked.

"Yes, of course. I have reporters keeping tabs on both Jesse and this Braden guy. Apparently Braden flew out to New York City the day before yesterday. From what I gather, he and Jesse have been friends for a while, but no one knew who Braden was. One day he's an unknown wannabe actor living in the shadow of his best friend; the next day everybody's talking about him. The power of publicity, right? As for Jesse . . . well, it's been less than a week since the story broke, but during that short time our Jesse's been busy. He's been spotted at Crown Bar with some blonde, then Les Deux with another girl. I guess someone's trying really hard to prove that he's over Jane."

"Interesting," Madison said, although really, it wasn't interesting at all. Who cared about Braden or Jesse? She wanted to get the subject back to what really mattered: *her.* "Listen. About our deal."

"Deal?"

Madison felt heat rising to her cheeks. "Yes, deal. You told me that if I got you dirt on Jane, you would put me in your magazine."

"Yes, yes, of course. I'll have one of my reporters call you first thing tomorrow. Oh, except . . . it's Christmas, right? Maybe the day after." Veronica cocked her head. "Funny, isn't it?"

"What?"

"That you, Madison Parker, are spending Christmas Eve plotting against one of your best and, as I understand, *only* friends."

Madison glared. "She's *not* one of my best friends. I

have other friends. Lots of them. Besides, Christmas Eve isn't over yet. I have plans."

"Of course you do." Veronica picked up her scotch and took a sip, never breaking eye contact with Madison.

Madison looked away, wanting so badly to say what she was thinking, which was that it didn't seem like Veronica had any warm, fuzzy Christmas Eve plans, either. But Madison knew better than to bite the hand she was hoping would feed her.

"Bitch," Madison murmured.

"What?" Derek rolled over from his side of the bed and gazed at her, confused.

Madison shook her head. "Nothing. Sorry. I was just thinking about this woman I had a drink with tonight."

"Oh," he said, glancing at the clock on her nightstand. "Damn. I've gotta go. It's almost midnight, and . . ." His voice trailed off.

"Don't worry about it. Go, go."

Derek stood up, picked up a dove gray Zegna dress shirt from the floor, and shrugged it on. "Hey, I left your Christmas present under your tree."

Madison grinned. "You did? Am I gonna love it?"

"You're gonna love it. Oh, and I mailed in your *other* Christmas present this morning. January rent."

"Awesome. Thanks, sweetie."

"No, I'm the one who should thank *you*." He leaned over, cradled her face in his hands, and kissed her.

Madison kissed him back, as always managing to (almost) ignore the cold touch of his platinum wedding band against her skin.

5

CHRISTMAS EVE WITH THE HARPS

"Could you pass the smoked trout, darling?" Scarlett's father said to her mother.

"Yes, of course, sweetheart. Scarlett, would you like another oyster with mignonette sauce?"

"Umm . . . sure."

Silence followed, filled with only the clinking of silverware against dishes. Scarlett glanced over her shoulder at Dana, who was making a frantic rolling motion with her hands, which Scarlett translated to mean, *Please keep the conversation going, already.* Any second now, she would be sending Scarlett another text: CD U TALK ABOUT CHRISTMASES FROM YR CHILDHOOD? ANY FUNNY STORIES? WHAT ABOUT THE BEST AND WORST PRESENTS U EVER GOT? WHAT ABOUT . . .

"So . . . skiing was awesome today, wasn't it?" Scarlett managed as she slurped down another oyster without grimacing. (Why did they have to have the consistency of snot?) She would normally ignore Dana's TMs, but she didn't want to come across as being even more awkward and conversationally challenged than her parents.

"Yes, excellent," her father agreed.

"A little crowded for my taste," her mother said.

More silence. Scarlett stared at the hideous all-white centerpiece (tall white candles, twinkling white lights, and a pair of fake white kissing doves nestled in a bed of white leaves and berries) and tried to think of something else to say.

Oh, yeah, the tricycle incident. "Remember when you got me that yellow tricycle for Christmas?" she said, forcing a laugh. "When I'd already taught myself how to ride a bike? That was hilarious, right?"

Her parents exchanged a confused glance. "I'm not sure I remember that," her father said. "Do you, darling?"

Her mother shook her head. "I don't."

More silence. Scarlett stirred in her chair, picking at the food on her plate. Why had she agreed to this? she wondered for what seemed like the hundredth time. Letting the show film her with her parents, of all people, on Christmas Eve, of all days?

But it had been so hard to say no—for Jane's sake.

Trevor had originally scheduled the cameras and crew to film Jane at home with *her* family on Christmas Eve. But as of yesterday, Jane was still missing. So when Dana had called Scarlett as soon as she'd landed in Aspen and asked if she wouldn't mind filling in for Jane, what could she say? "No?" Well, actually, that was exactly what she said, but after many phone calls they had worn her down, not-so-subtly reminding her that she had a contract. A contract that she was willing to honor for the few remaining episodes of the season. After that . . . she wasn't sure. Being on the show kind of sucked, in her opinion, and the (free) gorgeous apartment wasn't worth the invasion of her privacy and all the other little annoyances. She and Jane could happily move back to their rat hole by the 101. Well, she could, anyway. She wasn't sure how Jane was feeling about the show these days.

Soon after agreeing to the Aspen shoot, Scarlett had gotten the text from Jane saying that she was okay and that she was heading up to Santa Barbara. She had tried to call her a few times since then, but Jane hadn't picked up. Obviously, Jane wasn't ready to talk to anyone just yet. Which meant that she *definitely* wasn't going to be in the mood to have the *L.A. Candy* cameras in her face when she and her family sat down for their Christmas Eve dinner.

So Scarlett had decided *not* to inform Trevor or Dana that Jane was no longer MIA—or that they should move their shoot back to Santa Barbara, as originally planned. She had decided to give her best friend another few precious hours of space and privacy. She had even elected to try to be nice to her parents and put on a good show for the cameras. She could see the finished episode now:

"Christmas Eve with the Harps." *Gag!* The way it was going, the scene would be almost silent, with only the sounds of utensils clinking against china. She guessed that would end up being perfect for the way Trevor was editing her—the silent, pretty girl and her silent, pretty family.

See how much I love you, Janie? Scarlett thought drily.

What made it even worse was that her parents clearly had no idea how to behave in front of the cameras. Although on this count, Scarlett was sympathetic. It was definitely surreal, trying to act normal (well, as "normal" as the Harps could be) in your home (or in your rented condo in Aspen) with a crew of eight rearranging your furniture, plastering paper over your windows, and bustling around with their high-tech equipment. And then recording your every word and gesture for posterity—at least until Trevor edited the hell out of them.

The only—*only*—thing that was (almost) saving the day was the fact that Liam was here. Working, but still.

"Are we ready for the soup course?" her mother said.

"Fine with me," her father replied. "Vichyssoise?"

"No, lobster bisque. I had the caterer make it with skim milk, of course."

"Of course."

Scarlett slurped down another oyster (okay, so maybe they were kinda good) as she felt her cell vibrate in her pocket. Great, a Dana-gram. Obviously, the yellow-tricycle story hadn't cut it.

But when she glanced at the screen, she saw that it was a text from Liam.

DID THEY HIRE THESE PEOPLE 2 PLAY YR PARENTS OR R U ADOPTED AND DIDN'T TELL ME?

Scarlett stifled a giggle. She snuck a peek at Liam, who was behind the camera next to the massive stone fireplace. She could tell that he was trying to keep from laughing, too.

Underneath the table, she quietly typed: NEVER SEEN THEM B4. IM JUST HERE 4 THE OYSTERS.

Liam typed back: HOPE THEY TASTE BETTER THAN THEY LOOK!

WHY R U HERE? DID DANA MAKE U WORK? Scarlett typed.

A moment later, Liam typed back: BEN ASKED 4 THE DAY OFF AT THE LAST MIN SO I OFFERED 2 FILL IN.

Oh, Scarlett thought.

Staring at the bowl of lobster bisque that her mother had just set down in front of her (ew, pink soup?), Scarlett weighed Liam's statement. Liam had offered to work on Christmas Eve. Did he do this because he had nothing better to do? Or because he was a really, really nice guy and he wanted to help Ben out? Or because he wanted to be in Aspen . . . to be near her?

Stop it, Scarlett told herself. *You're being an idiot. Yeah, like the guy seriously gave up his holiday to work, just so he could watch your lame family eat pink soup and have nothing to say to one another.*

Her cell buzzed again. SO R U COMING 2 MY PARTY? Liam had typed.

Scarlett smiled. "Maybe," she said out loud, before she realized what she was doing.

"Maybe what, Scarlett?" her father asked her.

Scarlett glanced up sharply. Everyone in the room was staring at her, including Liam, who was obviously trying hard to keep a straight face.

"Uh . . . yeah . . . that is, maybe I'll have more of that, um, delicious soup," Scarlett managed to say.

Trying to recover her composure, she quickly tucked her phone back in her pocket. Texting with a cute guy in the middle of a shoot was way too dangerous!

6

CREATIVE EDITING

Trevor Lord leaned forward and studied the magazines fanned across his desk. Again. Each cover line and photo made him clench his jaw a little harder.

L.A. CANDY STAR
MORE TART THAN SWEET

JANE'S BETRAYAL

IS *L.A. CANDY* STAR
PREGNANT
WITH JESSE'S BABY?

DID JESSE'S DRUG HABIT DRIVE JANE
INTO HIS BEST FRIEND'S BED?

SEE JANE CHEAT!

And on and on. Each headline was insulting, attention-grabbing, and sure to sell issues. And sure to cause problems for the show.

How had everything spun *so* out of control? With his golden girl at the wheel?

He might've expected trouble from the other girls. Scarlett was stunningly beautiful, but she was way too smart, opinionated, and out-there to appeal to a general audience; Trevor had to edit out most of her real personality just to make her even remotely accessible. Madison was the perfect Hollywood cliché, with her dyed-to-the-max platinum hair and penchant for shopping, partying, and guys. But she was constantly bugging Trevor for more airtime; so far, he'd managed to keep her at bay with carefully worded compliments on the theme of "quality over quantity." Gaby had proven very entertaining, with her ditzy personality and natural talent for getting just about everything wrong. Sometimes she seemed too over-the-top even for reality television.

But Jane . . . Jane was his find of the decade. Sweet, natural, and vulnerable, she was a person everyone could relate to. She was pretty, but not too pretty. She liked to go out, but she didn't like to get wasted or do drugs. She worked hard. She was loyal to her friends. She came from a close-knit family.

Even her flaws were relatable. She procrastinated. She made mistakes at her job and got into trouble with her boss. She had arguments with her friends about dumb stuff. She didn't have the best judgment about guys and went on bad dates once in a while.

Right after the *L.A. Candy* series premiere in October, Trevor knew that he had a hit on his hands—and that Jane was largely responsible. Viewers loved her. After a couple of flops (fine, so everyone was sick of listening to amateurs sing Rihanna covers and watching strangers hook up on tropical islands), he was back on top as one of Hollywood's hottest reality producers.

Then things went from great to amazing when Jane and Jesse started dating, and with absolutely no intervention from Trevor. He couldn't have picked a better boyfriend than the bad-boy son of superstar actors Wyatt Edwards and Katarina Miller, who was always in some tabloid with a starlet on his arm. Jesse also liked to party hard. As in, in-and-out-of-rehab hard.

But Jesse had apparently cleaned up his act when he met Jane. It was love at first sight, and their chemistry was undeniable. Everyone seemed to want to tune in to their romance: Hollywood playboy falls for the girl next door. It was a reality producer's dream come true.

Trevor clutched his stress ball tighter. He had known that Jesse would eventually crash and burn. Once an addict, always an addict. But Trevor figured that if and when the time came, he would do some creative editing to make sure Jane and Jesse's romance continued its course, from breakup to makeup to breakup to makeup, without the unwholesome tarnish of Jesse's issues. The *L.A. Candy* cameras never showed Jesse misbehaving at clubs (drinking too much, disappearing to the men's room to do God knows what), and they never would.

But Trevor hadn't seen *this* coming: It was Jane who had screwed up. Big-time. Virtually overnight, the "reality producer's dream" had turned into a nightmare. With Jane and Madison gone, the shooting schedule was total chaos. Trevor and Dana were frantically improvising new and interesting ways to film Scarlett and Gaby: Scarlett Christmas shopping . . . Gaby taking a boot-camp fitness class . . . Scarlett checking out the spring courses in the USC catalog with a fellow student . . . Gaby taking her pint-size, overgroomed dog out for a walk. And filming the two girls together was beyond challenging, since most of those scenes consisted of Gaby having one-sided conversations while Scarlett mocked her and made sarcastic remarks under her breath.

How long would they be able to keep this up? Where the hell was Jane? (She'd been photographed at LAX yesterday, but she didn't seem to be at her apartment, and she still wasn't answering his calls. Her parents weren't answering his calls, either.) And what was he going to do with her when she finally resurfaced? He had a story line on his hands that everyone knew about but that didn't make sense for the show. There could be no mention of Braden, since he refused to sign a release. Which meant that there could be no mention of Jane cheating on Jesse with Braden. There could be no mention of the *Gossip* scandal, either. In the *L.A. Candy* universe, tabloids didn't exist. And neither did half-naked pictures of a nice girl like Jane.

"Trevor?"

He rubbed his eyes and glanced up. Melissa, one of the PopTV publicists, was standing in the doorway. He had ordered his entire team to put in overtime, and many were working today despite the fact that it was Christmas Eve. "Yes? What is it?" he snapped.

"Yeah, hello to you, too. Listen, you're gonna be a little nicer to me when you see this." She held up a file.

"What is it?"

"Ratings from the last episode. You know, the episode that aired after those, uh, lovely photos came out?"

Trevor stared intently at her. "And?"

"Our ratings nearly doubled."

"Let me see that."

Melissa handed the file to Trevor. He opened it and scanned the figures quickly. His pulse quickened, and he sat up straighter. Four-point-six million? Did it really say 4.6 million?

Trevor's lips curled up in a slow, satisfied smile. "You just made me a very happy man."

"Yeah, yeah. Until the next crisis," Melissa joked.

"No, no. The crisis was *good*. The crisis made our numbers go up."

"Any publicity is good publicity, right?"

"Something like that. Now, go back to your office

and break these down some more. I want them within the hour."

Melissa peeked at her watch. "It's almost eight and I've got a red-eye to New York to visit my family for Christmas."

"Well, you'd better get busy, then."

"Whatever you say, boss."

As Trevor watched her leave, he closed the file and thought about what this meant. As always, his brain operated simultaneously in two realities: the *real* reality and the *L.A. Candy* reality. Trevor realized that at this moment in time, these two realities were actually working in sync and in his favor. The *real* reality (Jane, Braden, Jesse, the *Gossip* scandal) boosted and would continue to boost ratings, while the *L.A. Candy* reality airbrushed—and would continue to airbrush—over any and all the ugliness, painting Jane in the same soft, golden glow that had morphed her into "America's sweetheart."

This was good—*all* good. Now all he needed was to find Jane. And figure out how to choreograph the next few episodes.

Trevor picked up the phone and got back to work.

7

IT'S KINDA COMPLICATED

Lacie hit the Pause button and pointed to the giant plasma screen. "Oh, yeah, *that* dude," she said, cracking up. "Did you ever go out with him again?"

"He seems like kind of a dork," Nora piped up. "But he's H-O-T."

Jane sighed and leaned back on the couch, where she was sandwiched between her two baby sisters. Lacie, sixteen, was to the right of her, wielding the remote. Nora, fourteen, was to the left, hugging a massive bowl of nacho-cheese-flavored popcorn. It was Christmas night, and the three girls were watching episode after episode of *L.A. Candy* in their family room. Lacie and Nora had TiVo'd all of season one so far, and were now making Jane sit through them as they grilled her about various details.

"Yeah, that's Paolo," Jane said, wishing she didn't have to relive *that* particular date. They'd had zero chemistry—and to make things worse, she had partied too much at

Madison's the night before and had thrown up on the way home. "No, no second date."

"See, I *told* you," Lacie said triumphantly to Nora.

"Yeah, well, she's gone on second dates with dorks before," Nora shot back. "Remember that guy she went to the Homecoming dance with? And what's-his-name from the track team, Rob, Bob?" She shook with laughter, practically rolling off the couch.

Great, Jane thought. *Why do little sisters have to remember everything?*

"How come your new boyfriend isn't on the show?" Nora asked. "Braden?"

Jane managed to fudge an explanation about Braden being too busy (and to add that Braden was *not* her new boyfriend) because she didn't feel like explaining that Braden had steadfastly refused to sign a release to be filmed. And as far as Trevor was concerned, if someone couldn't be filmed, that person didn't exist. Sometimes Jane would mention Braden while filming, but they would never use any of that footage.

On the floor nearby was the carnage from this morning's present-opening frenzy: wads of brightly colored wrapping paper, ribbons and bows, empty boxes, and stray gifts. Across the room, the eight-foot-tall tree looked as beautiful and Christmassy as always, decorated with family ornaments. She especially loved seeing the angel she'd made in second grade, out of white felt and cotton balls, hanging in its coveted spot on a high-up branch.

Still . . . Christmas felt different this year. Lacie and Nora had been their usual giddy selves this morning, ripping open presents and screaming about their new cell phones, iPods, Sephora gift certificates, and the rest of it. Their parents had tried to put on their best happy faces—her mother oohing and aahing over the diamond earrings from her father, her father modeling the goofy apron from Nora that said, DANGER: DAD GRILLING ON BARBECUE. But Jane had caught the two of them sneaking glances at her, looking stressed and worried. And disappointed. That was the hardest part, the disappointment. Jane had let her parents down by cheating on her boyfriend and causing a national media scandal.

Lacie hit Fast-forward, then Play. Gaby appeared on the screen, answering phones at Ruby Slipper, the PR firm where she worked.

"Okay, so what about your friend Gaby?" Lacie said. "She seems nice, but is she really that dumb?"

"Like that episode where she microwaved her True Religion jeans because the dryer was broken? Did the show *tell* her to do that, to make people laugh?" Nora asked.

"Gaby's really sweet," Jane said vaguely. "Hey, you guys wanna watch a movie or something?"

"*Movie?*" Lacie burst out. "Are you crazy? We have more episodes to watch! And we have soooo many questions to ask you!"

"Alanah and Ainsley might come over later, 'cause they wanna talk to you about the show," Nora added. She picked a piece of popcorn out of her purple-tinted braces. "Oh, and they want Jesse Edwards's autograph. You can get that for them, right?"

Lacie craned her head to glare at her little sister, her hazel eyes blazing. "Nora! Are you slow or what?"

"Lacie, *be nice*!"

Jane glanced up and saw her mother standing in the doorway. Maryanne Roberts frowned sternly at Lacie, who pulled her long blond hair over her face and mumbled, "Sorry," under her breath.

Maryanne was wearing a salmon-colored silk robe, Jane's Christmas present to her, as well as a pair of fuzzy pink slippers from Lacie. She set a tray of steaming mugs on the coffee table. "Hot chocolate," she announced to her daughters. "What are you watching?"

"*L.A. Candy*, what else?" Nora replied. She pointed to the screen. "Hey! Ha! That's when Jane gets drunk at that club and flirts with that Australian guy!"

"*Austrian*," Lacie corrected her.

"I did *not* get drunk!" Jane scoffed. Did Nora seriously have to say that in front of their mom?

"Okay, girls, enough," Maryanne snapped. "Jane could probably use a break from all this stuff. Why don't we watch one of the twenty thousand DVDs Santa brought you for Christmas?"

"Santa, right." Nora rolled her golden brown eyes.

"Good idea," Jane said quickly. "I'm gonna change into my jammies first. Back in a sec."

Her mom was right—she did need a break from all this stuff. Five days in Cabo hadn't done the trick, after all. Seeing her family was a lot harder than she thought it would be. Not to mention seeing them watch the show.

She hadn't had much time to herself since driving up to Santa Barbara in the middle of the night two nights ago. Her parents had been so happy and relieved to see her, but they had a lot of questions: Was she okay? Where did she disappear to? Had any reporters followed her from L.A.? Later, after dinner (their family had a tradition of making a Swedish feast together on Christmas Eve, because her mom was half Swedish), her dad had called her aside and asked her if she was having second thoughts about being on the show. Jane hadn't had a good answer. All she'd managed was, "I don't know, Dad. Maybe?"

Which was the truth.

The second Jane got to her bedroom, she closed the door and flopped down on the bed, which she'd forgotten to make this morning. The breeze through the open window was pleasantly cool and carried with it the sounds of the surf outside. Her cell was on her nightstand, with a full mailbox. She used to love her phone; now she hated it. Over the last couple of days, she'd somehow managed to listen to all thirty-one messages that had accumulated during her time in Cabo, as well as a few more that she had received since then. They were basically variations on the same theme: her parents, Trevor, Fiona, Scar, and others asking her where she was and if she was okay and could she please call them *immediately*? There had been some messages from Diego among the bunch, saying he was so, so, so sorry that he hadn't known about the photos of Jane and Braden being leaked to the magazine until it was too late. D worked as Veronica Bliss's assistant at *Gossip*, and from the sound of it, she wasn't a very nice boss. Or, Jane could now attest, a very nice person.

Reporters had called, too, offering her the chance to tell her side of the story. Yeah, right. Likely they just wanted to trick her into saying too much about Jesse and/or Braden, then twisting her words and printing more crazy headlines.

In addition to her daily "where/how are you" messages, Scar left a few confusing ones about Madison. Jane remembered the note Scar had left at their apartment, saying, *I have to talk to you about Madison ASAP.* What was that about, anyway? Jane figured she would find out soon enough. She planned to return to L.A. the day after tomorrow. Maybe Scar would be back from Aspen by then, and they could talk in person? They were long overdue for a heart-to-heart.

There were no messages from Jesse. Or Braden. None. Jane had checked and double-checked, and bitten back her disappointment each time. Why hadn't they tried to contact her? On the other hand, why was she so surprised?

She wasn't sure how she felt about either guy these days. She missed Jesse, missed the way things were before everything fell apart. But she couldn't deny that she was also attracted to Braden.

Not that she was in a position to choose one or the other. Jesse was likely never going to speak to her again. And Braden's silence spoke volumes. He was a low-key person who valued his privacy. Why would he want to be friends with—much less date—a publicity magnet like her, especially after what had happened?

Jane glared at her phone. She knew she was being kinda (well, definitely) irresponsible, not returning anyone's calls (although she *had* sent Scar that one text message). But she wasn't ready. She would be soon. Just not today.

As if on cue, her phone began ringing. "Go *away*!" Jane said out loud, as she looked at the screen to see which friend, producer, boss, coworker, or reporter was hounding her now.

Jane stopped when she recognized the number, which was still familiar to her after seven months of not seeing it appear on her screen.

It was Caleb. Caleb Hunt.

Caleb had been her first love and her first real boyfriend. They'd dated for a couple of years in high school. When he left to go to Yale the summer before last, they'd decided to try a long-distance relationship. She had been fine with it. He hadn't. At the end of his freshman year, he'd told her that he wanted to take a break. He'd spent the summer volunteering in New Orleans while she prepared to move to L.A. with Scar—and while she tried to get over him. Which hadn't been easy, although meeting Braden, then Jesse, had certainly helped.

Jane hadn't seen—or heard from—Caleb since their breakup back in May. Why was he calling her now?

Don't pick up, Jane told herself. *Just let it go to voice mail.* But then she remembered her mailbox was full. She grabbed the phone on the fifth ring and pressed Talk. "Hello?"

"Janie?" Caleb was the only person who ever called her that, besides Scar. "Hey. Am I catching you at a bad time?"

"Oh, hi, Caleb," Jane said casually. Although casual was the last thing she was feeling. The sound of his voice could still make her heart race, after all this time. "Nope, I'm just hanging out."

"You home for the holidays?"

"Yeah. Are you?"

"For now. I'm leaving tomorrow morning for Vail, though."

"Sounds fun."

"Hope so. Listen, Janie," Caleb said. "I'm calling because I'd heard some stuff, and I was worried about you. Are you doing okay?"

Jane realized that Caleb had seen the *Gossip* pictures. Along with everyone who had internet access or a TV set or who stood in grocery store checkout lines. "Oh, thanks, Caleb," she said, meaning it. "Yeah, I'm doing okay."

"You want me to beat anybody up?"

Jane laughed. "Yeah, maybe."

"Just say the word."

"Thanks. How's Yale?"

There was a pause. "It's . . . you know," Caleb said after a moment.

What does that even mean? Jane thought.

"How's Hollywood?" Caleb asked her.

"It's . . . you know," Jane mimicked him.

Caleb laughed. "Yeah, funny. So I guess you're with this Braden guy now?"

Why was he asking her this? "No, we're not together."

"Oh. So you're still with that Jesse guy?"

"Um, not exactly. It's kinda complicated."

"It always is with you, Roberts."

"You seeing anybody?" Jane asked him, wondering why they were quizzing each other on their love lives.

"Not exactly. It's kinda complicated." This time Caleb was mimicking her.

"Ha, ha."

Someone banged on her door. "Helllooooo?" It was Nora. "Everyone's waiting for you! We're gonna watch *Twilight* on Blu-ray!"

"Be there in a sec!" Jane called out. "I gotta go," she said into the phone.

"Nora-Bora's being a pain in the butt, huh?"

"Yeah, kinda. I haven't seen them in a while."

"No worries. I'll talk to you soon, okay? Call me if you need anything. Merry Christmas, Janie."

"Merry Christmas, Caleb."

As Jane clicked off and put her phone back on her nightstand, she wondered about his parting words: *I'll talk to you soon.* They hadn't talked at all in seven whole months. Why would they be talking anytime soon? And why was she supposed to call him if she "needed anything"? Had something changed? Of course, she was on TV now, but Caleb didn't care about that kind of stuff. He wasn't the type to track down an old girlfriend for a chance to be closer to a so-called celebrity.

Forget "kinda complicated"; everything in Jane's life was downright confusing.

8

YOU'RE TWO OF MY BEST FRIENDS

Scarlett sat cross-legged on her bed, clicking through channels, wondering what to do with the rest of her evening. She'd always hated Sundays. Sundays meant weekend over, back to school, back to work. These days, Sundays also meant receiving the upcoming week's shooting schedule from Dana. This week, Scarlett was scheduled to meet Gaby for lunch at La Crêperie . . . and at Kinara for a spa day . . . and at the Standard for a launch party for the Marley twins' new perfume.

It was two days after Christmas, and Jane and Madison were still not back. Which was why Trevor and Dana were (obviously) continuing to scrape the bottom of the barrel and force Scarlett and Gaby into social situations just so they had something to tape. She knew they were desperate for material, since the season finale was coming up in a month or so—and season finales were supposed to be full of drama and cliff-hangers, not scenes of faux friends eating crepes or getting mani-pedis. But that wasn't Scarlett's problem.

If only Jane would come home already. Then everything would return to normal. Well, sort of normal. How long did she plan on staying in Santa Barbara (or wherever she was these days)? How long did she plan on not picking up her phone or answering her emails?

"Scar?"

Scarlett muted her TV. *Jane?* She jumped to her feet and ran into the hallway. "Janie?" she called out.

"Yeah, it's me!" Jane's voice came from somewhere in the front of the apartment.

Scarlett ran down the hall and found Jane in the living room. She had obviously just walked through the door. Dressed in a pale yellow top and skinny jeans, her hair tied back in a messy knot, she was holding an overnight bag in one hand and a big shopping bag in the other filled to the brim with what appeared to be Christmas presents and Tupperware containers of homemade cookies. She looked kind of lost, like a little girl all alone at a train station.

"Janie! Ohmigod!" Scarlett rushed up to her and gave her a big hug. "Where the hell have you been? I've been so worried about you! Ohmigod, I am so happy to see you!" She hugged her again.

Jane hugged her back. "I'm glad to see you, too! Did you have a good Christmas?"

"What? No, it was lame. I'll tell you later. First, what about *you*? Are you all right?" Scarlett had a million questions to ask her; she didn't know where to begin.

Jane shrugged wearily. "I guess." She set her bags on the floor and walked over to the couch, sinking down.

Scarlett was right behind her. "Where did that psycho take you in Mexico? What did she say to you? Did she—"

Jane pulled back, her blue eyes wide. "Uh, Scar?" she said slowly. "I know you don't like Madison, and I respect that, even though I don't really understand it. But she's been a really good friend to me. So I'd appreciate it if—"

"*Friend?*" Scarlett cut in, practically shouting. She took a deep breath and forced herself to lower the volume. "Janie? Listen carefully to me, okay? I'm really, really sorry to have to tell you this, but Madison is the one who gave those pictures of you and Braden to *Gossip*."

There. She had said it. She sat back, waiting for Jane's reaction. Would Jane burst into tears? Start screaming? Pick up her phone and call Madison and end their friendship right then and there?

But Jane did none of those things. Instead, she gave Scarlett an icy smile. "Oh, really? You know what's funny? Madison said the same thing about you. I'm getting tired of your stupid feud. You're two of my best friends. Can't you at least *try* to get along? It's getting old, Scar."

You're two of my best friends? Scarlett heard the words but couldn't quite process them. When had Madison become one of Jane's best friends? She, Scarlett, was Jane's best friend. Madison was the enemy.

Scarlett took another deep breath. She *had* to get Jane to believe her. "I can prove to you that Madison did this."

"You can prove it?"

"Yes! See, right before you guys took off for Mexico, she told me that Jesse gave the photos to *Gossip*. So I went over to his house to confront him, right? But when I got there, he told me that *Madison* was the one who did it. He said she showed him the pictures earlier and tried to get him to deliver them to some woman at the magazine—you know, what's-her-name, D's boss. Veronica."

Jane was silent for a moment. "Why would he say that?" she said finally.

"Um, because it's the truth? Why would he lie about something like that?"

"I don't know. Because he wasn't thinking straight after those pictures came out? Because he was drunk . . . or on something? Because he doesn't like Madison? Or maybe because I just cheated on him with his best friend in the world and he wanted me to feel the same betrayal? There are a million reasons he would say that." Jane let out a frustrated yell. "I just want to forget about the pictures and get on with my life. *I'm* the one who messed up here. Not Jesse. And definitely not Madison. She pretty much saved my life, do you know that? If she hadn't gotten me out of here and taken me to her parents' condo in

Cabo, I don't know what I would've done."

"But—"

Jane held up her hand. "Let it go, Scarlett."

"Seriously—"

"No more." Jane took a deep breath and smiled the icy smile again. "Now, tell me about Christmas in Aspen."

Scarlett opened her mouth, then closed it. She could see that Jane didn't want to hear the truth about Madison. She would have to find another way to get through to her . . . to prove to her that Madison had manipulated her and lied to her from day one.

"Yeah. Right. So Trevor actually sent cameras to film our Christmas Eve dinner, can you believe it?" Scarlett said, figuring she should go along with Jane's attempt to change the subject.

"Seriously?" Jane glanced at her nails, distracted.

"Yeah. And I'm pretty sure Dana was texting my parents during the shoot. . . ."

Scarlett went on, describing the crazy Harp Christmas Eve dinner. But she could tell that Jane's mind was elsewhere. She knew her best friend—loyal to a fault. Scarlett had totally alienated her by going off on Madison.

Scarlett tried to bite back the sadness welling up in her—the sadness over this distance in their friendship that she couldn't seem to bridge. Sure, Scarlett hadn't told Jane about her noncrush on Liam . . . yet. Not that there was anything to tell, because nothing had actually happened between her and Liam. Still, Scarlett wasn't used to keeping secrets from Jane, big or small. Keeping secrets felt too much like telling lies.

How am I gonna fix this? Scarlett wondered miserably. And for once, the girl with all the answers didn't have a clue.

9

CRAZY GIRL

Just before 9 a.m. on Monday morning, Jane pulled into her usual parking spot behind Fiona Chen's building. She turned off the engine and carefully searched the entire lot through the window. Good—no photographers. She'd had to fend off two of them outside the apartment earlier. They were so obnoxious, shouting questions at her about Braden and Jesse—"Jane, why did Braden move to New York?" "Jane, what do you think of Jesse's new girlfriend?"—and snapping picture after picture of her while she gritted her teeth and tried to ignore them. She hadn't heard anything about Braden going to New York or Jesse having a new girlfriend. But she knew better than to talk to paparazzi.

Still . . . the thought of Braden and Jesse moving on without her, and so quickly, made her heart feel heavy. Neither had tried to contact her since the *Gossip* story broke. She knew she had to reach out to them at some point. She owed Braden an apology—for hooking up with him when she was so mixed-up about everything, and for inadvertently getting him involved in this whole mess. And she owed Jesse an even bigger apology. She had no idea how she could possibly make things right after cheating on him, and in front of the whole world, too.

There was one guy she didn't owe anything—and he seemed to have no problem getting in touch with her: Caleb. He had texted her yesterday, from Vail—something about the awesome powder, and did she remember when they went to Tahoe during her senior year, and she wiped out on her new snowboard, like, twenty times? A few minutes later, he had texted her a photo of her lying in a pile of snow and laughing hysterically. Jane had no idea why he was sending her this stuff. It was nice that he was thinking about her. But confusing. And she didn't need "confusing" right now, on top of everything else.

Riding up to her office in the crowded elevator, Jane felt butterflies in her stomach. And not the good kind. She hadn't been to work in over a week, and she was really nervous about facing Fiona. She had sent her boss a quick email yesterday, saying that she would be back in the office on Monday. Fiona had responded right away, writing simply: *See you tomorrow at 9 sharp.*

So what was in store for Jane at 9 sharp? A furious Fiona waiting with a long lecture? A pink slip, telling her that she had two weeks to find new employment? Maybe one followed by the other. *Can't wait.*

To make things worse, the *L.A. Candy* cameras were

up there already, prepared to shoot Jane's return to work. When Trevor had called Jane yesterday, Jane had felt compelled to pick up after ignoring him for so long. He asked her if it would be okay for them to shoot her at work the following day. After going MIA on him, what could she say but yes?

Much to her surprise, Trevor had been really sweet on the phone and didn't sound angry at all about the *Gossip* thing or her disappearing to Cabo. Which was weird, since he'd sounded so stressed in his messages. He told her that he was happy she was back, and that everything was going to be fine. He said that he'd been thinking about how to present "recent events" on the show, and thought her story line should be that she had cheated on Jesse (without naming Braden, of course), and that she wasn't sure who had spilled the news to Jesse. Maybe she could confess to someone, like her coworker and friend Hannah Stratton, that she felt really bad about the whole thing. It would be Jane's opportunity to tell her side of the story. He promised her that after people saw her side, everything would be better. And that was that. Trevor added that he would talk to each of the girls—Madison, Gaby, Scarlett, and Hannah—to clue them in on his ideas.

Jane was relieved that Trevor was being so nice about everything. At the same time, she wasn't sure how she felt about his interpretation of "recent events." Trevor's story line wasn't exactly accurate. On the other hand, it sounded a lot more PG—and more protective of Braden's privacy—than what had really happened.

Jane also didn't like the idea of Trevor talking to Hannah about his ideas. Hannah wasn't one of the main girls on the show—just someone who was lucky or unlucky (depending on your perspective) enough to have a desk across from Jane, which meant that she was almost always shot as part of the office "scenes." Hannah wasn't used to dealing with Trevor and Dana. Couldn't he leave her out of this?

Trevor had also emailed Jane some short scripts he wanted her to record later that day, at the recording studio. They were the voice-overs that Jane always narrated for the show, recapping previous episodes for each new episode. Months ago, before the series premiere, Dana had told Jane that she had been chosen for the voice-overs because she was thought to be the most relatable of the four girls. Whatever that meant.

Jane pulled out her BlackBerry, opened the email, and glanced over the lines briefly as several people got out on the fourth floor. (The elevator was moving soooo slowly today—and Jane didn't want to be late on her first day back.) One of the lines caught her attention: *Last week at the gym, Scarlett and Gaby met a couple of cute guys from Texas. Will there be a double date in their future?*

What? Scar and Gaby were going to the gym together now? Scar couldn't stand Gaby, or at least, that was what she had always claimed. Jane couldn't picture Scar and Gaby working out together—much less going out on a double date together. Had the world turned upside down while she was in Cabo?

The elevator doors finally opened on the fifth floor, and Jane stepped out. She was disoriented for a moment when she saw that the waiting area—usually so peaceful, with its dark gold walls, soft lighting, and miniature Zen garden complete with trickling waterfall—had been overrun by the PopTV crew. A couple of guys were running around with equipment, while Dana and Matt, one of the directors, were having a conversation by the receptionist's desk.

Dana snapped to attention when she saw Jane. "Good morning, Jane! Hope you had a great Christmas. Not to rush you, but we gotta get a mike on you right away."

"Not to rush you"? "Good morning"? Had someone slipped a Prozac into Dana's morning coffee?

"Fiona's all ready for you in her office," Matt added. Matt was a nice guy, even though Jane had been confused by his presence the first time they met. After all, *L.A. Candy* was a reality show. Why was a director necessary? Like someone had to "direct" her getting a cup of coffee or chatting with her friends? Jane had quickly figured out that he was there to direct the shots, not the girls. His job was to watch all the cameras at the same time on his portable screen and make sure they got the necessary footage.

Matt frowned into his headset. "Or . . . not. What, Ramon?" he said to the person on the other end. "Well, fine. Let me know when she's done with hair and makeup."

Jane knew that Fiona called in her own hair and makeup stylist on shooting days. The boss lady pretended not to care about things like her TV image, but she did.

One of the crew members came over and handed Jane a small silver microphone attached to a wire. "You wearing a bra under that?" he asked, nodding at her pale blue halter dress. That question used to make Jane blush. But she was used to it by now.

"No, it's got, like, this built-in bra. But I can tape it onto the dress."

"Great. You know the drill."

As Jane worked on the mike (it created a little humpback under her dress, which she covered with her hair), she saw the receptionist out of the corner of her eye giving her a little wave. Naomi was petite, blond, stylish, and whispered most of the time, not because she was naturally soft-spoken but because she was terrified of Fiona and took her boss's philosophy of keeping a calm, tranquil atmosphere very literally. Which was pretty hilarious, given the chaos Jane and the PopTV crew brought to the office. Jane waved back. It was nice to see a friendly face.

"Okay, Fiona's ready for you now," Matt called out to Jane. "Let's get a quick shot of you coming out of the elevators and saying hi to Natalie."

"Naomi," Naomi whispered.

"What?" Matt frowned.

"Her name's Naomi," Jane said helpfully.

"Naomi. And then Naomi will tell you that Fiona wants to see you, and you'll head on back," Matt went on.

After shooting the exciting scene for twenty minutes—they had to let several crowded elevators go by, and then a FedEx delivery guy wandered into the frame, requiring a retake—Jane was ready to go face Fiona. Well, ready*ish*.

Fiona sat behind her desk, busily typing on her computer. Two camera guys were in opposite corners of the room, filming. Forty-something and striking, Fiona was wearing one of her trademark all-black ensembles. Her freshly done hair and makeup looked lovely, especially with the help of the muted lighting, which Jane knew had taken the crew about two hours to achieve. They always had to go through this when filming in Fiona's office. The fact that she insisted they leave her office exactly the way they found it meant they couldn't leave the enormous lights in there and had to bring them in and out every time they filmed.

"Good morning, Fiona," Jane said with a nervous smile.

Fiona stopped typing and glanced up. "Good morning, Jane," she said simply, nodding toward the chair on the opposite side of her desk.

Jane sat down on one of Fiona's prized Eames chairs, set her bag on the floor, and waited. She mentally braced herself for the worst: *Your behavior has disgraced this entire company! You've made one mistake too many! You're fired! You're—*

"I have a new assignment for you," Fiona announced. "Crazy Girl has hired us to do a Valentine's Day party to launch their new drink flavor. I'm putting you in charge of it, and Hannah will be helping out. Ruby Slipper will be doing the PR, so you and Hannah will be coordinating with Gaby Garcia."

Jane was stunned. No chastisement from Fiona for leaving without notice? It was as though nothing had happened. It was business as usual. And a new assignment? With a major client like Crazy Girl?

Also, how was it that she was going to be working on the assignment with Gaby, who happened to be on *L.A. Candy*, too? Had Trevor intervened somehow?

"The budget will be . . . Why aren't you writing this all down?" Fiona demanded sharply.

"What? Oh, I'm sorry!" Flustered, Jane reached into her bag and pulled out a small notebook and pen.

Despite the unanswered questions in her mind, Jane couldn't help but feel kind of excited. Crazy Girl was a new brand of energy drink designed to appeal to a female market that might be put off by seemingly macho energy drinks like Katapult and Dragon Fuel. Even though it was new, the Crazy Girl name seemed to be all over the place. Now it would be all over a Valentine's Day party organized by her, Jane Roberts. It was pretty amazing.

Fiona proceeded to give Jane more instructions about the assignment, while Jane took notes in her nearly illegible shorthand. When Fiona was finished, Jane said, "Great. I'm on it. I'm really excited about working on this project."

"Crazy Girl is a very important new client for us, Jane. I need your full attention here."

"Absolutely."

"I haven't had a chance to discuss this with Hannah, so please fill her in."

"No problem."

As Jane put her notebook away, she remembered something. "Isn't . . . didn't we have another party scheduled for Valentine's Day? Anna Payne's wedding or recommitment ceremony or something?"

"Recommitment ceremony. And no, that's been canceled. She and her husband split up."

"Really? What happened?"

"Apparently she cheated on him with his best friend while he was in rehab."

Jane felt heat rising to her cheeks. "Okay, well, um . . . is there anything else?"

"No, that will be all," Fiona said without looking up from her computer screen.

As the camera guys started to move their equipment to film in her and Hannah's office, Jane gathered her stuff and stood up. And sat back down again. She had a few minutes between scenes, and she had something she wanted to say to

Fiona off-camera. She waited as the room slowly emptied.

"Um, Fiona?"

"Yes?" Fiona picked up her cell and began punching in a number.

"I'm . . . well, I wanted to apologize. For everything that happened, and for disappearing last week. It was really unprofessional of me, and I'm really, really sorry."

Fiona stared at Jane, then clicked her phone shut. Her dark eyes softened. "Apology accepted," she said gently. "You've been through a lot. I'm sure it hasn't been easy for you. But you're a strong, smart girl, and you'll survive this. I have faith in you."

Jane blinked. Had Fiona, the world's scariest boss (in Jane's opinion, anyway), just decided to be human?

"Thank you," Jane gushed. "Thank you so much, it's really nice of you to—"

"Yes. Well, sorry, but I've got to take this," Fiona cut in as she brought her phone to her ear. Her voice was hard again.

Jane scrambled to her feet. She'd better get out of there before Fiona decided not to be so understanding, after all. No point in pushing her luck!

"I'm so glad you're back. Things haven't been the same without you," Hannah said. She hooked a long strand of honey-blond hair over her ear. "Did you have a good Christmas?"

"Yeah, it was nice to see my parents and my sisters,"

Jane said. She glanced briefly at the two camera guys filming in the corners, then at the top of her desk, which was cluttered as always with files, fabric swatches, and magazine clippings. There was a vase of frilly peach tulips next to her Mac. "Where'd these come from?"

"Oh, I picked them up on my way in. I thought they'd cheer you up."

"Wow. That was really sweet. Thank you!"

"You're welcome!"

Jane smiled at Hannah. Hannah had started working at Fiona Chen Events shortly after Jane had. She was one of the nicest people Jane had met in L.A., and she was a good listener, too. In fact, Jane used to confide in her a lot about Jesse—not just because of her listening skills but because she was one of Jane's only friends who actually *liked* Jesse. Madison, Gaby, Scar (especially Scar), and even Braden had all advised her to stay far away from him because he was trouble. Hannah was the only person who had encouraged Jane to follow her heart. And back then, before everything blew up, Jane's heart had told her that she was falling for Jesse. That they belonged together.

"So we're gonna be working on the Crazy Girl party together," Jane said. "It's gonna be amazing."

"Definitely," Hannah agreed.

"We need to go over some details, then set up a meeting with Ruby Slipper."

"Yes! Anytime is fine with me. My schedule's pretty clear." Hannah peered at her computer monitor. That girl was always on IM at work.

Jane felt her phone vibrating and fished it out of her bag. It was a text from Dana.

CAN YOU SAY GABYS NAME WHEN YOU TALK ABOUT RUBY SLIPPER? Dana had written.

Jane ignored the text and shoved the phone back into her bag. *Guess that's confirmed,* she thought. Trevor had obviously intervened, convincing Fiona to pair Jane and Gaby up for the Crazy Girl party. The PopTV cameras would be all over their entire event-planning process from beginning to end.

"Soooo. Have you, um, talked to Jesse lately?" Hannah asked, breaking the silence of the room.

Jane shook her head. "No. I've been meaning to call him, but . . ." Her voice trailed off.

"You really should call him," Hannah told her. "I'm sure he wants to talk to you."

"I'm pretty sure he doesn't," Jane said. "I don't think he'll ever forgive me."

"You made a mistake. Everyone makes mistakes."

"Yeah, well, this wasn't just a mistake. I really screwed up, Hannah."

Then, before Jane knew what was happening, her eyes welled up. She wiped a tear off her cheek. "I really screwed up," she repeated, whispering.

Hannah got up from her desk and hurried over to Jane. She wrapped her arms around Jane's shoulders and gave her a big hug. "We all screw up once in a while," she said.

"Call Jesse. Apologize to him. You're gonna feel so much better if you do."

"I'll think about it," Jane said, wiping away another tear.

Jane remembered then that the cameras were still rolling. She had just confessed to Hannah on-camera how bad she felt about cheating on Jesse. This was what Trevor had told her to do when they spoke on the phone last night, wasn't it? Did that mean he'd put those words into her mouth? No, they were *her* words. So why did she feel a strange sense of . . . what? Being directed somehow? And had Trevor directed Hannah, too? *No, that's crazy,* she told herself. Trevor's suggestions were no different from Dana's text-messaged requests. They were simply meant to help shape the girls' conversations while they were on-camera. To make things more interesting for TV. After all, they couldn't just sit there and talk about nothing, right?

Right?

10

WHAT I NEED IS THE TRUTH

Scarlett touched the mike taped to the inside of her bra, making sure it was secure, before walking into STK. It was Monday night, and she had about a million things she'd rather be doing than attending some lame launch party for Cüt (pronounced "cute"), a new clothing line by the Japanese-American pop star Mika. When did pop stars start designing clothes? She blamed J.Lo. And Gwen Stefani. The party was a last-minute add to the shooting schedule, and Scarlett had tried to get out of it, telling Dana that she already had plans (i.e., an evening at home with some take-out Thai food and *Wuthering Heights*, which she'd been meaning to reread since Liam had brought it up).

"Scarlett, let's get a quick picture!"

A photographer was standing by the small white backdrop with the Cüt logo all over it. Scarlett had learned these backdrops were called step-and-repeats. Since being on the show and being forced to attend so many launches, openings, and premieres, Scarlett had learned a lot of new things, like that they were all basically the same event. They were at the same locations, with the same guests, and with the same photographers and reporters asking the same questions. The only things that changed were the logos on the step-and-repeat and gift bags for the guests to take home afterward. Scarlett hated posing for photos, but she was here at the party—might as well follow the party rules, which included smiling pretty for photographers and acting like she was really, really glad to be there in support of some here-today, gone-tomorrow teen idol's idea of fashion. Besides, the night was young. There was still plenty of time for rule breaking.

Inside, STK was crazy crowded. Several of the tables normally used for dining served as stages for models wearing what Scarlett assumed were clothes from the line. She saw that they had set up a DJ booth near the front door, filling the room with techno music. Waiters maneuvered their way through the thick crowd while balancing trays of tiny beef sliders and skewers of chicken satay.

Scarlett glanced around, searching for Jane. After their awkward conversation yesterday about Madison, Jane had puttered around the apartment unpacking and doing laundry, talking to her goldfish, Penny, and in general basically ignoring Scarlett. And this morning she had left for work early. Scarlett had texted her at lunchtime, asking her if she planned to be at the Cüt launch, and Jane had written back, YES. Not, YES, U 2? Or YES,

U WANNA GO 2GETHER? Just YES.

Scarlett noticed Madison at the bar, talking to some guy and looking for all the world like a high-priced hooker in her animal-print minidress and coordinating metallic platform stilettos. Scarlett felt her face go hot. She hadn't seen or spoken to Madison since before Cabo, but she had some things she wanted to say to her now. She didn't care that the cameras were there. Nothing she said to Madison would make the cut, anyway. Trevor had called last night and filled her in on his little plan for presenting the whole Jane-Braden-Jesse-*Gossip* fiasco. The sentiments Scarlett had in mind for Madison most definitely didn't fit Trevor's plan.

Scarlett crossed the room in a dozen quick strides, aware that the *L.A. Candy* cameras were following her every move. (No Liam today, though. *Sigh.*)

"Madison," Scarlett said, tapping her shoulder.

Madison turned around and looked a little surprised to see Scarlett there.

"Hey, Scarlett." Madison gave her a fake smile. "Jane didn't tell me you were coming. You want a drink?"

"I don't need a drink, you pathetic, two-faced, lying bitch. What I need is the truth."

Madison's fake smile never left her face. "About what?"

"About the fact that you gave those pictures to *Gossip*. I want to know where you got them. And why you did it."

Madison looked away, chuckling. "Guess I was wrong

about you needing a drink. You're already drunk—or crazy—or both."

"No, *you're* the one who's crazy," Scar spat out. "How could you do that to Jane?"

"I didn't do anything to Jane. I love her like a sister. I already told you"—Madison glanced at the camera—"Jesse's the one who gave those pictures to *Gossip*."

"I talked to him about it, and he said it was you."

"Oh, so you're gonna believe what Jesse says? Of course he's gonna lie about that. He's covering up for what *he* did."

"The only one who's covering up is you, you scheming—"

"*Hey!* What's going on?"

Scarlett jerked around at the sound of Jane's angry voice. Jane and Hannah, that girl from her office, were standing there. Scarlett wasn't sure what to think of Hannah. Was she friend or foe? She had met her only once, at Jesse's twenty-first birthday party at Goa. But she had seen Hannah on several *L.A. Candy* episodes, giving Jane encouraging advice about Jesse. Which was bizarre. Didn't Hannah know about Jesse's messed-up past? Had she ever even talked to him? Or was she too mesmerized by his (even Scarlett had to admit) gorgeous face to care?

At the moment, Hannah looked anxious as her brown eyes shifted between Scarlett and Madison. Jane looked . . . well, pissed off. But she would get over it once Scarlett forced Madison to come clean.

"Janie, I'm so glad you're here! Madison and I were just talking about why she likes to ruin the lives of her 'friends,'" Scarlett said, jabbing a finger in Madison's direction.

"You're insane," Madison shot back. "Jane, she's insane."

Jane frowned at Scarlett. "Scar, cut it out. Please just drop it."

"I am *not* gonna drop it! Madison's lying to you! She's trying to hurt you, and I'm not gonna—"

"Hey, what'd I miss?" Gaby pranced up to the group, patting her smooth light brown updo. "You all seem kinda stressed. Did they run outta gift bags or something?"

"Hi, Gaby, I'm Hannah." Hannah spoke up quickly, clearly trying to defuse the situation by acting as if nothing were wrong. "I don't know if you remember me, but we met at Goa."

Gaby nodded. "Oh, yeah. At Jesse's birthday party. Aren't you that girl he was flirting with?"

Hannah blushed. "Um, no. I'm Jane's friend from work. In fact, we're all gonna be working on the Crazy Girl party together."

"Cool," Gaby said, her gaze wandering to a passing waiter who was carrying a tray of Cosmos. "Ohhhh!" She reached over and took two.

"I really like Mika's designs," Jane said, her own attempt at changing the subject. "Especially her dresses. I love that one with the beaded neckline."

"You would look soooo pretty in that," Hannah said eagerly. *She's just trying to help Jane steer the topic away from Madison,* Scarlett thought, annoyed. *Which at this point puts her in the "foe" category.*

"So would you!" Jane exclaimed to Hannah. "And what about the shirt with the yellow—"

Jane stopped abruptly. The color drained from her face as she stared over Hannah's shoulder at something—or someone—across the room.

Scarlett followed Jane's gaze to see what had thrown her, and saw Jesse Edwards posing at the step-and-repeat with some brunette hanging all over him. Behind the official photographer were several other photographers, jockeying for position to get a clear shot of Jesse and his date.

Hannah and Madison took note of Jesse's arrival, too. Hannah looked worried and whispered something in Jane's ear as she reached down and squeezed her hand. Madison looked . . . What *was* that expression on her face? Panic? Scarlett allowed herself a brief moment of satisfaction. She knew she was right about Madison. The girl was terrified that Jesse was going to tell everyone the truth about what had happened. In front of Jane. On camera (not that Trevor would let it make it onto the air . . .).

Finally, Scarlett thought.

As for Gaby, she was oblivious to what was going on around her. "Ohmigod, look at that pretty dress!" she said, pointing to the piece of sea green dental floss wrapped around Jesse's date. "Do you guys think I could pull off that color?"

"Excuse me," Jane mumbled. She started pushing through a crowd of people, toward the ladies' room. She was obviously upset. Scarlett started to follow her, except that Madison actually *blocked her way* and then shouted, "Wait, Janie! I'm coming with you!"

Jane stopped, turned, and smiled gratefully at Madison. She stretched out her hand. "Thanks, Madison."

Madison threw a triumphant smile in Scarlett's direction as she took Jane's hand, and the two of them headed to the ladies' room together.

Scarlett knotted her fists. *Janie? Did Madison seriously just call Jane Janie?*

11

MY IMAGE NEEDS TO BE SAVED NOW?

"Soooo," Gaby said, picking at her manicure. "Who was that girl Jesse brought to the party last night? Does anyone know her name?"

Hannah stared at Gaby, stunned. Jane sucked in a deep breath.

Gaby, Hannah, and Jane had just spent the better part of their morning in the massive reception area at Ruby Slipper brainstorming ideas and locations for the Crazy Girl Valentine's Day party (on-camera, of course). Unfortunately, Gaby had a very short attention span and kept steering the subject to other stuff, like how cute her office decor was ("look at my cute phone!"). If only Dana would text Gaby as often as she seemed to text Jane, telling her to focus on work, already. Of course, Jane would rather talk about how Gaby had told her boss that everything on her desk *had* to be cute than about Jesse's date last night.

"Weren't you kinda bothered when she and Jesse were

making out?" Gaby asked Jane.

Jane reached up and twirled her hair around her index finger. It had been a nervous habit since she was little. Why was Gaby bringing this up? And on-camera, no less?

Last night had been bad enough. Jane had hidden out in the ladies' room at STK with Madison for what seemed like forever, though it was probably closer to fifteen minutes, trying to recover from her shock at seeing Jesse (with a *date*) and to gather the courage to approach him and apologize. Madison had been so great, holding her hand and giving her a pep talk. She'd advised Jane to hold off on talking to Jesse—she thought it was too soon—but Jane had decided to go for it anyway. Madison had looked genuinely concerned.

Except . . . when Jane emerged from the ladies' room and headed in Jesse's direction, their eyes locked . . . and then he turned to his date and kissed her.

Worst of all, the cameras had captured *everything.*

Gaby's phone rang. She frowned and picked it up. "Hey, Edgar. Huh? 'Kay, I'll be right there." She hung up.

"What's up?" Jane asked her.

"Dunno. My boss wants to talk to me about something. Back in a sec."

After Gaby left, Hannah leaned forward and touched Jane's arm. "Hey, are you okay?"

"Yeah." Jane shrugged. She glanced at the artwork that covered the walls: several framed photos of different pairs of red shoes and one of the oversize stills from the movie *The Wizard of Oz*. The red ruby slippers. "It's just hard . . . you know, seeing Jesse with someone else."

"I know," Hannah said. "But that girl wasn't like his new girlfriend or anything. You could tell he wasn't even into her. I saw him looking at you. It's obvious that he misses you and is trying to make you jealous. You hurt him and now he's trying to hurt you back."

"Doubt it," Jane said, even though she wanted to believe Hannah's words. "How could he miss me, after what I did?"

"Maybe he's ready to forgive you. You two love each other. You belong together, right?"

"Hmm. I don't know." Which was the truth. These days, she had no idea what—or who—she wanted.

"Seriously!" Hannah persisted.

Jane looked at Hannah and smiled sadly. "New Year's Eve's the day after tomorrow. It's like, out with the old, in with the new, right? I should move on. Date new guys."

"But are you really ready to move on from Jesse?" Hannah asked.

"I'm not sure," Jane said after a moment. "Maybe."

"Hmmm . . . that's convincing." Hannah grinned at her teasingly. "I think you've just got to get up the nerve to talk to him."

"Yeah, well, that didn't go so well last night," Jane said drily. She pulled her BlackBerry out of her bag. She wanted to focus on work, which was a lot easier than focusing on her messed-up love life. "I think I have the Tropicana event contact person's number. Maybe we could go by there later today or tomorrow and check out the space?"

"Good idea."

But as Jane pulled up her address book, her thoughts drifted back to Jesse. Okay, so she did miss him. A *lot*. The problem was, she was still more than a little hung up on his best friend. The whole thing was a total mess.

Last summer, during Jane's initial interview-slash-audition with Dana and a casting person about *L.A. Candy*, they had asked her why she moved to L.A.—and she had said, "To be uncomfortable." She had explained that she was eager to challenge herself and push the boundaries of her safe, comfortable existence.

She felt like screaming, *Okay, enough!* Things had gotten as uncomfortable as she could possibly stand.

The question was, *Now* what? The good news was, she still had her job. And, for better or for worse, she still had a place on the show. Even though she continued to have mixed feelings about being on TV, she had committed to finishing out the season, at least. After that . . . who knew? It might be nice to go back to her *real* real life, when her closest friends weren't also her costars and she didn't have to see her massive, smiling face on billboards up and down Sunset Boulevard as she drove to and from work. Not to mention getting her privacy back.

The bad news was, her love life was a train wreck. Her friendship with Scar wasn't going so well, either. And as far as she knew, the world continued to think of her as "Jane Ho."

She needed a miracle.

On her way home from work that night, Jane's phone rang. She glanced at the screen and saw that it was D. *D!* She still hadn't called him back from last week, but she *did* want to talk to him.

She picked up on the third ring. "Hey! Hi!"

"*MISS JANE!*" D screamed. "*OMFG!*" Jane pulled the phone away from her ear. "I've worn out my keypad trying to reach you!" he went on. "Where have you been? No, ignore that. First, are you okay? I've been so worried about you, I gained, like, five pounds with all the stress-related binge eating I've been doing. I used to think that diamonds were a girl's best friend, but now I realize it's carbohydrates. Seriously, I have a French baguette at home sporting a matching friendship bracelet."

"I'm fine," Jane reassured him. "I went to Cabo and then to my parents' for Christmas."

"Are you still mad at me?"

"Why would I be mad at you? The pictures weren't your fault."

"No, but I should've known Veronica was up to

something," D said bitterly. "I've gotta tell you, sweetie, I've been digging around trying to figure out how she got those pictures."

Jane gulped. Did she want to hear this, or didn't she? "Did you find anything?" she said hesitantly.

"Nothing. She's super-secretive. Like, FBI-and-CIA secretive. But I'm working on it. I promise I'm gonna get to the bottom of this."

"'Kay, thanks."

"Another thing. Listen, baby cakes, you've gotta whip your publicist into shape. I know you've got a lot going on right now. But those covers and headlines are killing you. No offense; ya know I'm just looking out for you."

"Yeah, I know," Jane replied. "I don't have a publicist, but PopTV has a publicity department, and I'm sure they're taking care of the—"

"*WHAT?*" D screamed. "No, no, no! The network's publicist looks out for one client and one client only: the network. *You* need your *own* publicist who looks out only for *you*."

"Um . . . okay?"

"Your agent should be able to hook you up with one ASAP."

Jane laughed. "Um . . . I don't have an agent."

Jane pulled the phone from her ear again as D began screaming. After he'd calmed down, she said, "Okay. So I need to find an agent and a publicist right away. How am I supposed to know how to do that?"

"Jane! This is an emergency! You can't be as big a star as you are and not have representation—especially with the media barracudas circling you. What are you doing New Year's Eve?"

"I think we're all going to a party at h.wood. We're filming."

"Perfect, I'll swing by there, too. And I'll invite some friends to come with. R.J. is one of the best agents in the business. And Sam is a great publicist who is amazing at saving images."

"So my image needs to be saved now?"

"Jane, your image needs CPR. We're talking code red. Crash carts are being requested. We're . . . Well, you get the point. Just set aside five minutes for your old friend D Thursday night, 'kay? By the time we ring in the New Year, you're gonna be set up with the best representation in the business."

"Thanks, D."

"Don't mention it."

Jane couldn't help thinking about the phrase *New year, new you*, and how it might be taking on a whole new meaning for her.

12

NEW YEAR'S RESOLUTIONS OR SOMETHING

Madison glanced at her reflection in a window next to the h.wood bar, admiring the way her metallic dress appeared to have been poured onto her like liquid silver, leaving little to the imagination. She looked hot! She hoped that the guys working the cameras would notice and take lots of extra footage of her tonight. She had caught some of them checking her out in the past. Actually all of them except the one with the bandanna—Liam?—who never seemed to give her the time of day. Whatever. He was most likely gay, or nearsighted, or both. No matter, she didn't see him here tonight.

Madison picked up a glass of champagne from a passing waiter's tray and took a sip. She glanced around the dimly lit, very crowded room. They were filming at a table outside, but it was cold, so she was waiting inside until they finished setting up. Dana had sent out an email for them to bring jackets, but Madison wasn't fond of layers, and she knew skin was always the best accessory.

Gaby was at the other end of the bar, wasting her time with some emo loser. That girl had such foul taste in men. Still, Madison noticed that Gaby looked kind of pretty in her mauve flutter-sleeve dress and with her light brown hair arranged in loose curls. Madison actually sort of liked Gaby, who was easy and fun to hang out with. But lately she had been focusing all her attention on Jane, so she hadn't seen as much of Gaby as usual.

There was no sign of Scarlett. Good. She was a wild card and loose cannon, not to mention a bitch. Madison didn't need another situation like the one at STK. The girl had no manners. She didn't know how to act in a dignified manner and wasn't bothered by causing a scene. While Madison didn't mind all eyes on her, she didn't want Scarlett pointing any more fingers at her.

But where was Jane? Madison scanned the room and narrowed her eyes as she spotted her faux friend across the room, talking to two guys and a woman. One of the guys looked familiar: short, Asian American, sporting a shiny, seventies-style violet tux with wide black lapels. Was that . . . Veronica Bliss's assistant at *Gossip*?

Madison frowned. That wasn't good. She didn't need Jane getting close to anyone on Veronica's staff, much less her assistant.

Madison wasn't sure who the other guy and the woman were. The guy was fortyish, dressed in a navy suit, conservative-looking. The woman was super-tall, with a long, messy cloud of auburn hair and a well-tailored black dress. PopTV executives? Someone's parents?

Only one way to find out: go over and introduce herself. Why not, right? It was important for her to keep tabs on Jane, especially now that she was so close to convincing Jane of some crucial "facts." Such as, *Scarlett is mad because she wants to be your only friend in the world, and now you and I are friends, so she's trying to come between us.* And *Jesse's no good for you. He's moved on, so you should, too. You deserve way better.*

It was harder convincing Jane of the "fact" that either Jesse or Scarlett had given the pictures to *Gossip*. But that wasn't so important now, since Jane didn't seem to want to think about the pictures anymore. It had worked out nicely that way. All Madison wanted was to get more airtime on the show, and eventually the *most* airtime on the show, displacing Jane altogether. That meant keeping Jane close to her side and continuing to provide Veronica with dirt about the soon-to-be-former "America's sweetheart."

It occurred to Madison that the season one finale was coming up soon. Maybe if she worked efficiently and dug up lots of dirt on Jane, Veronica would run a couple of quick pieces on her in the magazine, boosting her visibility? Which would convince Trevor to give Madison more scenes in the season finale? *Perfect.*

Madison took another swallow of champagne and started heading toward Jane and her mysterious entourage. But as she was making her way over, she heard her cell vibrating in her tiny beaded clutch. She extracted it and checked the screen. It was a text from Dana to her, Jane, and Gaby: READY 2 START SHOOTING IN ABOUT 5 MIN. CAN U 3 GO TO UR TABLE & SIT DOWN?

Madison saw Jane's group disband with a flurry of cheek kisses and handshakes. Then Jane headed outside to their table. Madison noticed that Gaby was still hanging on the emo guy. Gaby wasn't very good about checking her cell or following Dana's directions, not because she was stubborn and rebellious (like Scarlett), but because her tiny brain really couldn't process too many thoughts at the same time.

Madison thought about grabbing Gaby but instead just headed outside, too. Jane, who was already seated, looked up and smiled when she saw Madison approaching the table. "Hey, Madison!" she called out cheerfully. "Happy New Year! Your dress is so pretty!"

"Thanks. Your dress is nice, too," Madison lied, because seriously, Jane didn't have enough up there to pull off a strapless. The piercing blue color *did* complement her eyes perfectly, though. "So what's going on? Make some new friends?"

"Huh?" Jane asked.

"I saw you talking to some randoms."

"Oh, yeah! That was my friend Diego. He was introducing me to some friends of his who want to represent me."

"Represent you? What are they, lawyers?"

"No. R.J.'s an agent. And Samantha—Sam—she's a

publicist. D told me I needed my own agent and publicist. I wasn't so sure at first; it sounds so Hollywood! But after talking to them, I'm kinda into the idea. They seem really great. R.J. says he can take a look at my PopTV contract. And Sam's got all these ideas about turning my image around in the magazines. I'd barely said hi to her when she started telling me about her plan for me. She's really smart."

Madison tried to keep her smile frozen on her face. *Don't do it,* she told herself. *Don't freak out.*

This was the worst news she had heard all day . . . or week. She had gone out of her way to destroy Jane's nice-girl image. Unfortunately, people like R.J. and Sam would work really hard to do the exact opposite. And they did this sort of thing professionally. This wasn't exactly Madison's first rodeo, but she still hadn't acquired the experience it took to cause the kind of damage she had in mind. This was not good.

"Hey, you okay?" Jane said, distracting her.

Madison nodded. "Mmm. I'm just tired. My trainer really worked me at the gym today."

"Wow, good for you." Jane peered over her shoulder. "Have you seen Scar? It's not like her to be this late."

"She probably bailed on the party because she's pissed off," Madison said. She had to stop thinking about the agent and publicist and focus on the here and now. Jane had just given her the opening to get in some serious Scarlett bashing. "I didn't wanna tell you, but the other night, after STK, she called me and yelled at me some more, telling me to stay away from you," she lied.

Jane frowned. "She did?"

"Yeah. I don't know what her problem is. Honestly, I think she's, like, obsessed with you and can't stand the thought of you having other friends. It's kinda weird. Doesn't she have any other friends?"

"Yeah." Jane looked in the other direction and began playing with her hair.

"Hey, girls!" Gaby sat down next to Madison. "Did they start filming yet? I want to check my makeup before the cameras start rolling."

"Not yet," Madison replied. "Any minute."

Gaby reached into her clutch for a compact. "So what'd I miss?"

"Jane has a fancy new agent and publicist. Isn't that so cool?" Madison faked a smile.

"Well, not exactly. I just met them tonight. I'm still thinking about it," Jane corrected her. "I wanna talk to my parents about it, too."

"What kind of agent? And I thought the show did our publicity," Gaby said, swiping a coat of glossy pink over her lips.

Madison's cell began buzzing, simultaneously with Jane's and Gaby's. Madison glanced at her screen. OKAY, WERE STARTING NOW. CD U GIRLS TALK RE NEW YEAR'S RESOLUTIONS OR SOMETHING? Dana had written.

Jane slid her phone over to Gaby so she could read

the message, too. "New Year's resolutions?" Gaby said, scrunching up her face. "You mean like, 'I'm gonna lose ten pounds' or 'I'm gonna try Botox' or 'I'm not gonna hook up with guys named Spike anymore'?"

"Spike?" Jane laughed. "Who's Spike?"

Madison was about to pipe up when she saw more bad news (although it was difficult to top the agent and publicist) walking through the door: Jesse Edwards—again. With another new girl on his arm. Twice in one week? Was it a coincidence, or had Trevor arranged for Jesse and Jane to "accidentally" run into each other at yet another club where they were filming?

Madison had managed to avoid him at STK. And keep Jane away from him. But could she avoid him again? The last time they'd spoken had been several weeks ago, when she'd shown him the pictures and tried to get him to deliver them to *Gossip*. In retrospect, maybe that wasn't the best plan she'd ever had.

Besides Veronica, he was the only other person in the world who knew for sure that Madison was behind the whole Jane-Braden scandal. And that was one other person too many.

"OMG!" Gaby cried out, pointing. "Jane, don't look, but Jesse's here!"

Jane immediately craned her neck to see. She bit her lip.

"Just ignore them," Madison said, touching her arm. "Pretend like we're having a really funny conversation."

Jane didn't reply. She seemed to be considering

something. "I'm gonna go talk to him," she said finally. "This time, I won't let him ignore me. I'm going to apologize, no matter what it takes."

"That is so not a good idea," Madison blurted out. "It's New Year's Eve. We're supposed to have fun. Talking to Jesse will only bring you down. Why don't we just have some champagne and—"

"I have to do this, Madison. I need to start my year fresh," Jane insisted. And before Madison could stop her, Jane rose to her feet and followed Jesse and his lady du jour, who had wandered inside.

Madison picked up her champagne glass and swallowed the rest of it, trying to fight the surge of panic swelling inside her. What if Jesse told Jane the truth about the pictures? Then what?

13

YOU'RE PERFECT JUST THE WAY YOU ARE

Scarlett leaned against the door marked 1C, listening, wondering if she should ring the bell again or just turn around and walk away. On her way out, she'd forgotten to grab the six-pack she'd bought earlier, so she was empty-handed. Maybe she should find a liquor store and come back? She could hear voices, laughter, loud music, an occasional noisemaker. It was twenty after eleven, forty minutes until the New Year. Maybe she should just bail . . . go home and curl up in bed with a good book . . . or rush over to h.wood, where Jane, Madison, and Gaby were shooting, and where Dana (no doubt) was calling Scarlett every ten seconds, demanding to know where the hell she was. Too bad Scarlett had turned off her cell. *Oops, sorry, Dana!*

The air was chilly outside, with just a touch of a breeze that made the palm fronds overhead sway gently back and forth. Scarlett glanced over her shoulder at Beachwood Drive. She had never been to this neighborhood before; it was kinda low-key, with nice, not-too-fancy apartment buildings as well as bars and cafés that looked more comfy than trendy. Scarlett liked it.

Or maybe she just liked Liam, so she would naturally like where he lived?

The door opened. "Scarlett?"

Scarlett spun around to find Liam standing there, smiling at her. Wow, he had a nice smile. His lips curled up just so, and his blue eyes twinkled like he and she were sharing a private joke that no one else in the world could possibly understand.

Do something! Scarlett told herself. *Say something!*

"Oh. Hey. Yeah, so I was thinking I should head over to the store, because I realized I forgot to bring anything," Scarlett said, lowering her gaze.

Liam reached for her arm and steered her inside. "No worries. We've got plenty of stuff. Come on in; I'll introduce you to everybody. I'm really glad you came."

"Oh. Okay."

Scarlett let Liam lead her into the front hallway, and then to the living room, all the while trying to ignore the slow heat that was gathering in the place where his fingers lightly touched her elbow. There were about thirty or forty people scattered around the sprawling apartment, which had wood floors, high ceilings, and an eclectic bachelor style straight out of a flea market. Black-and-white photographs in mismatched frames hung on the brightly painted walls, and stacks of books covered an assortment of vintage-looking tables. A few people nodded and waved as Liam and Scarlett walked past. No one seemed to be fazed by her, which was a refreshing change. Scarlett liked flying under the radar, especially after her first semester at USC, where half her classmates wanted to be her BFF (for being on TV) and the rest scorned her mercilessly (for being on TV).

"Can I get you a beer or something?" Liam offered.

"Um, no, I'm good." *Huh?* When did Scarlett Harp ever say no to a beer?

"Food? We've got pizza, wings, Chinese."

"Sounds great. I'm starving."

"Well, let's take care of that."

Liam loaded up a couple of paper plates in the kitchen, then guided Scarlett back through the thick crowd, introducing her to various friends along the way. He had apparently graduated from UCLA last spring, so a lot of the guests were fellow alums. Everyone seemed friendly, pleasant, interesting. But Scarlett couldn't help but tune most of them out. It was like Liam was the only one in the room with her most of the time.

Scarlett and Liam ended up on the back terrace, which overlooked a small yard. Tiki torches flickered in the darkness, illuminating some flowering shrubs and a stone path. They sat down on wooden patio chairs and began digging into their food.

"Mmm, cold shrimp-fried rice, my favorite," Scarlett teased.

"Yeah, well, we're pretty fancy here," Liam replied.

"So, what was your major at UCLA?"

"Film. Cinematography. I wanna get into movies someday."

"That's probably more interesting than filming a bunch of girls shopping for nail polish."

Liam grinned. "Yeah, but definitely not as interesting as filming a girl having Christmas Eve dinner with Mom and Dad in Aspen."

Scarlett laughed. "Now you know why I need about thirty years of therapy."

"You? Nah. You're perfect just the way you are."

At Liam's words, Scarlett felt the warm, nervous, giddy feeling in the pit of her stomach that she'd had during the packing-for-Aspen shoot. She picked up a cold egg roll and bit into it, trying to buy a few seconds of time so she could calm down. She tried to think of something else, something other than the warmth/nervousness/giddiness, and the way Liam's blue eyes were fixed on her face, like he knew exactly what she was thinking about (or trying *not* to think about).

Small talk, Scarlett told herself. *Try some small talk.*

"Yeah, so I'm in my freshman year at USC," she began.

"Really? You mean the same USC where I've been filming you for months?" Liam teased her.

Scarlett blushed. Of course he knew where she went to college. What was *wrong* with her? "Oh, yeah."

"Sorry. So you like it there?"

"You've been there with me the past few months—what do you think?" Before he had a chance to respond, Scarlett realized she didn't want him to answer that question, so she said, "It's okay," and shrugged. "My parents gave me a hard time about not going to a better school."

"Did *you* want to go to a better school?"

"I wanted to stay in the area, you know? I mean, Jane and I had a plan. We'd move to L.A. together, she'd get a job in event planning, and I'd go to school."

"So it all worked out, right?"

"Yeah, except signing on to do a TV show wasn't part of the plan."

"What, you're not into having your life 'created and produced by Trevor Lord'?"

"Exactly!"

Liam nodded. "From where I'm standing, it's like you're a character in a novel, and you're not sure you like the plot. In fact, sometimes you *hate* the plot. But there's nothing you can do about it, because you're not writing it."

Did the guy have to be so smart about everything?

About *her*? "Yeah, that's kinda how it feels sometimes," Scarlett admitted.

Liam leaned forward in his chair, until their knees were almost touching. "You could just think of the show as a learning opportunity," he said slowly. "You're learning what you want and don't want for yourself. You're learning what you want and don't want out of your friendships. You're learning about the wonderful world of television." He laughed. "And in the end, you can just bail if that's what's right for you, a lot smarter and a little richer, and you can even write a screenplay making fun of all us Hollywood assholes and become a whole *lot* richer."

"You're definitely *not* a Hollywood asshole," Scarlett said, impressed.

They stared at each other for a moment. There was a sudden commotion inside the house, people shouting, "Ten! Nine! Eight!" But Scarlett barely noticed it, because Liam's face was so close to hers now, and she could smell the warm, musky scent of his skin, and maybe it would be a good idea if she stood up right now and said good night and went straight home. . . .

"I'm glad you don't think I'm a Hollywood asshole," Liam said softly. "Does that mean you're going to let me kiss you at midnight?"

"What?!" Scarlett started to say, but it was too late, because Liam's lips were already on hers, just as the party guests were screaming, "Happy New Year!" and the noisemakers were going off. As Scarlett leaned into the kiss, she realized she had never fully understood the meaning of the word "swoon" before. But now she did. She was swooning. And it was awesome.

14

CAN U EVER 4GIVE ME?

As Jane walked toward Jesse, she was barely aware of the other guests at h.wood, drinking champagne and laughing and dancing to "Pon de Replay" by Rihanna. Some of their eyes followed her, and she could hear people whispering. (Was it, "Ohmigod, it's that girl from the show"? Or was it, "Ohmigod, it's that slut from the magazines"?) She dropped her gaze as she walked through the crowd.

The room was so festive, with long silver streamers hanging from the ceiling; clusters of silver, gold, and black balloons floating up from the tables; and glittery confetti sprinkled across the floor. But Jane didn't feel very festive right now. She felt terrified. Her heart was racing. Because she was about to do one of the hardest things she had ever done in her life. On-camera. She wished the moment could be more private, but she didn't care anymore. She *had* to talk to Jesse, cameras or no cameras.

She went through a bunch of opening lines in her mind.

Hey, listen, we need to talk.

I know you probably hate my guts.

Are you okay?

I've been so worried about you.

I miss you. (No, scratch that one.)

I'm so, so sorry.

This was actually not the first time she'd tried to reach out to Jesse since the *Gossip* incident. Or the second time, if you counted Monday night at STK. She had started to text him on Christmas Eve—there was something about the holidays that made a girl emotional and sentimental about ex-boyfriends—writing, CAN U EVER 4GIVE ME? MERRY CHRISTMAS, JANE.

She had stared at the message forever, her fingers hovering over the Send button. In the end, she had just deleted it, wishing she could be braver, feeling dumb because she was such a coward.

And now . . . now she was about to face Jesse in person, and look him in the eye, and deliver the apology of her life. Because she was pretty sure that what she had done to him was the worst thing she had done to anybody, ever.

As Jane got closer to Jesse, she saw his date whisper something in his ear. (Could her hot-pink, obnoxious bubble dress be any shorter?) Giggling, Ms. Bubble Dress tucked her clutch under her arm and took off. Good, the coast was clear.

Ms. Bubble Dress had barely disappeared into the swarm of partyers—Jane saw her grab some girl's arm, and the two of them went off to the ladies' room, talking closely—when Jesse turned, cell in hand, and noticed Jane. He stared at her, and his beautiful, familiar light brown eyes lit up with . . . pure rage. Ugh. Jane wondered if he was going to storm off without giving her a chance to speak. But he didn't move.

"Hey." Jane approached him, giving him a tentative little wave. *Yeah, brilliant opening line.*

Jesse didn't say anything. He tucked his phone into the pocket of his sleek black jacket. Jesse always dressed so well, unlike Braden, who was always more at home in faded tees and jeans, yet who still managed to look hot anyway.

Jane stopped in front of him and tilted her head up to look at him. At five-foot-five, she was at least seven inches shorter than him. "Can I talk to you for a minute?" she asked him.

Jesse's jaw clenched. "What about?"

"I just wanted to . . . I wanted to say I'm sorry. I know you'll probably never forgive me, and I don't expect you to. But I wanted you to know how bad I feel about what happened."

Jesse glared at her, not saying anything. The volume in

the room began to rise—people were shouting, noisemakers were going off, the DJ was making an announcement—but Jane wasn't paying attention. Getting through to Jesse was all she could think about.

"It really hurt me when you were all over that girl at your birthday party," Jane went on. "Because I thought that you and I were . . . well, I thought that you really cared about me and . . . Anyway, after that night, I wasn't sure what was gonna happen to us. I was so mad at you. I know that's no excuse for what I did. I . . . I *have* no excuse, and . . . and . . ."

Jane's throat burned as her eyes brimmed with tears. She covered her face with her hands, shaking, trying to stop from breaking down in public, and with the camera guy standing just a few feet away from her, filming everything. It was all catching up to her now: these last few crazy months, meeting Jesse at his and Braden's house party, falling for Jesse, falling apart when she thought he wasn't the guy for her, after all . . . and then Braden coming over to comfort her, offering her a friendly hug that somehow turned into a kiss that somehow turned into more. . . .

Jane felt Jesse's hand on her shoulder. "Hey," he said in a voice that was gruff and tender at the same time. "You okay?"

Jane sniffed and nodded. She took a moment to try to compose herself. She needed to get this out.

"I know I don't have any right to ask this," Jane said, gazing up at him. "But do you think that we could be friends someday?"

Jesse looked away. "I don't know. Maybe. I'll think about it."

Jane nodded. At least there was hope. That was all she could ask for. She had no idea if she was meant to be with Jesse as *more* than friends. But she couldn't imagine not having him in her life. Friendship was better than nothing at all.

Wiping away a tear, Jane realized that everyone in the room was yelling, "Ten! Nine! Eight!" And then Jesse's date appeared out of nowhere and wrapped her skinny, spray-tanned arms around his neck. The countdown continued: "Three! Two! One! *Happy New Year!*" Confetti rained down to a symphony of noisemakers and popping champagne corks and that New Year's song they always played (what did "Auld Lang Syne" even mean?), and Ms. Bubble Dress stood on her tippy-toes and pressed her artificially plumped lips against his lips. Jane's heart sank even farther. She should go. But Jesse kind of drew back a little, even as Ms. Bubble Dress kept trying to kiss him, and then Jane realized that he was looking over the girl's shoulder at *her.* Their eyes met, and she mouthed the words, *I'm sorry*, again, as if she couldn't say them enough, which she couldn't, and he kind of smiled at her, as if he were trying to let her know that maybe, just maybe, things were going to be okay between them after all.

Which made this the best New Year's Eve ever. Even though her life was still a crazy, tangled-up mess.

15

LIE UPON LIE

Scarlett groaned and rubbed her eyes as sunlight flooded her field of vision. What time was it? She glanced over at the alarm clock, which flashed 11:25 a.m. Eleven twenty-five a.m.? How could it be so late in the morning already? Her head felt cloudy, like she had gotten only a couple hours of sleep.

Wait! WTF?

Scarlett did a double take. Where was her beaten-up, retro, turquoise blue alarm clock? This alarm clock was sleek and white and had an iPod dock on top. And now that she thought about it, she didn't own sheets the color of Cocoa Puffs, either.

She turned slowly, nervously, to check out the other side of the bed.

Liam was lying there, fast asleep.

Scarlett sucked in a deep breath, trying not to panic.

What was he doing there? Wait, no—what was *she* doing here?

She had to get out right now, before he woke up. She searched the room quickly, trying to locate her clothes. *Oh.* She was still wearing them. And upon closer inspection, she realized that Liam was still wearing his, too.

And then it all came back to her.

After the amazing kiss they had shared at the stroke of midnight, a bunch of people spilled out onto the terrace with bottles of champagne. She and Liam had escaped to his room and proceeded to stay up for hours, watching old movies on cable . . . and making out . . . and talking . . . and making out . . . and eating Ben & Jerry's out of the carton . . . and making out . . . and playing Wii tennis . . . and making out. She hadn't intended to spend the night with him; in fact, she remembered thinking at 1 a.m. (and at 2 a.m. and 3 a.m.) that really, it was soooo late and she should go, and that maybe Jane would be home from the lame h.wood party.

But obviously Scarlett had fallen asleep on Liam's Cocoa Puff–colored sheets instead. *With Liam.* After a long (and, admittedly, really fun) night of activities that were more "datey" than "casual hookup." They had talked a lot and she hadn't had a single drink. The problem was, Scarlett wasn't into "datey." She didn't even remember the last time she'd given a guy her real phone number, much less her real name.

Now all she had to do was make her escape before it was too late.

Scarlett glanced at Liam again. Still asleep. He looked really cute sleeping, and she was kind of tempted to lean over and kiss him.

Scarlett shook her head. She had to focus. The question was, should she just slip away? Or should she leave a note? Something casual and noncommittal along the lines of, *Had to run. See you around!*

She was carefully trying to slip out of bed when Liam's eyes blinked open. He smiled lazily at her. "Good morning."

"Oh! Hey! Hi! I was just"—Scarlett jumped out of the bed and started looking around the room—"leaving. I was trying to find my, uh, shoes. Oh, there they are! Shoes! Well, listen, thanks for everything, and, uh, I'll see you later!"

Liam sat up. "Wait, Scarlett? Do you want coffee, or—"

"No, I'm good. Thanks, but I've gotta go. I'm really, really late for this thing I forgot I had to do today. They're expecting me. Bye!"

Scarlett didn't even wait for his reply as she scooped up her sandals from the floor and bolted out of the room.

It was almost noon when Scarlett walked through the front door of the apartment. She found Jane curled up on the couch, watching TV in her sweats and drinking a glass of OJ.

"Hey," Jane called out. "Where've you been?"

Scarlett threw her keys on the front hall table and sat

down next to Jane. "What? I went to this party at a friend's house and I fell asleep on the couch." No reason to tell Jane *which* friend, or that by "couch" she meant "bed."

Jane gave her a strange look. "You know we were shooting at h.wood last night, right? Dana tried to call you, like, a hundred times. I tried to call you, too. Why weren't you answering your phone?"

"Battery died," Scarlett said, feeling increasingly uncomfortable piling lie upon lie with her best friend. "Ohmigod, I totally forgot about the shoot. I'd better call Dana and apologize. How was the party?"

"Soooo weird," Jane replied. She picked up the remote and began clicking through channels. "Jesse showed up."

"The man-whore? *Again?* He was at that party at STK, too. What, is he stalking you?"

"Hardly. But we talked. I apologized to him for, you know, for everything."

Scarlett, who didn't think Jane had anything to apologize for, since Jesse had screwed up first, arched her eyebrows. "And?"

"He started out really mad. But then he kinda . . . I don't know. I think that he came around."

An image of a couple kissing flashed across the TV screen. Scarlett winced. Déjà vu. It was a scene from one of the movies she and Liam had watched last night on cable: *Casablanca*. Jane was watching the television with a wistful half smile.

Scarlett was starting to get a bad feeling. "Janie? Be

honest. You're not seriously thinking about getting back together with Jesse, are you? I don't care how hot or charming or rich he is; you and I both know that deep down, he's a mess, and—"

"Scar!" Jane snapped. "Stop it! And stop saying mean things about him! He's my . . . he *was* my boyfriend, and I care about him, and it's really, really obnoxious of you to keep saying this stuff." She added, "Seriously, I'm so sick of your negativity lately. It's extreme, even for you. You need to lighten up."

Scarlett folded her arms across her chest, trying to resist the impulse to shake some sense into Jane. They'd argued about Jesse throughout much of his and Jane's (brief) relationship. No matter how hard Scarlett had tried to convince Jane of the very obvious fact that Jesse was a C-list celebuspawn who loved girls, drinking, drugs, and his own press more than he could possibly love Jane, her BFF had steadfastly defended him. She was still defending him now. "Okay, whatever. Sorry."

Jane sipped her OJ in silence and clicked to some random game show on TV. Scarlett could tell that she was still pissed. "So . . . how was the rest of your evening?" she said, trying to change the subject.

"Good," Jane replied, staring at the screen.

"What'd you do?"

Jane shrugged. "Madison and Gaby and I stayed at the party till, like, two thirty, and then we all went back to Madison's. And then a bunch of us went to Toast for breakfast. It was Madison's idea, even though she barely ate anything. Like two blueberries or something. She says she's on a diet, which is insane, since she's, like, a size negative two."

Madison, Madison, Madison. Scarlett wasn't sure whose name she hated hearing more—Jesse's or Madison's. Probably Madison's. Actually, *definitely* Madison's. Jesse might be a man-whore, but Madison was a sabotaging bitch who was out to ruin Jane's life.

Jane began clicking through channels again. "So tell me about your party. Who was throwing it?"

"Um, this girl from my English class last semester and a couple of her roommates," Scarlett said quickly. *Ugh.* More lies.

"Did you have a good time?"

"You know, I did." At least that part was the truth. "Just a bunch of us literature geeks debating about British novelists between vodka shots."

"Hmm, sounds pretty wild," Jane joked. At least she was smiling now.

"Yeah, things got a little out of control," Scarlett joked back.

"Any cute guys?"

Scarlett thought about Liam. Her breath caught in her throat. "Nah."

"Too bad."

"Yeah, well."

For a brief second, Scarlett was tempted to tell Jane

everything. But she couldn't bring herself to do it. For one thing, there was nothing to tell. Big deal, so Scarlett liked Liam. She accidentally spent the night with him. It wasn't like they were dating or in a relationship or anything like that. Last night was a onetime thing. She had no intention of repeating it.

The other thing was bigger: Scarlett felt strangely uncomfortable confiding in Jane. It was like she was watching their relationship change and she couldn't do anything about it. It used to be that they never kept secrets from each other.

And now they did.

16

FIFTEEN MINUTES

Veronica Bliss leaned back in her chair and gazed pensively through the glass-paned wall of her office, looking out onto her employees' cubicles. She'd had it mirrored on one side so that she could see them, but no one could see in, which helped to achieve the balance of privacy (for her) and lack of privacy (for her staff) that made *Gossip* the well-oiled machine that it was.

She glanced at her laptop screen and saw that Madison Parker had sent another email. Veronica opened it with a heavy sigh, guessing that Madison was throwing a tantrum about the latest issue of *Gossip*.

She was.

TO: VERONICA BLISS
FROM: MADISON PARKER
SUBJECT: WTF???

You promised me that if I got you pictures of Jane, you would publish an article about me. You call the tiny mentions of the grooming habits of "Jane Roberts's friend and confidante" an article about me???? WE HAD A DEAL.

Veronica rolled her eyes, annoyed that she had to waste even thirty seconds of her valuable time dealing with this. Quickly, she typed:

TO: MADISON PARKER
FROM: VERONICA BLISS
SUBJECT: RE: WTF???

That was your article. If you want another one, you need to get me more info ASAP. What is Jane up to? Is she dating anyone new?

What was Madison complaining about, anyway? The latest issue of *Gossip* featured a cover story about Jane's postscandal escape to Cabo: *L.A. CANDY* STAR HIDES IN MEXICO AFTER TWO-TIMING BF. The photographer had gotten pictures of Jane on the beach: downing a margarita, covering her face with her hands (probably to shield her eyes from the sun, although the readers didn't need to know that—better they believed she was sobbing in shame). And talking to Madison (whom the photo caption described as the "tan, skinny shoulder Jane cried on").

And now Madison was throwing a fit because . . . why? Because she wasn't the cover story? She was lucky to have gotten into the magazine at all.

A movement on the other side of the one-way window caught Veronica's eye. It was her assistant, Diego, hovering. *Ugh.* What was his problem? He was really getting on her nerves lately.

The reply email from Madison came almost immediately. The girl must be sitting at her computer or staring at her BlackBerry, waiting. Obviously, she didn't have a life.

TO: VERONICA BLISS
FROM: MADISON PARKER
SUBJECT: RE: RE: WTF???

Nothing new on Jane at the moment. She's back at work and she's not seeing anyone as far as I know.

Veronica exhaled sharply. Was Madison an idiot or what?

TO: MADISON PARKER
FROM: VERONICA BLISS
SUBJECT: RE: RE: RE: WTF???

FYI, "Nothing new," "back at work," and "not seeing anyone" isn't news. You can't get something for nothing.

Veronica swore under her breath. If Madison couldn't deliver, then she would have to cultivate other sources. Through the window, she saw Diego talking to himself. Honestly! She was surrounded by idiots. Did she have to do everything herself?

A small *ding!* from her laptop indicated a new email. She glanced at her mailbox quickly, guessing that it was another whiny response from Madison.

It wasn't. Veronica didn't recognize the sender's address, and there was no name attached. But the subject line intrigued her, and it was kind of a bizarre coincidence, considering.

TO: VERONICA BLISS
RE: MADISON PARKER

Madison isn't who she says she is. Interested?

Veronica read the message again. She rubbed her eyes, calculating. Reply or not reply? *Not reply,* she decided after a moment, slamming her laptop shut. It was probably just Madison pretending to have dirt on herself. Or some other nutcase, fishing for attention. It seemed that everyone wanted their fifteen minutes these days.

17

HOW TO ACT FOR THE CAMERAS

It was a beautiful night in Los Angeles—stars glittered in the sky and a warm breeze carried the scent of jasmine and eucalyptus. But Jane had no time to enjoy any of it as she hurried into Beso, trying to avoid the photographers whose flashbulbs popped like firecrackers as they shouted questions at her:

"Jane, how 'bout a smile?"

"Jane, are you and Jesse getting back together?"

"Jane, can I get an over-the-shoulder?"

Jane wished, fleetingly, that Sam were with her—Sam the publicist, whom Jane had decided to sign with (along with R.J. the agent) after discussing it with her parents over the weekend. Jane still wasn't 100 percent sure that she needed a publicist, but she got the feeling that if Sam were with her right now, she would usher Jane through this gauntlet of paparazzi like a pro.

As Jane entered the restaurant and greeted the hostess, she spotted several PopTV camera guys in the dining room, ready to film. She wondered if Jesse was already there, or if she was the first to arrive. *Deep breaths*, she told herself. *So you're having dinner with your ex-boyfriend. On-camera. The same ex-boyfriend you cheated on, a mistake that millions of people know about. No big deal.*

After Jane had been miked in the alley behind the restaurant, Matt, the director, had rushed up to her and given her instructions on how she should walk to the table. (Apparently, he had a great shot from the second floor.) Jane saw Jesse sitting at a table surrounded by bright lights in the center of the massive room. He saw her, too. His face lit up, and he gave her a small wave. He actually seemed glad to see her, which was a relief.

When he'd texted her yesterday, asking if they could get together for dinner tonight, she hadn't known why or what to expect; she just knew she had to see him. She'd already had a shoot scheduled—just her and Scar at the apartment. Unfortunately, the rest of Jane's week was equally jam-packed. So she'd called Trevor and asked if they could postpone the shoot, explaining the reason. He'd immediately suggested that they shoot Jane and Jesse's dinner out instead, even naming Beso as a location, saying that he liked the lighting and the cooperative management there. Jane had said no at first—she wanted to have some privacy, and she figured Jesse would, too. But

Trevor had been so convincing, insisting that it would be a way for PopTV viewers to see that Jane and Jesse had moved on. Jane had finally agreed, and Jesse had agreed as well.

As for Scar . . . well, she had been less than happy about this change in plans (although normally she would have welcomed any excuse to get out of shooting), and made her usual negative remarks about Jesse, which Jane had basically tuned out—actually, *literally* tuned out, with her iPod headphones and Death Cab for Cutie.

A moment later, Matt told Jane they were ready for her. She took a breath, then wove her way through the room per Matt's instructions.

When she reached the table, Jesse rose to his feet. He looked . . . gorgeous. There was no other word for it. His charcoal gray button-down shirt complemented his light brown wavy hair, and his tailored black slacks accentuated his muscular build. Even his black Gucci loafers and silver TAG Heuer watch were perfect.

He smiled at her. "Hey."

"Hey." Jane slid into the seat across from him, quickly, because she wanted to avoid an awkward *should we hug or kiss each other on the cheek or what?* moment. "Sorry I'm late."

"Late? It's only five after eight. That's early for you."

"Ha, ha. True."

Jesse's gaze traveled the length of her, from her beige silk one-shoulder dress to her Jimmy Choo peep-toe pumps. "You look nice."

"Thanks. So do you." Jane shifted uncomfortably in her seat.

They looked at each other; then Jane dropped her eyes, fumbling with her napkin. She noticed that the glass in front of him contained mostly melted ice cubes. Obviously he had already polished off a drink.

The waitress came by. "Can I get you a cocktail to start?" she asked Jane. She turned to Jesse. "Another ginger ale for you?"

Jane raised her eyebrows. Ginger ale? Jesse? She'd figured scotch on the rocks or a gin and tonic, and that he was already halfway to wasted. . . . *Guess I was wrong,* she thought.

"I might switch to wine," Jesse told her. "Jane?"

"Um, just water. Thanks." Jane knew that, unlike the clubs where they usually filmed, restaurants were likely to card. And her fake ID had become increasingly difficult to use after people realized her name wasn't Jillian McManus.

"Red wine for me," Jesse said. "I'll try the cab."

"Sure thing," the waitress said before walking away.

Jesse leaned back in his chair and gazed at Jane. "So. How are you?"

"You know. Okay. Ish."

"Yeah, me too." Jesse was smiling as he said this, but

Jane couldn't help but notice a little sadness in his expression.

"So what'd you do for Christmas?" Jane asked, deciding to start with something positive.

"My mom invited a bunch of friends for dinner. It was like the who's who of Hollywood forty-somethings. My dad's filming a new movie in Australia, and he couldn't get away."

"What's the movie about?"

Jesse shrugged. "Not sure. I think it's some kinda indie-artsy thing. It's being directed by that Italian guy, Michaelangelo what's-his-name."

"Wow, cool."

"I guess. You know, if you're into indie or artsy." Jesse smiled at her. "So. What'd *you* do for Christmas?" he asked.

"I went home to Santa Barbara and hung out with my parents and my sisters."

"That must have been fun," he said sincerely. "You hadn't seen them in a little while, right?"

"Yeah, it was nice to see them."

Jesse picked up his menu, and Jane followed suit. But she had a hard time concentrating on it; she was so nervous, and yet at the same time oddly comfortable. As though she and Jesse had never broken up. As though the whole Braden thing had never happened.

Ugh, Braden. D had texted her on Saturday, saying that he'd read on a blog that Braden had gotten a part in some new show based on a book series. The news had finally given her an excuse to send the email she'd been meaning to:

Hey. I heard you got a part on a big show. Congratulations! That's huge.

If and when you're ready to talk, please call or text me. I feel so bad about what happened and I'm sorry you got dragged into all of this. I never wanted you to get hurt.

Love,
Jane

Braden still hadn't replied, nearly three days later. Would he ever? Was he so mad at her that he was never going to speak to her again? Could she really blame him? She had ruined his oldest friendship, with Jesse. And embarrassed him in the national media.

After the waitress came back with their drinks and took their orders, Jesse asked Jane how work was going, and she filled him in on the Crazy Girl Valentine's Day party at the Tropicana and how excited she was that Fiona was entrusting her with such a major assignment. By the time their food arrived, the conversation had shifted to the topic of . . . them.

"I'm glad we talked at the New Year's party." Jesse picked up his glass and watched the way the light danced on it.

"Yeah, me too."

"Because the truth is, I've kinda missed you."

"You have?"

"Yeah."

"Really?"

Jesse grinned. "Really."

"I've kinda missed you, too."

"Really?"

They both laughed, awkwardly, because they knew how silly they sounded. Jane wasn't sure what they were doing, talking about missing each other. She hadn't expected this. She had expected . . . what? Small talk. Catching up. Thinly veiled hostility. Her apologizing some more. Jesse saying that he forgave her. The two of them insincerely promising that they'd stay in touch as they air-kissed good-bye.

Jesse reached across the table and laced his fingers through hers, tentatively, as if he were uncertain as to whether she might pull back. She didn't. She was still so confused about everything—about Jesse, about Braden, even about Caleb—but she knew for sure that she liked the feel of his hand on hers, so she held it tight.

"Hey." Jesse glanced toward the camera crew. "You wanna get out of here?" he asked her quietly.

Jane hesitated for a moment. Then nodded.

"Good. Me too."

Jesse signaled to the waitress for a check. A split second

later, Dana came rushing up to their table. When did she arrive?

"You guys are doing great! But could you hang out here for a min while we set up outside to film your exit? Awesome, thanks!" With that, Dana was gone, speaking rapidly into her headset.

Jesse's eyes twinkled. "See, you *can't* go out with any other guys besides me, because I'm the only one who'll put up with her telling us what to do on dates."

Jane shrugged and smiled at him. "That's what I like about you—you're very obedient."

"Seriously. I mean, what other guys are cool with being miked every time they walk into a place with you? You're lucky I'm so understanding," Jesse teased her.

"Yeah, it's such a huge burden, having to be on TV all the time," Jane teased him back.

Jane watched as the camera guys hauled their equipment through the dining room and out the door. She and Jesse were now officially off-camera—at least for a "min."

There was something she had been meaning to talk to him about. Maybe this was her chance.

Or maybe she should just drop it.

Just do it, she told herself. She leaned forward, lowering her voice. "So there's something I have to ask you. I'm really sorry to have to bring this up. But it's about those pictures."

Jesse's smile vanished, but Jane forced herself to go on.

"Madison thinks either you or Scar gave them to *Gossip* magazine. Which is crazy, I know, but—"

"Madison?" Jesse cut in. His jaw clenched angrily. "She said that? Are you fucking kidding me?"

Jane was stunned by Jesse's furious response and wished she could go back to three minutes ago, before she had said anything. "Okay, okay," she said, holding up her hands. "I'm sorry I brought it up." She had been 99.9 percent sure of his innocence before. She was 100 percent sure now.

"Madison's the one who should be sorry. She's lying to you; don't you know that? *She's* the one who gave the pictures to *Gossip*. Didn't Scarlett tell you?"

Jane sighed. Obviously, Jesse and Scar still shared the same delusional ideas about Madison. Just as Madison had *her* delusional ideas about Jesse and Scar.

This was getting to be too much. Her friends had to stop fighting and making up horrible stories about one another. Besides, Jane was more convinced than ever that the pictures were the work of some random (evil) photographer. After all, Madison had totally been there for her through all the recent craziness, proving she was too good a friend to do something so low. And Madison was so wrong about Scarlett (and Jesse, too). Even though Jane and Scar weren't exactly getting along these days, Jane knew Scar would never do that to her.

Jesse was still bad-mouthing Madison when Jane interrupted.

"Okay, okay," Jane said, giving Jesse a look that (she

hoped) conveyed to him that the subject was now off-limits. Forever. "Can we just go?"

Jesse's expression stayed stern. "Sure," he said coldly.

As Jesse paid the check, Jane peered at her phone and saw a text from Dana, saying that the camera guys were ready. Jane slid her phone over to Jesse so he could read the text, too.

Jesse rose from the table, helping Jane out of her chair and then taking her arm and leading her to the door. As they wove through the dining room, a group of young women snapped pictures of them with their cell phones. Jane heard one of them say, "I thought they broke up?"

Outside, she saw the *L.A. Candy* guys in position, filming her and Jesse's exit—and then, a few feet behind them, the paparazzi. Dana was standing there, not yelling at them to scram as she usually did, but simply watching Jane and Jesse and talking quietly to someone on her headset. What, had the *L.A. Candy* crew formed some sort of an alliance with the tabloid photographers? As soon as she and Jesse walked out of frame, the paparazzi came toward them at once.

"Save me," Jane whispered to Jesse, who nodded and handed his ticket to the valet, then placed his hand protectively on the small of her back. Jane felt, as she sometimes did, trapped, as they stood on the sidewalk, waiting for Jesse's car while the paparazzi's cameras circled them, recording her every move. The weird thing was, she was good at this. She knew, without being told by Dana or anyone else, to do exactly what she was doing: fake-smiling, making small talk, pleasantly and patiently killing time until she and Jesse could escape in his Range Rover. Scar, on the other hand, would have lost her temper by now, or given someone the finger, or made some funny, sarcastic comment and stormed off.

Not Jane. She knew enough to smile and be polite, even though it terrified her to be surrounded by flashing lights and faceless photographers who had no respect for her personal space.

"Car's here," Jesse announced. More flashbulbs popped as he helped Jane into the front seat.

"How 'bout a kiss, Jesse?" one of the photographers shouted.

Yeah, right. Jane waited for Jesse to close her door and go around the car to the other side. But instead, he leaned in and kissed her on the lips—not just a quick, friendly kiss, but a long one. The cameras went crazy.

It was so nice kissing Jesse again . . . or it would have been, anyway, if it weren't for the fact that they were not alone. They were the absolute opposite of alone. *Guess Jesse knows exactly how to act for the cameras, too,* Jane thought.

18

WHO SAYS WE'RE DATING?

Sitting cross-legged on her bed, dressed in nothing but a white tank top and black boy briefs, Scarlett hurled another pair of rolled-up socks at the TV screen. It was laundry day (at this point, laundry *night*), and as always, Scarlett had sorted and folded all her clean clothes in neat piles. Unfortunately, the neat piles were quickly coming apart. And it was all Trevor's fault.

The sock hurling had started when she made the mistake of turning on the TV during the sorting and folding part, to watch *L.A. Candy* on TiVo. It was the "Christmas Eve with the Harps" episode (or that's what she called it, anyway), and it was really, *really* pissing her off.

After their initial, deer-caught-in-the-headlights silence in front of the cameras, her parents had warmed up to them and started opening their mouths.

Mom: So how was your first semester at USC, darling?

Scarlett: It was okay.

WTF? Scarlett threw another pair of socks at the screen. She recalled exactly what she'd said in response to her mother's question. It *wasn't*, "It was okay." It was, "It was okay, if your idea of a good education is being taught by professors who have lower IQs than you do." Sure, maybe that was a little harsh and not totally true, but why had Trevor reduced her sentiment to, "It was okay"? Was he trying to make her sound vapid?

The painful scene droned on.

Dad: Have you thought about your future?

Scarlett: Sure. I guess.

More socks. Except that Scarlett had run out of socks, so she hurled some rolled-up panties instead. *Sure. I guess?* What she had said to her father was, "Sure. I guess. I was thinking I would drop out of school and maybe go back to my old job grilling chickens at El Pollo Loco or maybe dance at a strip club." Now she was *sure* Trevor was trying to make her sound vapid.

Mom: Oh, by the way, I meant to tell you we ran into

your old boyfriend Dave the other day. He was asking about you.

Scarlett: Really?

Panties, tank tops, hoodies. They hit the TV screen and fell in a soft heap on the floor of Scarlett's otherwise tidy room. This one was the worst bit of Trevor-izing yet. Her mother—her real mother, her off-camera mother—knew better than to bring up the subject of her love life, such as it was. Dana had obviously told her to do so.

What Scarlett had said was, "Really? You mean Dave, *Jenn Nussbaum's* boyfriend? I just hooked up with him at her eighteenth birthday to piss her off. Yeah, well, be sure to tell him hi the next time you see him. Where is he these days—working in the surf shop and living with his parents? He didn't strike me as the Most Likely to Succeed type, at least from what I could tell during the twenty-three minutes of our relationship."

Okay, yeah, so maybe that wasn't exactly PG-rated material. Still, did Trevor have to chop her words to the point of making her sound like a lobotomized Barbie doll?

"Asshole!" she yelled.

The doorbell rang.

Scarlett sat up abruptly. She glanced at the clock. *Crap!* That must be Liam. And she wasn't even dressed.

It wasn't like her to lose track of time like this. Jane must be rubbing off on her.

Liam had texted her that morning, asking if she wanted to check out a French double feature at the New Beverly Cinema, and she had replied, SURE, before she'd had a chance to think it through. She hadn't seen him since leaving (or rather, catapulting out of) his apartment last Friday. She had hoped and prayed that he wouldn't call her or text her after that, telling her how much fun New Year's Eve had been and could they do it again and all that BS. And he hadn't. Which had been kind of confusing. By Sunday night, she had actually found herself checking her phone to make sure she hadn't missed any messages. This morning, when she saw his text pop up, she had actually giggled—giggled!—responding to his invitation.

What was wrong with her? Scarlett Harp didn't giggle. She laughed, usually at the expense of other people.

Scarlett clicked off the TV, scrambled out of bed, and dug through the pile of freshly laundered clothes on the floor. She found a clean pair of jeans and a slightly wrinkled tee and pulled them on. She didn't bother with makeup or her hair, because she never did (unless Jane forced her to, for a shoot). She grabbed her wallet and keys.

The doorbell rang again. "Hang on!" she yelled. "I'm coming!"

A minute later, she opened the door. Liam was standing there, looking . . . well, quite hot in a pair of distressed jeans and a blue polo that matched his eyes.

He smiled at her. "Hey."

"Hey."

"I'm not early or anything, am I?"

"Nope. I was just finishing up the laundry. Ready to go?"

"Yup. Car's just outside."

A few minutes later, they were in Liam's silver Prius, listening to the radio and driving along Beverly Boulevard with the windows down. Scarlett put her bare feet up on the dash and leaned back in the seat, enjoying the feel of the air tossing her long black hair. She was quite content. This was much better than staying at home doing the laundry (or launching laundry at the TV), moping because Jane had gone out to dinner with her loser boyfriend turned ex-boyfriend turned sort-of-boyfriend again, instead of hanging out with her. (It would have been on-camera, but still . . . it had been a while since the two girls had spent a night in together.)

"So." Liam turned to glance at her. "Not to get serious on you, but I think we should talk about something."

Scarlett stared at him. "What?"

"Crew and talent aren't supposed to date."

Scarlett arched her eyebrows. "Did you just call me 'talent'? Besides," she continued, hitting his arm playfully, "who says we're dating?"

"Yeah, well, whatever you want to call it. It's just . . . I could get fired for this."

"So we're not dating. They can't fire you for being friends with me, can they?"

"I'm not sure if the network makes those kinds of distinctions. Point is, I think you're cool and I want to keep seeing you, but it would be better if we didn't tell anybody about us."

Us? What did he mean by *us*?

"I knew from the schedule that Jane was out tonight, which is why I was able to pick you up at your apartment," Liam went on. "You can't talk about this with anyone, okay? Not even Jane."

"No problem," Scarlett said breezily. "I'm good with secrets."

"Yeah? Well, hopefully, you're better at keeping secrets than you are at Wii tennis."

"What are you talking about? I destroyed you!"

"You're delusional."

"*You're* delusional."

As they bantered, Scarlett thought about what Liam had just said. She was actually glad that she couldn't tell anyone about him. Truth was, she didn't *want* to tell anyone about Liam, because she didn't even know what she would say. She had never felt this way about a guy before, and trying to explain it out loud would make it seem too real. She had no words to describe her emotional state these days ("irrational" and "unstable," maybe?). She wanted to linger in this irrational, unstable, and, if she had to admit it, kind of awesome limbo of her noncrush on Liam for as long as possible—not going forward, not making a commitment, just . . . being there. She couldn't see their relationship continuing, but she couldn't see it *not* continuing, either. So for now, she would just enjoy whatever it was they had—without labels, without promises, and without telling anyone about it. Not even Jane. Scarlett had already *not* told her about New Year's with Liam. Might as well keep the half-truths rolling—that was the state of their union these days anyway.

Plus, the season finale was coming up soon. After that, who knew what the future held? Maybe Scarlett would leave the show. And then Trevor Lord couldn't Trevorize her anymore, or tell her what to do, or who to date. She could just focus on school (classes were resuming next week) and make some decisions about the next academic year. Like, should she transfer to a different college? Or should she pursue another path altogether? The future was wide-open.

"Ready to sit through four hours of subtitles?" Liam said, pulling into a parking space.

"Who needs subtitles? I speak French."

"You do not."

"Oui, je parle français."

"Show-off."

Scarlett laughed at him and kissed him on the lips. She wrapped her arms around his neck. Just then, some guy passing by yelled, "Get a room!" through the open window. She and Liam pulled apart, laughing.

"I thought we weren't dating," Liam said, caressing her arm.

"We're not."

"Yeah? You always kiss your friends like that?"

"Yep. That's why I'm soooo popular."

As they walked into the theater, Liam took her hand in his. *What the hell,* Scarlett thought, and then let him.

19

CD U AND HANNAH PLZ TALK ABOUT SOMETHING????

Jane took a sip of her Coffee Bean & Tea Leaf vanilla latte (yum) and jotted down a note to check out some roller-skating websites to get ideas for the Crazy Girl event. Skating to Valentine's Day was a bit of a stretch, but she knew that Crazy Girl had sponsored several athletic events, so maybe there was something there? Although . . . roller-skating events sounded good in theory, but really, you ended up with a crowd of people drinking alcohol, with wheels attached to their feet. Injuries were inevitable. *Love hurts, though, right? Hmm.*

"Good morning!" Hannah walked into the office, looking fresh and put-together in a cream wrap dress and camel-colored wedge shoes. "How was your weekend?"

Jane noticed that Hannah didn't even glance at the two PopTV cameras in the corners, which she used to do in the beginning. *We're all getting to be such pros at this,* she thought. "It was fun. How was yours?"

Hannah sat down at her desk and tucked her purse away in the bottom drawer. "Kinda quiet. I went to the movies Saturday night."

"Cool! Who'd you go with?"

"A couple of friends," Hannah said vaguely. Hannah never mentioned her friends by name. It was weird how she never opened up about herself. Jane really liked her, but she felt like she knew nothing about Hannah's nonwork life. Was she just a private person? Or maybe the cameras intimidated her more than she let on? Jane had invited her out a few times, but other than coming to Jesse's birthday party at Goa, and the Cüt launch at STK, she usually had other plans . . . with her mysterious friends/dates/boyfriends/ex-boyfriends, no doubt.

"So what did you do?" Hannah asked her.

Jane smiled and blushed. "Jesse and I hung out."

"Really?"

"Yeah." Since dinner at Beso last Monday, Jane had gone out with Jesse almost every night. They'd spent most of the weekend at his spacious house in Laurel Canyon, watching movies and swimming in his pool and cooking dinner together. When she and Jesse were dating before, she had been to the house only a couple of times, mostly because Braden lived there, and it would have been awkward running into him in the mornings, wearing nothing but one of Jesse's white shirts. Even though nothing had happened between her and Braden back then, there was that unspoken *something* between them, and besides, she knew he didn't approve of her dating Jesse.

Now Braden was gone, and Jesse hadn't brought him up. Not once. Jane figured it was best that way. Even though she wished Braden would respond to her email (from *nine* days ago), already. Or was their friendship totally dead? The thought made her sad. Really sad.

Hannah glanced at her computer monitor, then began typing. "So how are things going with him?"

Jane frowned, confused. Why was Hannah asking about Braden? And then she remembered that they had been talking about Jesse. "Really great," she gushed. "He's so sweet to me. Do you know what he did Friday night? He TiVo'd *The Notebook* because he knew it was one of my favorite movies, and then he made me dinner and we watched it together. Seriously, things are better than ever with him."

"Wow, that's amazing. I'm so happy for you."

Jane stared at Hannah. She didn't sound happy. She sounded . . . worried.

Jane turned back to her computer, biting back her disappointment. She wanted to share her good news about Jesse with a friend. One who didn't hate him. Which left Hannah. But for some reason, Hannah wasn't interested in talking about Jesse today. Maybe she was just in a bad mood?

Jane began punching keys, checking out skating sites, when her computer made a little *ding!* noise, and she saw that she had an email from Sam. She opened it eagerly.

TO: JANE ROBERTS
FROM: SAMANTHA SUTHERLAND
RE: THINGS ARE LOOKING UP!

Hey, sweetie. Check out these links. We're on a roll!
Love, Sam

The first linked to an item about Jane and Jesse going to a video-game launch party together. The next was all about Jane's fabulous job as the assistant to one of the biggest event planners in the business. Then a picture of Jane attending a charity fashion show to benefit children's leukemia.

None of them mentioned Braden. None of them even hinted at scandal.

Sam really *was* a miracle worker.

When her phone buzzed a few moments later, she wondered idly if Sam was making sure she'd seen the email or maybe it was another text from Caleb, who had sent her another message this morning "just saying hi," whatever that meant.

But it was from Dana, who had written, CD U AND HANNAH PLZ TALK ABOUT SOMETHING????

Jane glanced up. Dana was standing in the doorway, gesturing wildly with her hands for Jane and Hannah to resume their fascinating conversation.

Jane turned to face Hannah. "Yeah, so we have a meeting with Gaby today, right?" she said hastily.

Hannah nodded. "Gaby from Ruby Slipper?"

Jane remembered that Dana had asked them to mention Gaby's name whenever they talked about Ruby Slipper. But why was Hannah saying it like that—like she was in a commercial or something? She really *was* in a strange mood today. "Yes, Gaby at Ruby Slipper. We have to go over the list of DJs for the party."

"Sounds good."

Silence. Hannah gazed pensively off into space. Jane heard her own phone buzz again, then Hannah's phone. Dana was probably about to lose it with the two of them, wasting precious airtime with . . . well, dead air. Jane was tempted to ask Hannah if something was wrong.

But knowing Hannah, Jane was not likely to get any answers.

20

POISON APPLE

Madison sat back in the sleek white pedicure chair and dipped her feet into the warm, rose-scented water. "Mmm, this is just what I needed."

Jane, who was in the chair next to her, smiled. "Yeah. Thanks for inviting me. I really needed this, too."

"Your nails were nasty, huh?" Madison joked.

Jane laughed. "It's nice to relax, that's all. I've been working hard, and things are a little crazy."

"Yeah, me too. We have to start doing this girls' stuff every week."

"Definitely."

Madison fell silent, digesting Jane's words. "Things are a little crazy right now" probably referred to her renewed and, from Madison's perspective, disastrous romance with Jesse. Although maybe it wasn't as awful as she had feared? From what she could tell, Jesse either hadn't told Jane about Madison being behind the *Gossip* pictures, or he had, and Jane hadn't believed it. Either way, Madison seemed to be off the hook—at least for now. Jane was as friendly and nice to her as ever, and since Jane didn't seem capable of ulterior motives, Madison assumed it was sincere.

Still, Jane's being with Jesse was not good news for Madison for other reasons, namely because Trevor was weirdly obsessed with their relationship (and with not-very-pretty, not-very-exciting Jane, Plain Jane—*why?*), and would likely focus on them for the rest of the season. And maybe next season, too—if there *was* a next season, and if the Jane-Jesse love-fest hadn't expired by then.

How was she going to turn this around?

Patience. She would continue to stay close to Jane in order to get what she needed for Veronica, in exchange for more pieces in *Gossip* (like pictures of Jane and Jesse fighting or Jane the morning after too many margaritas). And in order to get more airtime on *L.A. Candy*, too. The math was simple. Jane got the most airtime of all four girls, so being Jane's BFF would mean . . . well, getting *almost* as much, since there would be lots of scenes with both of them. And since Scar was on the outs with Jane these days, the BFF position was available.

In fact, Madison had been thinking lately that it would be so incredibly awesome if she and Jane could become roommates someday. She could imagine the cameras now, capturing all their predate closet raids, postdate couch convos, and more. The possibilities were endless.

Although . . . where were the cameras tonight? Madison had texted Dana that she and Jane wanted to get mani-pedis. In response, Dana should have cleared a salon and scheduled a crew. Instead, Madison got a text from Gaby that they were filming her and a couple of her coworkers at some stupid event at the Thompson Hotel. Lame.

Madison turned to Jane, faking a smile. "Soooo. How are things with Jesse?" She forced herself to sound as chatty and girlfriend-y as possible. "You know I worry about you with him. Did you see the trash he hauled into STK?"

"I know, I know." Jane sounded uncomfortable. "He was just doing that because of what happened with . . . ya know."

"So are you guys, like, officially back together? Or are you kinda taking it slow and dating other people?"

"We're back together."

"Seriously? You don't think he's seeing other girls?"

"No. Why are we talking about this?" Jane snapped. "And why am I constantly defending him? Why can't my friends be more supportive?" She picked up a magazine and began flipping through the pages.

Madison reached over and squeezed Jane's arm. "Sweetie, you know I'm just looking out for you."

Jane frowned. "Yeah, but . . . it's just that I wish my friends would at least pretend to be *happy* for me. Why do you all assume the worst about him? If you knew him like I did, you'd feel differently."

Okay, time to shift gears, Madison thought. *Otherwise, Jane's gonna dump both me and Scarlett and find a whole new BFF.* "Well, then, maybe I should get to know him better," she said brightly.

Jane's face lit up. "Really? You mean that?"

"Yeah, why not? This is nothing that three or four rounds of martinis can't solve."

"That would mean so much to me, thank you! I wish Scar felt the same way."

Score. Madison pictured Scarlett's red face when Jane told her about Jane, Madison, and Jesse hanging out.

"How *are* things going with you and Scar, anyway?" Madison said, her voice full of fake concern.

"I don't know. Not great. She's so . . . *negative* these days. She didn't used to be this bad."

"I'm so sorry." Madison leaned toward her. "You know what? Living together can sometimes ruin a good friendship. Especially if the friendship's got issues to begin with. Like if one person is kind of possessive or controlling about the other person. You know what I mean?"

Jane sighed. "Yeah . . . I guess I kind of do."

"You guys might think about taking a break for a

while. Like, live apart. It might help you get your friendship back on track."

Jane looked thoughtful. "Hmm. Maybe."

This is too easy, Madison thought smugly.

A couple of aestheticians dressed all in white came into the room. One of them knelt on the floor by Jane's chair. "What color would you like today?"

"Maybe a dark purple?" Jane replied.

"That would be so pretty on you. We have a few different shades."

"And you?" Madison's aesthetician asked her.

"Same as last time," Madison replied. "That really deep red. I think it's called Poison Apple."

"Of course."

Madison's phone vibrated with a new text. She knew there was a no-cell-phone rule in the salon, so she had just silenced it, because she was expecting some important calls.

"Hot date?" Jane teased her.

"Dunno. I'm checking." Madison punched some keys.

There was only one text, from a private number. Madison read it.

I'VE BEEN WATCHING YOU ON TV AND I KNOW WHO YOU REALLY ARE.

There was no name or other ID.

Madison's fingers tightened around the phone. *It's just*

a prank, she told herself, trying to regain her composure. *It's just a prank.*

"Madison? You okay, sweetie?" Jane sounded concerned. "Who was that?"

"What? Oh, nobody." She plastered an Emmy-caliber smile on her face, turned off her phone, and tossed it on the counter. "It was a wrong number."

21

I DON'T EVEN KNOW YOU ANYMORE

It was almost 10 p.m. when Scarlett walked through the front door and tossed her backpack onto the floor. What a long day. The new semester had started on Monday after a monthlong winter break. In an effort to challenge herself academically, Scarlett had registered for some upper-level classes, including a couple of literature seminars, one of which involved reading novels in their original French. Sure, she did this on her own sometimes, just for the hell of it. But it was another thing altogether to do it in a classroom, and with a super-picky professor to boot. She'd stayed up most of the night trying to get through the first few chapters of Marcel Proust's *À la recherche du temps perdu*, aka *Remembrance of Things Past.* Yikes. Her online French–English dictionary was going to get a serious workout over the next few months.

Scarlett yawned as she made her way into the living room, then the kitchen. Sleep. What an appealing idea.

She didn't mind pulling all-nighters once in a while, but she'd stayed up most of the night on Monday as well as Tuesday—not reading Proust, but hanging out with Liam. It was all catching up with her now.

Still, a smile tugged at the corners of her lips at the thought of Liam. He'd taken her out to dinner Monday at a funky little fish shack in Malibu; afterward, they'd gone for a long walk on the beach. She couldn't decide which was more amazing: their marathon conversations about everything under the sun, or the way it felt when they kissed, their lips and bodies fitting together perfectly as though they were two halves of the same—

Stop it! Scarlett scolded herself. *You're starting to sound like one of those pathetic romance novels! Puke!*

She grabbed a bottle of water from the fridge, then plopped down on the couch and glanced around. No TV. No music. No sounds of Jane rifling through her insanely messy closet, looking for a missing designer whatever. The apartment was too quiet.

"Janie?" she called out. No answer. They had barely seen each other since New Year's Day, when they'd had that awkward conversation about Jane talking to Jesse at h.wood. Scarlett wasn't sure, but she thought Jane and Jesse might be back together. Jane hadn't come home a couple of nights last week, and she hadn't been around most of the past weekend. And Scarlett had seen some tabloid covers with photos of Jane and Jesse looking cozy. She knew full well that those magazines were capable of distorting anything, but she was pretty sure that this time they were telling the truth.

She and Jane had always shared the most intimate little details of each other's lives, like when they were eleven and Scarlett told Jane about her fear that her chest was lopsided, or when they were thirteen and Jane told Scarlett about how she'd practiced kissing on one of her dolls. Now it was as though they existed on parallel planes. It felt so bizarre.

Scarlett was the same old Scarlett. It was Jane who had changed. What happened to the old Jane? That Jane would never go out with someone like Jesse Edwards. A couple of dates, maybe. But a relationship? Especially after he showed his true man-whore colors at his twenty-first birthday party? And the old Jane would never be friends with Madison Parker, either.

Scarlett heard the front door open with a jingling of keys. A moment later, Jane walked into the living room, wearing a navy blue wrap dress and wedges. She was carrying a to-go bag from Koi in one hand and a large white leather tote with some files spilling over the top in the other. She set the items down on the dining room table, very gingerly, then held up her hands, studying them with a worried expression.

"Hey," Scarlett called out. "What's wrong with your hands?"

"Madison and I got mani-pedis, then sushi after," Jane replied. "I *think* my nails are dry." She frowned.

Madison and I got mani-pedis, then sushi after. Scarlett took a swig of her bottled water, forcing herself to count to ten so she wouldn't make a rude comment. "Yeah? Definitely sounds like one of Dana's brilliant ideas" was the best she could manage.

"Nah, the cameras weren't there. It was just a girls' night," Jane replied. "Hey, how's school going? Classes started this week, right?"

"'Just a girls' night'? Seriously?" The words tumbled out before Scarlett could stop herself. This counting-to-ten stuff was crap. "Was Gaby there, too? What, have I been kicked out of the club?"

"No, Gaby wasn't there. Madison invited me out. I don't get it. You keep telling me how much you hate Madison. Now you wanna hang out with her?"

"No, I don't wanna hang out with her. And I don't want you to, either."

"Scar, please don't lecture me about Madison again. She's my friend. You need to accept that."

"She's *not* your friend. Don't you see? She's a crazy, lying bitch, and she's got you wrapped around her finger! She's—"

"Scar!" Jane put her hands on Scarlett's shoulders. "This. Has. Got. To. Stop. Do you understand? I can't take it anymore!"

Scarlett pushed Jane's hands away and stood up abruptly. "Why won't you *listen* to me? Why would you trust some girl you've known for all of four months instead of me?"

she demanded, her voice cracking with anger and also hurt, because no matter what she said, she couldn't seem to get through to Jane. "Would you listen to me if I had proof? I could go to Madison with, like, a hidden microphone, and get her to confess about how she sold those pictures of you and Braden to *Gossip* magazine."

"No!"

"Why not?"

"Because, Nancy Drew, you sound like a crazy person right now."

Scarlett knotted her fists. She felt like punching a wall. She *had* to calm down. "Yeah? So what does your boyfriend think of your new best friend?" she said sarcastically.

"She is not my new best friend. Although my old best friend is never around anymore, so it's good I've got new friends to hang out with."

"What do you mean, *I'm* never around anymore?" Scarlett burst out. "*You're* the one who left the country!"

Jane ignored her. "And to answer your question, Madison was just saying tonight that she wants to get to know Jesse better. You know, like a fresh start. Which is something we could *all* use," she added pointedly.

"What's that supposed to mean?"

"I mean I'm sick of all your negativity about Madison—and Jesse, too. You need to learn how to be nice to them. Or, if you *can't* be nice to them, at least stop being such a bitch all the time."

"No! I'm *not* going to be nice to them, and I'm *not*

going to stop being bitchy about them. Someone's gotta look out for you, because you're being really, really stupid about those two. I don't know why, but you are."

"What is *wrong* with you?" Jane cried out. "I can't believe you're saying these things. Seriously, I don't even know you anymore!"

"That makes two of us, because I don't know you anymore, either!"

Jane got up and paced around the room. After a moment, she stopped and turned around. "Well, maybe we should take a break from living together," she said in a trembling voice.

"Fine!"

"Fine!"

Jane looked as though she was about to say something else. But instead, she turned and ran down the hall toward her room. A second later, Scarlett heard a door slamming.

And another second later, Scarlett did something she never, ever did.

She burst into tears.

22

MOVING DAY

"It's the last door on the right," Madison told the movers. "And be careful going around corners and through doorways. I don't want any scratches or marks on my walls. Got it?" As she spoke, she turned ever so slightly toward the soft light filtering through the paper-covered windows. She wanted to make sure that the PopTV camera crew captured her at the most flattering angle possible.

"Yes, miss," one of the guys in the bright orange MOVE IT! INC. tee said. He wiped his brow as he and another guy maneuvered Jane's queen-size mattress past one of Madison's lipstick-red chairs. "What about the fish? Which room does he live in?"

"Penny's a she! Bedroom, please!" Jane called out. She was carrying a potted ficus tree strung with tiny lights. She set it on the living room floor and sat down next to it, swigging from a sports bottle. The cameras pivoted toward her.

Madison hoped Jane didn't plan on leaving her sorry

Wal-Mart plant in that spot, so close to the ten-thousand-dollar Italian leather couch. Seriously, she was beginning to have second thoughts about letting her move in. The girl had so much crap. Madison believed in what one of her old (and older) boyfriends called "one percent decor": that is, furniture and artwork that only the top 1 percent income bracket could afford. She had been very careful about what items to choose for her prized penthouse—or rather, what items to let Derek, her current (and older) boyfriend, choose for *his* prized penthouse, which he was kind enough to share with her.

Not that he was around often. Mostly, he was at his other home in Pacific Palisades with his wife (who didn't know about the penthouse) and their new baby.

Still, he was going to be a problem. Or rather, Jane was going to be a problem where he was concerned. When the call came from Jane four days ago, saying that she'd had a fight with Scarlett and needed to find a new place to live ASAP, Madison had immediately invited her to move in with her—for a week, for a month, for a year—however long she needed. And Jane had accepted gratefully. Madison couldn't have planned it better herself, and she wondered if her remark that day at the spa had actually set this in motion.

Madison had called Derek right away, telling him that the network was forcing her to let Jane move in temporarily for a certain story line they had in mind. He hadn't been happy at first, but she had convinced him that it would be okay to meet elsewhere for a while—maybe their old suite at the Beverly Hills Hotel?—and he had agreed. Men. They could never say no to her.

But this little lie was bound to catch up to her if Jane stayed longer than a few weeks or months . . . or if Derek (who watched *L.A. Candy*, or rather, whose wife watched *L.A. Candy*, and he watched with her, because it gave him a stupid, secret thrill to do so) eventually figured out that there *was* no "certain story line" having to do with Madison and Jane being roommates. Although Jane moving into her apartment *would* make an awesome season finale—wouldn't it?

One crisis at a time, Madison thought. *I'll figure it out later. I always do.*

She moved over to the Italian couch and perched on the armrest, making sure to push her shoulders back in a way that made her cleavage look . . . telegenic. She was glad she had worn her formfitting pink tank top today. "You doing okay, sweetie?" she said to Jane, who was still sitting on the floor.

Jane took another swig from her sports bottle, then put it down next to her sad little plant. She rose to her feet and joined Madison on the couch. "I feel like I *just* moved," she complained good-naturedly. "I *did* just move. Twice. In August, Scar and I moved from Santa Barbara to our first apartment by the 101. And in September, we moved from there to the Palazzo."

"Moving day is always super-stressful," Madison agreed.

"When'd you move into this place? It belongs to your parents, right?"

"Yeah. I've been here for, like, a year?"

"It's soooo amazing!"

"Thanks!"

Jane glanced around. "How come there aren't any pictures of them?"

"Of who?"

"Your parents."

Madison forced a smile, mostly to buy herself the split second she needed to craft a plausible story. She hadn't been prepared for this question. "I have them on my laptop," she improvised. "I'm soooo bad about ordering prints and putting them in frames and stuff. Plus, to tell you the truth, my parents are kinda camera-shy. They *hate* people seeing pictures of them."

"Guess you didn't inherit that from them," Jane teased her.

Bitch, Madison thought.

Jane sat up abruptly as one of the movers passed by, carrying a coffee table. "Hey, that's Scar's!" she said to Madison. "That's my roommate's!" she said to the guy, then corrected herself. "I mean, my *ex*-roommate's."

"Sorry about that! We'll return it to your old apartment once we're done here," the guy apologized.

"No problem." Jane turned back to Madison. "I didn't even say good-bye to her before I left."

"Whatever. You shouldn't be worried about her, after

the way she treated you," Madison said. "Seriously, that girl needs therapy."

"I don't know."

"Sweetie, you're way too understanding. You've gotta stop letting people walk all over you."

"Scar didn't walk all over me."

"She did! You're just too nice a person to see it."

Understanding. Nice. The words caught in her throat and practically made her gag. Still, Madison didn't want Jane doubting this new arrangement, even though she and her ficus and all the rest of her crap were cramping Madison's style. Besides, Trevor had called her yesterday and told her that she shouldn't hold back on expressing her opinions about Scarlett to Jane, if that was what she felt "compelled to do." Translation: Trevor was ecstatic that Scarlett and Jane were fighting, and he wanted to keep the tense friendship triangle going for as long as possible. Madison knew that he and the other producers had been struggling to find story lines for the totally unfilmable Scarlett. Her rift with Jane was actually good news for the show. And Madison was happy to cooperate.

Jane sighed. "I feel bad about the way we left things. Maybe I should call her?"

Jane was acting like she was having second thoughts about moving. Madison had to distract her from those thoughts. "No! You wait for *her* to call *you*. She owes you a huge apology," she said quickly. "Besides, I wanna talk to you about something. It's important."

"What?"

"I've been thinking. Now that you're living here, maybe we could think about getting a pet? Like a puppy?"

Jane's eyes widened. "*Whaaaat?* No way! I've always wanted a puppy! Ohmigod, Madison, are you serious?"

Madison grinned as she took in the sight of Jane's happy face. *Wow.* Jane had mentioned to her once how she couldn't have a dog growing up because of her mom's allergies. Madison knew the puppy idea would win her points with Jane. She had no idea that she would basically be hitting the jackpot.

"Yeah, I'm serious. What are you doing tomorrow? You wanna go dog shopping?"

"Yes! Madison, I love you!" Jane leaned over and gave Madison a big hug.

"Love you, too, sweetie!" As Madison hugged her back, she shifted a few inches to the right—just enough so that the cameras had *her* profile in their sights, and not Jane's. Monopolizing the frame was hard work, almost as hard as coming up with clever lies.

Fortunately for Madison, she was really good at both.

23

REMEMBRANCE OF THINGS PAST

"Let us explore the significance of the madeleine in Proust's novel," Professor Friedman said.

Scarlett slunk down in her seat and pulled her long black hair across her face, obscuring it. She knew that she would get a text from Dana any second now, telling her to sit up and push her hair back and act alive for the cameras. And normally she would be happy to engage in some spirited class participation, not for the sake of the show, but because she had actually started enjoying *Remembrance of Things Past* and discussing it with the very tough but very smart Professor Friedman (who looked like an older Kristen Stewart, and who seemed to favor cool black vintage dresses).

But not today. Scarlett was in a foul mood—for two very good reasons.

Jane had moved out of their apartment.

And Jane had moved into Madison's apartment.

Her cell buzzed. "Ugh," Scarlett muttered under her breath, ignoring it. It was no doubt Dana, begging her to behave.

As if that strategy ever worked.

The lit seminar on French novels was on the small side, around fifteen people. Scarlett didn't know most of the students, except for the girl with the elaborate tats on her arms (Vivian?), who had passed her a note at the beginning of the class saying, *Reality TV is for whores.* Nice. There was also the guy sitting next to her, whom she had mentally labeled Surfer Boy, who kept leaning in her direction for no good reason and trying to get into the shot. He had confessed to her last week that he wanted to be an actor, and could she introduce him to the PopTV producers? And maybe her agent, too?

There was another student in the class who kind of intrigued her, named Chelsea. Chelsea seemed supersmart, always making insightful comments and asking interesting questions. She and Scarlett had talked a few times, away from the cameras, and Chelsea had suggested that they hang out sometime, also away from the cameras. Scarlett planned to take Chelsea up on her invitation one of these days, when she had gotten over her bad mood about Jane and Madison. Which, at this rate, might be never.

Liam and another camera guy were wedged in opposite corners of the room, which seemed barely bigger than someone's kitchen. Dana was hovering in the hall, listening in on her headset. Liam had caught Scarlett's eye a couple of times, looking concerned, but she had tried to ignore him. She didn't want sympathy. Actually, she never wanted sympathy. Sympathy was for losers who couldn't deal, and she was most definitely not one of those.

"First of all, can anyone tell me what a madeleine is? More important, can one find it at Starbucks?" Professor Friedman said. A few students laughed politely. "How does Proust use it as a literary device?"

If Scarlett didn't feel so crappy, she would answer the professor's questions about the madeleine, which was a little shell-shaped cookie or cake, depending on your view. In *Remembrance of Things Past*, the narrator ate a madeleine with some tea, and the smell and taste of it unlocked all kinds of long-buried, wonderful, interesting memories.

Scarlett loved the idea of sensory experiences invoking memories. Like how hearing some song from the summer of 2005 could suddenly take you right back there. Or how smelling a certain cologne could make you think of an old boyfriend. There were all kinds of sensory experiences that Scarlett associated with her and Jane's life back in Santa Barbara. The coconutty scent of sunscreen. (Beach, checking out guys, commiserating about the previous night's bad dates.) The taste of blueberry pancakes. (Jane's dad made them really well, and the two girls used to eat way too many of them on Sunday mornings, after sleepovers.) Seeing constellations in the night sky. (When they were eight, Scarlett taught Jane the names of the constellations, including her favorite, Orion the Hunter.)

And now . . . she and Jane weren't even speaking to each other.

How could their friendship go from so great to so . . . not there?

Scarlett listened but didn't speak for the rest of the class, occasionally typing notes on her laptop and continuing to disregard Dana's increasingly insistent texts. When it was time to go, she scooped up her belongings, stuffed them into her backpack, and made a beeline for the door. As she passed Liam packing up equipment, he reached out his hand as if to intercept her, but then jerked it back as he noticed Dana approaching.

"Scarlett? A word?" Dana snapped. Her face looked even more stressed than usual.

"Love to stop and chat, but, um, I have an appointment with my adviser," Scarlett improvised. "We'll talk later."

Scarlett escaped into the hallway—and practically ran smack into a familiar figure.

"Hey, Scarlett!" Cammy was standing there, waving like a maniac, dressed in super-short denim shorts and a maroon USC baby tee that barely contained her very fake, oversize chest. "How's it going?"

Talk about a blast from the past—the recent past, anyway. Scarlett had met Cammy during her first week of the fall semester . . . and had been dodging her ever since.

Which wasn't easy: Cammy had become determined to befriend her once she saw the *L.A. Candy* cameras.

"I'm great, Cammy," Scarlett replied, fake-smiling. "See you around! Bye!"

"Wait!" Cammy grabbed her arm. "I've been soooo worried about you."

"You have?"

"Yeah, 'cause I heard that your best friend, Jane, moved out?"

Scarlett frowned. Jane had moved out all of two days ago. News didn't travel *that* fast—did it?

"Uh, Cammy? How do you know that?" Scarlett asked.

Cammy ignored her question. "You guys had a big fight, huh? Personally, I think it's that girl Madison's fault, don't you?"

Scarlett stared at her. And then she stared at Cammy's very fake oversize chest. Scarlett could just make out the outline of a wire in the general area, running down and around her torso.

Cammy was miked.

Scarlett glanced around the crowded hallway and spotted the other camera guy (not Liam) standing nearby, his lens pointed at the two girls. This was a setup. A Dana (and Trevor?) setup.

Assholes!

Scarlett turned her attention back to Cammy. "Actually,

Madison is one of my BFFs," she said with another fake smile. "She's not doing very well, though."

Cammy scrunched up her face. "Huh?"

"Madison has this condition that makes it difficult for her to control her bowel movements," Scarlett explained. "That's why Jane moved in with her temporarily. To take care of her."

Cammy's eyes grew huge. "Oh!"

"Yeah, it's pretty serious. Anyway, gotta go. Bye!"

"Wait! Scarlett!"

Scarlett started down the hall, along the way ripping off her mike pack and tossing it to the camera guy (who barely managed to catch it, or the finger she flipped him). She saw a door for the women's room and rushed in, finding an empty stall.

She sat down and put her face in her hands, sucking in a deep breath. What a crappy day. What a crappy week. What a crappy month. What a crappy year.

Maybe she should just get off the show. And maybe she should leave L.A.? But then what? Go back to Santa Barbara? Not an option. Transfer to another school after all? Maybe. Jane was the real reason she was living here to begin with. And now that they were on the outs, Scarlett had nothing tying her to the city.

Except for Liam.

Her phone buzzed. *Damn Dana,* Scarlett thought irritably and fished her phone out of her pocket to turn it off.

But she saw that this latest text was from Liam, not Dana.

HEY R U OK? he had written.

Scarlett was anything but okay. She hit Reply and typed, IM FINE.

ANYTHING I CAN DO? he wrote.

NOPE, she replied.

WE STILL ON 4 TONITE?

Scarlett hesitated. Liam was taking her out to dinner at his favorite French restaurant tonight because he thought she would enjoy practicing her French on the fluent staff. He also just wanted to cheer her up after everything she'd been through lately.

CANT, SORRY, Scarlett typed finally. RAIN CHECK.

Liam didn't reply.

Now I'm being the asshole, Scarlett thought.

But she couldn't help it. She willed her guilty conscience to go away. The last thing she needed was to have Liam trying to cheer her up or save her or whatever. She wasn't some sort of helpless little victim. She could get through this mess on her own. She had always managed alone in the past. And she would continue to manage alone in the future.

24

BE GOOD

"Okay, can you two stop making out?" Gaby giggled. "The show's PG, remember?"

"We're *not* making out," Jane said, blushing as Jesse kissed her neck. Jane leaned back on the comfy leather couch, enjoying the atmosphere at Teddy's. The room was dark and intimate, with high, arched ceilings and a stylish chandelier glittering over the upholstered leather bar. The effect was very old-style Hollywood glam. "I really like it here. I've never been before, have you, Jesse?"

"A couple times," Jesse replied. "But never with you—so it's like the first time all over again." He gave Jane his *I know I'm a cheeseball* smile and took a sip of his Jack and Coke, swishing the ice cubes around in the glass. Jane noticed that after a few weeks of soft drinks (and some wine and beer here and there), he was back to cocktails. "Friend of mine is a promoter, and he does a night here. Quentin Sparks."

"Quentin, I know Quentin!" Jane said. "D introduced him to me at the series premiere party at Area."

"Is he cute?" Gaby asked eagerly.

Jesse laughed. "His boyfriend, Todd, thinks so."

Gaby shrugged and proceeded to scope out the scene. "I'm sure there's some hot guy here tonight who can't wait to buy me a drink."

The mostly B-list, well-dressed crowd was dancing to a jazz band that played everything from Billie Holliday and Etta James to Norah Jones. Jane wondered if any of them were miked, or if it was just her, Jesse, and Gaby tonight—and Madison and Scar, if and when they made it.

Trevor and Dana had arranged for the girls to attend the event, which was for some new magazine called *Alt*. Jane had noticed the *Alt* logo all over the step-and-repeat when she and Jesse walked in, and again on the cool-looking metallic blue gift bags that some stressed-out assistant named Emily was arranging on a table. (Jane had felt an instant wave of sympathy for Emily, being an assistant herself.) Trevor was actually here tonight, along with Dana and the rest of the crew. Jane wasn't sure if he was here for the party or for work, and whether she should talk to him or ignore him.

Jane didn't know what she should do when she saw Scar, either—she hadn't seen or talked to her in almost a week—not since she'd moved into Madison's apartment. What would Scar do when she eventually showed up at the party? Would she be polite to Jane? Cold? Bitchy? All of the above? Having Jesse and Madison there definitely wouldn't help things. Jane just prayed Scar wouldn't pick a fight with them, especially with the cameras present.

She felt Jesse's warm lips brush up against her ear. "Can we leave yet?" he whispered.

Jane punched him playfully on the arm. "No! Be good!"

"I *am* being good. I just wanna see what you're wearing under that little black dress."

"Shhhh!" Jane knew the mikes wouldn't pick him up at that low volume, but still!

"Hey, kids!"

Jane's head shot up. Madison, clad in a gold minidress with a narrow V-neck that plunged down almost to her belly button, was approaching their table. She smiled at Jane, Gaby, and Jesse—especially Jesse.

"Hi, Maddy!" Gaby stood up and air-kissed her on both cheeks. Jane used to think the two were best friends, but lately she hadn't seen them hanging out together much. "You want a Cosmo? They're really good here."

"Sure, sweetie. Please don't call me that. Hi, you lovebirds," she said, sliding onto the couch next to Jesse. "How's the party?"

"This place is beautiful," Jane said, her gaze shifting nervously between Madison and Jesse. Jesse wouldn't acknowledge Madison, and his expression was tense. "Have you been here before?"

"Ohmigod, all the time. Hey, Jesse? Can I talk to you privately?"

Jesse turned to Madison, looking surprised. "What? Why?"

"One minute. That's all I need."

"Uh . . . okay." He turned back to Jane and flashed his *WTF?* smile—he had a lot of different smiles, and Jane was getting to know them all.

Jane watched as Madison and Jesse wandered off, weaving through the crowd. What was *that* about? Madison had promised her that she would try to get along better with Jesse. Maybe she was going to apologize to him?

"Uh-oh. Madison's trying to steal your man," Gaby warned her.

"I don't think so," Jane said, wishing Gaby wouldn't say stuff like that on-camera. She knew it was too easy for Trevor to use it out of context. "Hey, you and Hannah and I have a meeting tomorrow, right? I can't believe the Valentine's Day party's less than a month away."

"Why are we having a meeting? Didn't we decide everything already?" Gaby said, scanning the room. "We've got a venue, we've got a sponsor, we've got the DJ. What else is there?"

"Uh, Gaby? Like everything?" Jane reminded her. "We've gotta decide on a menu, come up with the guest list, design invitations. Not to mention figure out gift bags and the guest list. We've gotta—"

"Okay, okay! I hear you! This is soooo much work, it's

giving me a headache," Gaby complained. "It's a lot more fun checking out guys. Like that guy over there, by the bar. He's hot!"

Jane followed Gaby's glance. The guy in question was thirtyish and balding. He was, in Jane's opinion, the polar opposite of hot. Although he was probably rich, since his custom Armani suit had likely cost a small fortune. Gaby did have eclectic taste in men. Then Jane spotted Jesse and Madison, who were walking back in the direction of their table with linked arms. Madison was saying something to him, and he was . . . laughing. Laughing! Jane couldn't believe it. Seeing the two people she was closest to getting along made her smile. She had no idea what voodoo Madison had performed, but whatever it was, Jane was grateful.

Jane was about to call out to Jesse and Madison when someone caught her eye. She watched as he made his way through the crowd—and felt her heart lurch in her chest.It was Braden. And Willow, his girlfriend (or ex-girlfriend, or not-girlfriend, depending on who you asked).

Jane closed her eyes and wished she'd left a few minutes ago, when Jesse wanted to. She didn't want to have to see his *oh, hello, former best friend and guy my girlfriend hooked up with* smile. She didn't want anyone else to see it, either.

25

SOMEONE LIKE HIM

Scarlett hesitated outside the Roosevelt Hotel on Hollywood Boulevard, wondering if she should head inside for the party at Teddy's. There was a small crowd on the sidewalk waiting to get in; luckily, there were no paparazzi. For a moment, Scarlett's thoughts flashed back to the night in August when she and Jane had to wait nearly an hour in line to get into Les Deux. Now they could just waltz into any club they desired. Not that she and Jane were doing any clubbing together these days. The only times she saw Jane at clubs was when it was for a shoot, and they always arrived separately.

Scarlett had originally planned to skip this thing, because she didn't feel like having a showdown with Jane and/or Jesse and/or Madison. Then she had changed her mind, thinking that she might use the opportunity to make up with Jane somehow.

Then she'd changed her mind again.

And again.

And again.

And now she was standing there in her usual fancy getup (jeans, black tank, light makeup, no purse), feeling like an idiot because she couldn't decide whether or not to go inside. Her indecision was about more than Jane, though. It was also about Liam, who was working cameras tonight. After she'd blown off their French-restaurant date on Monday, he'd sent her several (really sweet) texts, telling her that he was thinking about her and that he would be waiting for her call, if and when she was ready to talk—or just hang out and not talk.

Scarlett hadn't written back. And she wasn't entirely sure why. She just couldn't bring herself to do it. It wasn't that she didn't miss him. She did—a *lot.* She missed their conversations about books and music and movies and politics. She missed his kisses. She missed the way he wrapped his arms around her, making her feel so desired and so protected at the same time. She missed his face. She missed his eyes. She missed everything about him.

So why was she ignoring him? Part of it was that she was in a funk, and she didn't like sharing her funks with another person. She also didn't like how much she missed him, which seemed crazy and upside down, but there it was. Crazy and upside down seemed to be her hallmarks these days.

"Going inside?"

A young guy was holding the door open for her, eyeing her appraisingly. He looked like every other Hollywood club-scene wannabe: cute, dark hair, stubble, nice build, designer clothes. Scarlett was used to getting hit on by guys like him—and guys, period. In another lifetime (as in, before Liam), Scarlett might have hooked up with him, just for the hell of it. But tonight she had no interest.

"Guess so." Scarlett headed through the door. She had made her decision to attend the *Alt* party, after all—or rather, the decision had been made for her by this random stranger.

"I'm Matteo. You look familiar."

"Scarlett."

"Scarlett, Scarlett. Hmm. You're a model, right? Listen, can I buy you a drink?"

"No, thanks. I'm meeting some people."

"Okay, lemme know if you change your mind."

Scarlett smiled briefly at him before heading through the hotel lobby to Teddy's. She didn't get very far into the dark, opulent club (she'd heard that Marilyn Monroe used to frequent the place) before she realized that some sort of commotion was happening. A ton of people were standing around a couple of guys who appeared to be . . . fighting? *Uh-oh.* A red-haired girl was hanging onto the arm of one, while a blond girl was pulling at the arm of the other guy.

Scarlett did a double take. The blond girl was Jane! She was clinging to Jesse, who was drawing his fist back to deliver a right hook to . . . OMG, it was Braden! The red-haired girl was what's-her-name, Willow, who was not Braden's girlfriend, exactly, but more of a friend with benefits. (The arrangement was likely his idea, not hers. Scarlett had seen the possessive look Willow gave Braden whenever there was another girl around. Clearly, she didn't like to share.)

Jesse punched Braden in the mouth. Jane and Willow both screamed.

Near the back of the room, Scarlett spotted Trevor talking to someone on his cell, his face bright red and furious-looking. He must have been having a heart attack witnessing this scene unfold. Trevor loved conflict for the cameras, but not conflict involving Braden, who refused to be on the show, and not with this crowd present. Dana was nearby, also shouting into her phone.

Jane. Scarlett had to rescue Jane. She shouldered her way across the line of ogling partygoers with no plan of what to do in order to extract her BFF from this insane mess. (Scarlett didn't care that they weren't speaking to each other—Jane was still her BFF.) But before she could reach Jane, she felt someone bump into her, hard.

"Hey!" she yelled.

"Sorry!"

Scarlett recognized the fake-blond hair as the girl swept past her. Madison. She turned briefly to lock eyes with Scarlett before running up to Jane and grabbing her hand, pulling her away from Jesse. At the same time, a couple of the *L.A. Candy* crew members, and what looked like Roosevelt Hotel security, appeared and separated Jesse from Braden.

"How fucking dare you!" Jesse was yelling at Braden. "How fucking dare you show your face in this town, after what you did?"

"You're a drunk asshole!" Willow was yelling at Jesse. She looked like she was crying.

Braden said nothing, merely swiped at his bloody lip, his eyes blazing angrily.

Jane was crying, too, her mascara streaking down her cheeks. Madison draped her arm around her shoulders and escorted her through the crowd, whispering in her ear. A couple of random girls tried to follow, but Dana, for once in her life being useful, blocked their way.

Shit, Scarlett thought, watching Jane going off with Madison just like she'd managed to do at STK. *Shit, shit, shit. That she-devil has totally taken over Jane.*

"Do you think Jane's gonna get back together with Braden now?" Gaby said to Scarlett.

"Can we talk about something else?" Scarlett snapped. "Another one, please," she added to the bartender.

The bartender raised his eyebrows at her before pouring her a shot of Patrón. This would be her fourth. Or fifth? Or sixth? She had lost track. But she didn't care.

She wanted to obliterate the last hour from her memory. No, not just the last hour but the last few days, weeks, and months of her dying friendship with Jane.

Jane had left Teddy's, along with Jesse. If she ever saw Scarlett at the party, she gave no indication. Frankly, she seemed too upset to notice anyone or anything. Madison was gone, too, as were Braden and Willow. (Scarlett overheard a couple of guests saying that Willow was a contributing writer for *Alt*, which explained why she and Braden had shown up at this particular event.) The PopTV camera crew lingered, mostly because Dana had wanted to try to salvage the night by getting some footage of Scarlett and Gaby "hanging out" at the bar.

Yeah, right. Good luck with that, Scarlett thought.

Liam was stationed in a corner near the bar, filming Scarlett and Gaby. Scarlett had steadfastly avoided looking at him, even though she knew that he was looking at her, and not just professionally through the lens. In fact, he had sent her a text a few minutes ago—WANNA GRAB A LATE DINNER AFTER?—but she hadn't responded. She didn't want to have dinner with Liam. She didn't want to have dinner with anyone, not with the mood she was in.

Gaby gave up on Scarlett and started flirting with some older guy to her left, having finally picked up on Scarlett's *don't talk to me* vibe. (Tonight's Very Special Episode of *L.A. Candy,* when it aired, would no doubt start with a brawl between Jesse and a blurred-out guy and end with Gaby making out with some dude who was a member of

AARP.) Maybe now Scarlett could just slip away and head home and go to bed, in anticipation of the massive hangover that would surely be waiting for her in the morning.

"Hey? Scarlett, right?"

Scarlett turned to the studded leather bar chair on her right. The guy from earlier—Matthew?—was sitting down, Corona in hand. "Yeah. Hey."

"Are you here for the *Alt* party?" he asked.

"What's left of it, anyway."

"I write for the magazine. Matteo," he reminded her. "It's nice to meet you. Again."

"Oh. Yeah, likewise."

Matteo didn't seem to have picked up on her *don't talk to me* vibe, because he started telling her all about *Alt*, about being a writer, about his pain-in-the-ass coworkers (including Willow). Scarlett had no idea if he was miked or not. She didn't care. It was almost pleasant listening to his numbingly boring monologue about his job. It was definitely better than replaying the endless mental loop of her problems with Jane, with Liam, with the show. Or drinking more tequila. As if she hadn't killed enough brain cells tonight.

Scarlett wasn't sure if five minutes had passed, or fifteen, or more. But all of a sudden, Matteo was leaning close to her and saying, "Hey, you wanna get out of here? Maybe grab a drink somewhere more . . . private?"

"Yeah, why not?" Scarlett said, before she could stop herself. Getting away from the cameras sounded like a great idea. She stood up from her bar chair, a little unsteadily, and tried to figure out where the exit might be. The room was wobbly. She was wobbly. She saw in her line of vision the PopTV camera pointed at her, and the man behind it, his posture completely rigid. Liam. She couldn't see his face, but he could see hers. And he could see the fact that she was leaving Teddy's with some stranger, on-camera, on *his* camera, instead of with him. God, when had she turned into such a bitch? But she couldn't stop herself, any more than she could stop herself from drinking all those tequila shots. She was in pain. And her answer to pain was not crying on someone's shoulder or talking about her feelings. It was diving deeper into the darkness. And at the moment, that darkness consisted of tequila, hooking up with Matteo or someone like him, and breaking the heart of the nicest guy she'd ever met.

"This way," Matteo said, taking her arm. His touch felt all wrong, not like Liam's at all. "You okay?"

"Never better," Scarlett lied.

26

IT WAS GREAT SEEING YOU

Jane walked through the restaurant doors that led to the open-air seating, squinting into the sunshine and digging through her bag for her sunglasses. The outdoor area at Barney Greengrass was packed, with a mostly older crowd of agents discussing deals over expense-account Cobb salads and middle-aged women enjoying a lunch break from shopping. The restaurant was located on the top level of Barneys, and Jane knew that the photographers waiting for her in the parking lot wouldn't be able to shoot her up here. The store's management never allowed the paparazzi to bother customers.

Jane took a seat and picked up a menu. It was cooler than usual for late January, and she was glad she had worn a white sweater over her floral-print dress. She peered at her watch. Noon, exactly. For once, she was on time. Normally it would have amused her, except nothing was really funny to her today. She was still upset about what had happened last night at Teddy's. Just thinking about it made her stomach twist.

And, of course, she was more than a little nervous about her lunch date.

"Hey, you."

Jane glanced up. Braden was walking up to their table, car keys in his hand. "Sorry I'm late. God, I've been away for, like, a month and I already forgot about L.A. traffic."

Jane smiled. "No worries."

Braden sat down, which took a moment because he was super-tall (six-foot-three), and the tables and chairs on the patio were placed pretty close together. Jane noticed that he didn't try to hug her or kiss her on the cheek. She wondered what this meant, then wondered why she cared, either way.

"Nice place," Braden said, looking around. "A lot nicer than Big Wang's, huh?"

Jane laughed. And it felt good. Braden had always been able to cheer her up. "I guess we are moving up in the world."

"Yeah, well, speak for yourself. I'll always love Big Wang's—it's the dive bar where I met the famous Jane Roberts, after all."

"Ha, ha," Jane said. "I thought *you* were the big TV star now. You got a part in a new series, right? Isn't that why you were in New York?"

"Actually, that kinda fell through. The pilot didn't get

picked up. My agent's lined up some other stuff for me, though. That's why I came back."

"Oh . . . Are you back for good?"

"Yeah. New York was just temporary, anyway."

"Oh!" Jane felt an unexpected wave of relief and happiness at this news. Maybe she had missed him more than she realized?

The waitress came by to take their orders but they weren't ready yet. While Braden studied the menu, Jane studied him. She hadn't really had a chance to do that last night at Teddy's, during all the commotion. He looked mostly the same as before, but upgraded. Braden 2.0. His messy, longish dirty-blond hair was shorter, neater, more styled. He had shed a few pounds from his already slender frame. He wore a white James Perse button-down shirt instead of his usual ripped tee (although the shirt *was* untucked and a little wrinkled). He seemed to have traded in his black-rimmed glasses for contacts. His bottom lip was slightly puffy from where Jesse had punched him. Jane winced at the memory and at the fact that the only communication between them in over a month was the note he had left on her door the morning after they'd hooked up—*I'm not sure what last night meant, but I'm not sorry. Please call me later*—which she'd never replied to, and her email to him, which he'd never replied to.

After the waitress took their orders and left, Braden turned his attention back to Jane. "So. It's nice to see you."

"It's nice to see you, too. Are you . . . okay?" Jane pointed to his mouth.

Braden touched the swollen lip. "Yeah. It looks worse than it feels. I promise."

"That's good."

"You probably wanna know why I asked you to lunch today."

"Um, yeah." *Especially after you never responded to the email I sent weeks ago,* Jane added silently.

"I want to apologize about last night. If I'd known you and Jesse were going to that party, I would never have gone."

You could've just picked up the phone, Jane thought, wondering why he had elected to see her face-to-face. Maybe he had missed her, too? *Wishful thinking, Jane.*

"Why *did* you go? You hate parties like that." Braden had always been Mr. Anti-Hollywood. Unlike Jesse, he avoided star-studded events like the plague. He wasn't chasing fame. His dream in life was to be an obscure indie actor in artsy films. He had considered jobs in commercials, TV shows, and mainstream movies only because he knew that he had to pay the bills somehow.

Braden shifted uncomfortably in his chair. "Willow invited me. She works for *Alt*, so I thought I should go."

"Oh. I guess you guys are still together, then." Jane felt an unexpected stab of jealousy. Why? She was with Jesse now.

"Well, we aren't exactly 'together.'" Braden hesitated.

"She was pretty pissed off at me after the . . . you know, and anyway, she's over it now, and she asked me to the party, so . . ." His voice trailed off.

Jane was silent. Braden and Willow had been dating on and off for three years. When she met Braden, he and Willow had definitely been "on." That was one of the reasons he and Jane had stayed just friends, despite what appeared to be their mutual feelings for each other—or that was what Jane had told herself, anyway.

And they had remained just friends until that fateful night when the photographer had taken those pictures.

"And I'm sorry I didn't return your email," Braden said. "It's just that . . . things were really bad after you took off for Mexico. My phone was ringing nonstop. Photographers followed me everywhere. I was really mad at you because I felt like you left me to clean up your mess."

Jane gasped. "Oh, God, I'm sorry. That wasn't what I was trying to do."

"I know, I know."

The waitress interrupted, bringing them their iced teas and salads. Braden waited until she was gone before continuing. "So I had to get out of L.A. immediately," he said. "I couldn't stand it anymore. My agent got me this audition in New York, and I just packed up my stuff and moved out of Jesse's house and headed east. My friend has a place in the Village, so he let me crash on his couch.

If the series had worked out, I was gonna find my own place there."

Jane picked at her salad. "So where are you living now?" At Willow's, she guessed.

"I'm, uh, crashing with a friend. I'm looking at apartments, though."

"Well, you could always move in with Scar," Jane said sarcastically, although she knew that the joke wasn't very funny. "She's probably looking for a roommate."

Braden frowned. "You and Scarlett aren't living together anymore?"

Jane told him an abbreviated version of the story, still a little shocked that this was her life she was talking about. "So I moved in with Madison," she finished. "Her parents own this huge condo. Oh, and we're getting a puppy!"

"No way. Seriously?"

"Yeah. I can't wait. She took me to a couple of breeders last weekend to look at these cute little poodle mixes. But I told her we should go to the shelter and adopt a dog from there. They're the ones who really need homes, right?"

"No, I mean . . ." Braden hesitated. "Yes about getting a dog from the shelter, but I mean, Scarlett thinks Madison was responsible for the pictures? That's kinda random."

"It's crazy, right? There's no way Madison would ever

do anything like that. She thinks Scar did it, which is obviously not true, either. It was just some horrible paparazzo. I *hate* them," Jane said emphatically.

"I'm with you there."

They continued talking for a while, catching up on their lives and the show and his upcoming auditions. Jane noticed that neither one of them brought up the pictures again, or him and Jesse, or her and Jesse . . . or, for that matter, her and Braden. They were finally talking, which was good, but were they really saying anything to each other?

A little after one o'clock, Braden got the check so Jane could rush back for a 1:30 meeting at the office. Fiona had many pet peeves, one of which was lateness. Jane had been on the boss lady's good side lately, and she wanted it to stay that way.

"Soooo," Braden said as he walked her to the elevator. "I don't know if it's a good idea to tell Jesse that you and I had lunch."

Oh, so we are gonna talk about Jesse, Jane thought. She hesitated before replying. She had given this a lot of thought, and there were no easy answers. On the one hand, judging from what had happened last night, Jesse might react badly. On the other hand, she didn't want him to find out from anyone else. Then he would *definitely* react badly.

"No, I have to tell him," she said after a moment, trying to sound more decisive than she felt. Bottom line was, she didn't know how or what she was going to tell him, but she didn't want to keep any secrets from Jesse. "You okay with that?"

"Yeah, of course. I'm not worried about me, Jane."

"Oh," she said. "Thanks, but I'll be fine. *I promise.*" She gently bumped into him.

"Of course you will." He smiled at her wistfully. "So are we still friends, or what?"

Jane stopped at the elevator doors, fumbling through her purse for her keys. She tilted her head up to look at him. "What do you think?"

"Does that mean yes?"

"Yes!"

"Good."

"We'd better go down separately," Jane suggested. "There are a few photographers outside of valet."

"Sure."

Braden reached down and hugged her. Jane started to pull away—she wasn't sure if it was okay to hug him, after everything that had happened between them—then changed her mind and hugged him back. It was . . . nice. His arms felt strong and warm around her body, and she had forgotten how much she loved the wonderful, beachy smell of his skin. She closed her eyes, and for a moment she let herself remember that night, how he had kissed her and she had kissed him and they hadn't been able to stop.

What would have happened if those pictures hadn't been published? Or if she and Jesse hadn't gotten back together? Would she and Braden be together instead? Was he the one she was meant to be with, after all? Not Caleb, not Jesse, but Braden?

Then the moment passed, and Braden broke away from the hug. "Yeah, so, it was great seeing you," he said, sounding flustered. "Take care, okay?"

"You too," she said, wishing she could've stayed in that moment a little longer.

27

HANGOVER

"Okay, on the floor! Give me another set of planks!" Deb ordered Scarlett.

Scarlett shot her personal trainer her best *what did I ever do to you?* look before getting down on the ground and into position. She hated this particular exercise. Actually she hated most exercise that took place inside of a gym. She just preferred to be a little more . . . imaginative with her workouts.

Although she was especially unenthusiastic about her session with Deb today. She wasn't in the mood for any form of physical activity. She wasn't in the mood to do anything, except maybe crawl into bed and nurse her deadly hangover and feel really, really sorry for herself.

It was Friday afternoon, and the gym was pleasantly uncrowded. Nearby, a couple of girls in maroon USC tees were working out on the gravity machines. Scarlett could just make out their conversation, which had something to do with a party they were hosting that night at their apartment, and whether or not some cute guy named Ethan, who was apparently "super-hot," would show up. Roommates, obviously. Scarlett thought about Jane and felt a pang in her heart.

"Hey, you're cheating! Get that knee off the ground!" Deb reprimanded her.

Scarlett glared at her again, then took a deep breath and did as instructed. Maybe one of Deb's famously brutal workouts was exactly what she needed today. Maybe pain, sweat, and sheer physical exhaustion would make her forget about last night.

"You're halfway there! You can do this!" Deb shouted.

As Scarlett struggled to complete her next rep, her thoughts drifted to last night at Teddy's . . . or what she could recall of it, anyway, in the wake of so many tequila shots. She couldn't decide what was worse: Madison being all besty-besty with Jane, or her own behavior. She had acted like an attention-starved slut when she left the bar with Matteo while Liam watched.

Although she *hadn't* hooked up with Matteo. Fortunately for her, she had come to her senses once they had hit the sidewalk, and she'd taken off in her own cab without even saying good-bye.

But Liam didn't know that. He was probably still under the impression that she'd gone home with the guy. It was probably the way Trevor would edit the scene, too, when the episode eventually aired.

"Two and . . . one. Great job!" Deb shouted. The woman was always shouting. Usually, this helped motivate Scarlett. Today, it only made her head hurt even more than it already did.

The USC girls were throwing a medicine ball back and forth now and talking animatedly about ex-boyfriends. Scarlett wished she had someone to talk about ex-boyfriends with. Not that she had a lot of those in her personal history. Unless you counted Liam. Could one call him an ex-boyfriend, since he had technically never been her boyfriend? He was definitely an ex-*something*, after her behavior last night. She hadn't heard from him, and she didn't expect to.

"Sweetie, what's up with you today?" Deb asked as she handed Scarlett a towel. She wasn't shouting anymore; she sounded concerned. "Are you sick? You're not yourself."

"Nothing, just had a bad night," Scarlett replied. She sat up on the exercise mat and wiped her face.

"Boy problems?" Deb asked with a knowing smile.

"Well, I think *I'm* the problem." Scarlett shrugged.

"Aw. Listen, what are you doing tonight? A bunch of us are going out for margaritas. You wanna come? It'll be fun."

Scarlett made a sour face. "Ew, don't mention margaritas to me—or anything containing tequila, for that matter. Besides, *you* drink them? You seem like more of the organic-sea-kelp-smoothie type of girl."

Deb laughed. "Hey, you gotta have fun once in a

while. As long as you work hard, to compensate. Speaking of which, let's grab some tens and move on to chest flies." She added, "We're going to a bar called Velvet Margarita. It's up the street from Big Wang's. Come by if you're not doing anything."

Big Wang's. That was one of the first bars Scarlett and Jane had gone to when they moved to L.A. It was also where they met Braden.

She couldn't believe that was less than six months ago. Had so much really happened in such a short time?

"Scarlett! Chest flies! Come on, come on, come on!" Deb ordered.

Scarlett sighed and followed Deb over to the free-weight rack. Maybe she *should* go out with Deb and her friends tonight. It was better than sitting at home alone. Maybe it was time for her to start making some new friends.

28

LIAR

Jane peered nervously out the glass doors of Katsuya. She counted five photographers outside. There had been only one earlier in the evening, when she and Jesse had arrived for dinner. Tonight of all nights, she didn't want press. Not with Jesse in the kind of mood he was in.

Of course, his mood was completely her fault.

Obviously she should have listened to Braden.

Jesse, who had lingered behind to speak to the maître d', now swept past her and headed outside without stopping to reach for her hand or even to look at her. Flashbulbs popped brightly as he cut through the group of paparazzi toward his Range Rover, which the restaurant had (generously) offered to retrieve in advance so he and Jane wouldn't have to wait awkwardly at the valet stand—a situation that would have been even more unpleasant than usual tonight.

"Jesse, over here!"

"Jesse, any comment on what happened at Teddy's last night?"

Jane could see Jesse's shoulders stiffen with anger as he reached the car, thrust a crumpled bill at the attendant, and got inside. Did he plan on leaving without her? *God, what a nightmare,* Jane thought as she pushed open the glass doors and half walked, half ran toward the curb, keeping her eyes on the ground.

More flashbulbs, more shouts.

"Jane, did you know Braden was going to be at Teddy's?"

"Jane, are you and Jesse breaking up?"

Jane tried to tune them out as she climbed into Jesse's car and shut the door. She was grateful for the tinted windows, which insulated her from the crazy commotion outside.

Although now she was alone with Jesse in the chilling silence *inside*. She wasn't sure which was worse.

Jesse started the engine and pulled onto Hollywood Boulevard, not saying a word. He didn't even turn on the CD player, like he usually did. Jane rested her head against the window and stared out at the passing scene. It was Friday night, and everyone was out: sitting in bars, walking down the street, laughing, holding hands, kissing. They looked so happy.

She glanced in Jesse's direction. His profile was completely rigid, and his knuckles were white as he clenched the steering wheel. Why wasn't he saying anything? She felt as though his silence were going to suffocate her.

She couldn't stand it anymore. "Look, I'm sorry. I just wanted to be honest with you," she blurted out.

Jesse shot her a look of disgust. "Yes, Jane, I know how important honesty is to you," he said sarcastically.

Jane winced. Clearly, telling him about lunch with Braden had stirred up some of his anger from the original incident. And clearly, this was how he dealt with it—by trying to make her feel just as bad as he did.

As soon as she had opened her mouth at Katsuya and told Jesse about the lunch, explaining that Braden had wanted to apologize about the *Alt* party, she had regretted her decision. Not because Jesse had made a scene—in fact, it had been the opposite of a scene. He had simply stared at her and said nothing—and then flagged down the waiter to order a whiskey, and another a few minutes later, and another after that. Their spicy crab rolls and Kobe beef had gone untouched. She'd tried to explain, but after a few minutes it was clear he wasn't willing to talk about it. The silence had been deafening.

Five whiskeys later, he was driving them home. Jane should have insisted on driving instead, but she wasn't about to bring it up in front of a group of photographers. And now she just didn't have it in her to fight with him about it.

Jesse reached into his pocket, pulled out a pack of cigarettes, and shook one into his mouth. Jane hadn't seen him smoke in weeks. But she didn't have it in her to fight with him about that, either. "Everybody thinks you're so sweet and perfect," he sneered as he turned onto La Brea, fumbling for the lighter. "It's such bullshit."

"I've never claimed to be perfect, Jesse. I—"

"No, you're far from perfect, Jane. You're a slut."

Jane gasped. She knew he was mad, but she couldn't let him speak to her that way. "Jesse, I didn't do anything but have lunch with him. I'm just trying to be honest with you."

"You didn't do anything?" Jesse spat out. "I'm sorry, Jane. You go and cheat on me with *my best friend*. Then, after I forgive you, you go and hang out with him again. Don't sell yourself short—I think you've done plenty."

Jane didn't reply. She didn't know what to say. There was no point in arguing with him when he was so drunk—and so furious with her.

"What's wrong, Jane? You know I'm right! You just can't admit it!" Jesse was yelling now. "Admit it, Jane—you like him!"

"No, I don't." Jane tried to keep her voice level. She tried to believe her own words.

"Sure, you do. You slept with him," Jesse insisted.

"No, I didn't!"

"I know you did. Everyone who walked by a newsstand last month knows you did!"

Jane sighed in frustration. "I didn't sleep with him. You know I didn't!"

"All I know is that you're a fucking liar!"

He punched down on the accelerator, sending the car five miles over the speed limit. Then ten. Then fifteen. He seemed unconcerned about the other cars on La Brea as he swerved erratically into the left lane and then back again.

"Jesse, watch where you're going!" Jane cried out, reaching over to straighten the wheel in his hands. Why was he acting like this? He was even angrier than he had been after the fight with Braden at Teddy's. He was mad then, yes, but he hadn't taken it out on her. Instead he'd apologized for causing a scene and ruining her night. She'd really thought everything was on its way to being okay.

He pushed her hand away, dropping his lit cigarette on the floor. "Get the hell away from me!"

"Jesse, slow down!" Jane pleaded, instinctively gripping the sides of the leather seat. This was all her fault. She should definitely have listened to Braden.

"Not until you admit you're a liar!"

Twenty-five miles over.

Jane pressed her body against the back of her seat, now in a full state of panic. "Seriously, Jesse. Stop it!"

"Admit you're a liar!" Jesse demanded.

Thirty miles over.

Jane could feel her heart pounding in her chest. "Jesse, *please*!"

"Say you're a liar!"

People honked their horns as Jesse began weaving aggressively between cars. "Jesse, please slow down. You're scaring me!" Jane begged.

"Say it! Say you're a liar!" Jesse swerved, narrowly missing a sleek black BMW. The driver blared his horn at them.

Jane began crying. "Jesse, please stop the car! Please! You're gonna kill us!"

"Say it!" Jesse roared. Through her haze of tears, Jane watched in terror as the Range Rover careened toward a line of cars that had stopped at an intersection. The blur of red taillights rushed at them.

"Say it!"

"I'm a liar! I'm a liar!" Jane sobbed. "Please just stop! I said it! I'm a liar!"

The Range Rover screeched and careened sideways across two lanes, in the direction of the curb. *Oh my God, he's going off the road!* Jane thought, horrified, squeezing her eyes shut and bracing for the crash.

She felt the slam of brakes as the car came to a sudden halt. Then nothing. Slowly opening her eyes, she realized that Jesse had pulled onto a side street off La Brea.

Jane raised her tear-streaked face to look at him—slowly, cautiously. His gaze was locked angrily on her.

"Get out," Jesse spat. "Get out of my car, liar."

Jane began shaking. She was terrified—even more terrified than when she thought he was going to crash.

"Seriously, get the hell out of my car!"

Without saying anything, Jane grabbed her purse and jumped out of the car. She had barely shut the door before he sped off, leaving her alone on the quiet street.

She dropped onto the curb, unable to stop shaking. And just sat there, feeling completely numb. And it was silent again.

Jane fumbled through her purse for her cell phone. She was still miles away from home and didn't have any way of getting there. She instinctively began scrolling to Scarlett's number . . . then stopped. She knew she couldn't call her. She could call Madison—or maybe Gaby—but they already hated Jesse, and she didn't want them to know he had just dropped her off on a street corner. She didn't want anyone to know.

Then she took a deep breath and reluctantly called the only person she knew would understand.

Braden picked up after three rings. "Jane?" he said, sounding surprised. She must have come up on his caller ID.

"Hey, Braden, I'm so sorry to bug you, but I didn't know who else to call." Jane tried to hide the fact that she was still crying.

"Are you okay?" Braden asked quietly. Jane could hear voices in the background.

"Umm . . . I'm sorry. I shouldn't be bothering you. I—"

"Jane, what's wrong?" Braden said, more urgently.

"I told Jesse that we had lunch today, and we got in

a fight and he left me on the street." Jane started crying harder. "He was yelling and driving so fast, and—"

"Where are you? I'm coming right now."

Jane told him the intersection. She swiped at her face with the back of her hand.

"Okay, I'll be there in five minutes."

"Thank you, Braden."

"No problem. But . . . Jane?"

"Yes?"

"Please just trust me this time. If you're planning to make up with Jesse, don't tell him I took you home."

"Okay," Jane whispered.

Later that night—after Braden had dropped Jane off at her apartment and she'd gone straight to bed (alone), and after Jesse had left her twenty voice mails and texts apologizing profusely and telling her how much he loved her, how the thought of her being with Braden (again) had made him temporarily lose his mind—she decided to forgive him. Even though what he had done had been practically unforgivable, she felt she had brought it on herself. And it wasn't that she shouldn't have told Jesse about lunch with Braden—she should never have agreed to the lunch in the first place. How would she feel if Jesse had cheated on her with her best friend (Scar? Madison?), and then gone out to lunch with her, just the two of them? As though nothing had happened?

Especially if Jesse really did have feelings for that best friend—just as Jane had feelings for Braden?

Jesse was right.

She *was* a liar.

29

TIME BOMB

"Come here, doggy. No, stay away from Madison's shoes! Bad boy!" Jane scolded.

Madison bit her lip in exasperation as she watched Jane chase after the dog (correction, *mutt*) that they (correction, Jane) had adopted from the pound yesterday. The little furball was racing around the apartment, chewing on everything in sight, including Madison's brand-new Manolo snakeskin pumps that had cost a small fortune.

Why had she agreed to this . . . *animal*? When she had suggested to Jane last Saturday that the two of them adopt a puppy together, she had meant the small, fluffy, well-behaved kind that could be carried around in a purse—not some mixed-breed animal on steroids. This was ridiculous. She was just waiting for him to start peeing on Derek's favorite Persian rug.

Jane was saying something to her. Madison had no idea

what, because the psycho dog was barking loudly at the wall.

"Whaaaat?" Madison shouted, cupping her hands around her ears.

"What do you wanna name him?" Jane shouted back.

"How about Crazy?" Madison suggested.

"Whaaaat?"

"Never mind! *You* name him."

"I think he looks like a Tucker!"

"Sure! Whatever!" Madison watched nervously as Tucker sniffed the white leather couch.

"Really? You like it? Yay! Come here, Tucker!" Jane got down on her knees. The dog bounded over to her and knocked her down to the floor, covering her face with wet, slurpy, nasty dog kisses. *Ew.* Jane didn't swat him away, but instead started giggling happily and speaking to him in some stupid-sounding doggy-speak: "Yesyou'resuchagoodboy! Yesyourmommiesloveyou!"

Madison rubbed her temples. She needed a couple of Advils and a martini—ASAP. Who cared if it was only 10 a.m.?

Still, it was kind of a relief to see Jane acting like her old self. When Jane came in on Friday night, she looked like hell, and she had obviously been crying. Madison had tried to find out what was up—maybe she and Jesse had finally had a big falling-out about the boy fight at Teddy's?—but Jane hadn't wanted to talk, instead going straight to her room. Madison had emailed Veronica with news of the fight and her immediate reply had been, *Tell me something I don't know.* The problem was, Veronica seemed to know everything. Madison had yet to unearth a single newsworthy fact about Jane that hadn't already been in *Gossip*.

Jane had been quiet and pensive yesterday morning, too. It wasn't until yesterday afternoon, when they'd made the excursion to the SPCA and adopted the hound from hell, that Jane had perked up. Actually, "perked up" was an understatement. Madison had never seen her so giddy with happiness.

Eventually, the *thing* exhausted himself with all his barking and running around in circles. He curled up in the brown corduroy bed Jane had bought for him at some discount pet store on Santa Monica Boulevard and went to sleep, twitching and thumping his tail. (Madison made a note to herself that she had to replace the bed *immediately* with something more in keeping with the decor.)

Jane sank onto the couch next to Madison, beaming. "Isn't he soooo cute?" she gushed.

"Hmm."

"They said he was, like, part German shepherd and part collie and part something else, right?"

"Hmm."

"Are you hungry? I could make us breakfast. How about some pancakes? My dad always used to make blueberry pancakes on Sunday morning."

"No, thanks," Madison replied. "I'm trying to lose a

few pounds." *And you could stand to lose more than a few pounds,* she thought, eyeing Jane's figure. "Soooo. How are you doing?"

"I'm good."

Madison decided to press. Maybe Jane was finally ready to talk about whatever had gone down on Friday night. "Everything okay between you and Jesse?" she said gently.

Jane reached up and tugged at a lock of her hair. "Um . . . well . . . you know."

Good. It was an opening. "He's still pretty mad about Teddy's, huh?" Madison guessed. "I can't believe Braden had the nerve to show up."

Jane bit her lip. "Yeah, well, Braden didn't know Jesse and I were gonna be there."

Madison raised her eyebrows. "Braden tell you that?"

"Yeah, at lunch."

"Lunch?" This was getting better and better. And was something Veronica didn't know.

"Yeah. We had lunch on Friday. It was Braden's idea."

"Where'd you go?"

"Greengrass."

"You met him at Barneys?"

Jane shrugged. "I didn't want . . . you know, photographers around."

"Got it. So why did Braden wanna meet you?"

"He wanted to apologize for what happened at Teddy's. Plus, you know, he wanted to catch up and stuff. His show fell through, so he's, uh, back in L.A.," Jane said casually, then looked away.

Madison couldn't believe it. Jane was still hung up on Braden. This was . . . *awesome.* This was exactly the kind of dirt Veronica wanted. This was also the ammunition she needed to pry Jane away from Jesse. If they broke up, Jane would have a lot more free time to spend with her. Madison could envision entire *L.A. Candy* episodes devoted to their girls' nights out, intimate talks, and more. Or maybe Madison would get a (disposable) boyfriend. Then *she* would have the main relationship on the show. She began to imagine crazy first dates, romantic vacations spent entirely in a bikini, and a dramatic, over-the-top breakup. The season one finale was coming up, so there weren't many episodes left. But there was sure to be a season two, right? Although Trevor still hadn't mentioned anything about that.

But first things first. "Did you tell Jesse about your lunch date?" Madison asked Jane.

Jane's expression darkened. "Well, it wasn't a date. But yes, that night, at Katsuya. He didn't take it too well."

"Oh, sweetie, I'm so sorry," Madison said, her voice oozing with faux sympathy. "What happened?"

"I don't know. We got into a fight. I told him it was just lunch, and Braden was just apologizing about everything. But he wouldn't believe me. It was pretty bad. . . ." Jane stopped.

Madison tried to hide her excitement. She couldn't

make this stuff up. *Wait'll Veronica hears about this,* she thought. *She's gonna do a huge spread about me, just me. No "Jane Roberts's friend and confidante" bullshit.*

She leaned over and squeezed Jane's arm. "Sweetie, I know you don't want to hear this. But that's the real Jesse. He's a total time bomb. You should get out while you can."

"No, no, I'm not gonna break up with him!" Jane protested. "I love him. And he loves me. Besides, it's my fault he's acting like this. I cheated on him with his best friend. This is on me."

"Okay. But he has to get over what happened between you and Braden. He can't go on punching people in clubs and stuff."

"Yeah." Jane looked like she was only half listening now.

Maybe she's starting to see the light about Jesse, Madison thought.

"Everything was going so well." Jane sighed, and Madison wondered if she had meant to add, *before Braden came back.* "Seriously, like, even you and Jesse were starting to get along better. Hey, I keep meaning to ask you—what did you say to him at Teddy's, anyway? I asked Jesse, and he said you apologized?"

"Oh, you know. I just worked my amazing charm on him. I told him I was sorry for any misunderstandings between us and could we be friends and blah, blah, blah."

"Wow. You're good!"

"Hey, I would do anything for you. You know that, right?"

Jane smiled gratefully. "Thanks. That means a lot."

Madison smiled back. It was easy lying to Jane. The girl was beyond gullible, or maybe she was just desperate for a friend. The truth was, Madison had called Jesse aside at Teddy's and told him—in a dark corner, with the two of them standing close enough for him to admire the view of her plunging V-neck dress, whispering so their conversation wouldn't be picked up by the mikes—that she had shown those pictures to him back in December because she had been hopelessly attracted to him and wanted him to break up with Jane. He had been just drunk enough to buy it, and to buy the convoluted story she told him about how, exactly, she had acquired the pictures and why she had tried to get him to take them to Veronica Bliss and how someone else entirely, she wasn't sure who, had ended up selling them to Veronica—and he was so obviously flattered by her confession to him that he hugged her (and continued hugging her for a second beyond what would be considered friendly), and let her link arms with him as they headed back to Jane and Gaby, joking and laughing. Really, the whole thing was genius. She wasn't exactly dealing with rocket scientists here, but she was pretty impressed with herself.

Madison's self-congratulatory reverie was interrupted by the sound of barking. *Ugh.* Tucker.

"Yay, he's up!" Jane said, suddenly animated again, as

if the mutt had barked away her troubles with Jesse. "Hey, you wanna take him over to the dog park? He'd love that, right?"

"Yeah, sure," Madison said amiably. Jane's news had put her in such an excellent mood, she didn't mind humoring her. Besides, long walks often led to long conversations. Maybe she could unearth more useful gossip about Jane's potentially scandalous lunch date with Braden.

30

I DIDN'T MEAN ANY OF IT

"I wanna surprise Jesse with a minivacation, to cheer him up," Jane told Hannah. It was Monday morning at the office. The *L.A. Candy* cameras were there filming, and Jane had just finished telling Hannah all about the recent events at Teddy's. "Like maybe Jesse and I could drive up the coast? I was thinking of renting a beach house or maybe checking into a cute B and B. It might be good for us to just get away for a few days."

Jane was careful to leave out any references to Braden. Yesterday, Trevor had called her in for a meeting to figure out how to handle what had happened at Teddy's. He said she owed it to viewers to tell as much of the truth as possible, without mentioning Braden's name. She'd had to tell Hannah things like, " . . . then the guy I cheated on Jesse with showed up at the club, and things got kinda ugly. . . ." Which was beyond awkward, but it was Trevor's orders. She was going to have to repeat similar lines when she recorded the voice-overs for future episodes. The whole thing was a mess, especially since he couldn't actually show Braden's face in the fight scene at Teddy's.

Hannah had been mostly silent, not responding to Jane's story with her usual sympathetic comments. This had been happening more and more—was Hannah mad at her?

"Hmmm." Hannah stared at her computer screen. "Hey, I was looking through those menus for the Valentine's Day party. They look really good."

"Yeah, I agree. So what do you think?"

"About what? The menus?"

"No, about the minivacation idea."

"Oh!" Hannah glanced quickly at the cameras. "I . . . uh . . ." She cut her eyes toward the cameras again, and then at Jane. She looked a little upset.

"Hannah?" Jane whispered. "You okay?"

Hannah didn't say anything, but instead rose from her chair and hurried out the door. *What is wrong with her?* Jane thought as she ran after her. Out of the corner of her eye, she saw the two camera guys scrambling to follow. She heard one of them swearing as he tripped on a cord, dropping equipment. Jane stepped into the hall and saw Dana. She looked a little frantic, probably wanting to know what the hell was going on.

Jane saw Hannah rushing into the ladies' room. *Good.* The camera guys wouldn't dare follow them in there. Jane went inside—and found Hannah leaning against the slick black sink in the empty bathroom.

"Hannah?" Jane's voice echoed in the bathroom. "Hannah, what's wrong?"

"Everything." Hannah looked at her with tears brimming in her eyes. Jane had never seen her like this. "I'm so sorry, Jane."

Jane blinked. "Sorry? About what?"

Hannah opened her mouth to speak, and then shook her head quickly. She reached into her shirt and extracted the mike taped to the inside of her bra. She unplugged it from the rest of the unit, and motioned for Jane to do the same. Jane reached around to her mike pack and flipped it off. Whatever Hannah had to say, she obviously wanted to say it in private.

"I have to tell you something," Hannah began.

"Sure."

"I . . . well . . . all those things I've been saying to you about Jesse? How you should be together? I didn't mean any of it."

"I don't understand."

"Trevor and Dana told me to say that stuff," Hannah blurted out. "They told me that I should convince you to stay with Jesse. They said that you could be kind of dramatic about your relationships, and that he was actually a great guy."

"What?"

"I'm so sorry!" Hannah cried out. "I went along with

it for a while because you seemed really into him. But then I started seeing that maybe he wasn't so good for you. It seems like he drinks a lot. And Saturday night I ran into him at Crown Bar with this girl."

"What?" Jane's heart dropped. Saturday was the day after she'd told Jesse about her lunch with Braden—and Jesse had almost crashed the Range Rover. "What girl?"

Jane heard someone opening the bathroom door. She quickly pushed it closed and twisted the lock. She ignored Dana's muffled voice calling out to her and Hannah from the other side.

"I think her name was Amber," Hannah replied. "Maybe it was totally innocent. I mean, I never saw them kissing or anything. But I just got this bad feeling."

Jane tried to think. On Saturday afternoon, she and Madison had gotten Tucker at the SPCA shelter. They had stayed in that night to help him settle into his new home. She and Jesse had made up over the phone in the morning, and he had told her that he was going to a Lakers game that night with his friends Howard and Zach.

"You deserve better," Hannah said, her voice insistent now. "In the beginning, I didn't care as much because I didn't know you. But now I know you, and I feel like we're friends. Real friends, not just pretend friends for the cameras." She reached for a tissue and dried the corners of her eyes. "I didn't know what I was getting into when I signed on to do the show."

"How could you have known?" Jane said, resting her head against the door. "It's not your fault your new job came with a TV show on the side."

The way Hannah immediately looked away when Jane tried to smile freaked her out.

"Hannah, what else aren't you telling me?" Jane asked. "You were just applying for the job, right?"

"I met Trevor at Coco de Ville," Hannah explained, "at a party I helped organize for a magazine launch, when I was working for David Sutton. Trevor asked me what I did, and I don't know how it happened, but we got to talking and I mentioned that I was looking for another job in event planning. Then one thing led to another, and he said he could probably get me in with Fiona if I wanted because he was friends with her. He also said that it just happened he was looking for another person for his show. Not like a fifth girl or anything, but someone to be in Fiona's office, sort of hanging out with you."

"Soooo . . . you came here to be on the show and pretend to be my friend," Jane said slowly.

"No! I mean, I was just so happy to get this job with Fiona! I liked working with David, but there wasn't any room for me to move up there. And then here comes this guy out of nowhere, telling me that he could get me an awesome new job *plus* a part on a cool new TV show. It sounded amazing—at the time."

"Yeah." Jane remembered the night at Les Deux, back in August, when Trevor had made a similar, equally irresistible pitch to her and Scar. He was definitely hard to say no to. And he was definitely a pro at changing people's lives—and trying to influence people's lives. No, not *influence.* More like control.

Dana's voice grew louder, and so did her knocks. They both ignored her.

"If you hate me now, I don't blame you," Hannah said miserably. "But I hope you can forgive me. Because I really do consider you a friend."

Hannah seemed to be genuinely sorry about it. And she seemed to care about Jane. Which was a rare commodity in Hollywood. Now that Jane and Scar were on the outs, it wasn't like she had a lot of close friends these days.

"Yeah, I understand," Jane said finally.

Hannah's face lit up. "Really?"

"Really."

As the two girls hugged, Jane thought about how the day that had started out like any other day had suddenly become really, really difficult. She and Hannah were going to have to face Dana's wrath once they emerged from the ladies' room. And, more important, Jane was going to have to have a serious talk with Jesse.

Late that night, Jane was woken up by a phone call. She sat up and rubbed her eyes, disoriented. The digital clock on her night table read 2:08 a.m. Who on earth could be calling her at this hour? *Maybe it's Jesse,* she thought.

She had called him earlier, right after work, but she had gotten his voice mail instead. She couldn't stop thinking about what Hannah had said about seeing him with "Amber." She knew that he'd had plans to go out with his friends tonight (or she knew that was what he'd told her, anyway) but had hoped he'd answer her call. She still hadn't seen him since their fight on Friday. Was he avoiding her?

When Jane picked up her cell and glanced at the screen, though, she didn't recognize the number. She decided to ignore it and let it go to voice mail.

Tucker was curled up at the foot of her bed, snoring quietly. She knew she shouldn't let him sleep on the bed, but she didn't have the heart to push him off.

Jane snuggled back under the covers, trying to get comfortable. Closing her eyes, she thought about the voice-over she'd recorded earlier that day, for the upcoming series finale. *After I apologized to Jesse on New Year's Eve, it looked like there might be hope for us after all. Now he wants to meet me to talk. Could a new year mean a new Jesse, too?*

Jane sighed heavily. She had been so full of hope that night at Beso. It had been her second chance with Jesse . . . a fresh start. And now look where they were. Who the hell was Amber? And where the hell was Jesse?

Just as she was slipping back to sleep, her phone rang again. *Ugh.* Whoever it was probably wouldn't leave her alone until she picked up. And she didn't want to turn off her phone, in case Jesse called.

"Hello?" she said, not bothering to hide the annoyance in her voice. "Who is this?"

"Jane, I am sorry to call you so late. I don't know if you remember me. It's Quentin Sparks. I got your number from D."

Quentin? D's promoter friend? Jane had first met him at the *L.A. Candy* series premiere party and had seen him around at clubs a few times since then. Why was he calling her in the middle of the night?

"Uhh. Hey, Quentin. What's up?"

"I'm at Teddy's, and I've got kind of a situation on my hands. I thought you should come down."

"What . . . sort of situation?"

"Your, uh, boyfriend's here, and he's, uh, had way too much to drink. He's not in any shape to drive. Photographers are out front, so I've got him in back. Can you come down and get him?"

"Ohmigod! Yes, I'll be right there," Jane said as she sat up quickly.

Quentin told her to meet him at the back valet. He was going to bring Jesse out from the Tropicana exit so that no one would notice. Also, one of Quentin's friends—a paparazzi magnet—had agreed to leave out the front at the same time, to divert attention.

"Thank you so much," Jane said as she rolled out of

bed. "It's so nice of you to do this for me."

"Hey, any friend of D's is a friend of mine," Quentin said. "Besides, I can't stand the idea of the press having a field day with this. No reason for people to get hurt."

"Thanks again. I'll be there as fast as I can."

Jane fumbled for the light switch and looked for her purse and car keys. Oh, and her clothes. She couldn't show up at the Roosevelt Hotel in her jammies.

Stay calm, she told herself. *Don't freak out.*

She once again found herself thinking, *How is this my life?* A year ago she was in a long-term, long-distance relationship with her high school sweetheart. Now she was running out of the house at two in the morning to save her boyfriend from himself and the paparazzi. Her hands were shaking as she picked up some jeans and a T-shirt from the closet floor and slipped them on.

As Jane hurried toward the door, she heard Tucker wake up and give her a sad little whimper. She turned and hugged him quickly. "What? You think I should break up with him, too? It's complicated, Tuck!"

Tucker whimpered again. Jane shook her head, feeling like a crazy person. Was she seriously talking to a dog about her love life? How desperate had she become?

Pretty desperate, she thought. Maybe she should ask Penny's advice.

Her friends had been warning her for months about Jesse. And now, all their worst predictions were coming true. He was spiraling out of control. And it was all her fault. How was she going to turn him around—turn *them* around—so they could get back to the way things were, before Braden?

Because she was in too deep with Jesse to get out now.

31

BEST FRIENDS ARE FOREVER

"Do you have, like, a minidress? You would look awesome in a minidress," Gaby told Scarlett.

Scarlett eyed (or pretended to eye) the contents of her very spare closet. She knew exactly what was in there: about twenty pairs of jeans and the same number of tees and assorted other tops, mostly black. "Nah, no minidress," she announced. "I thought I'd just go with jeans and a T-shirt. Party's casual, right?"

"You can't wear jeans to the season finale party!" Gaby gasped.

"Why not?"

"Why not? Because . . . 'cause you just *can't*, that's all. Wait, lemme think. Maybe I can call someone to rush-messenger an outfit."

Scarlett sighed. Maybe this was a bad idea, letting Gaby come over. It wasn't like she could blame Dana this time, either. Tonight it was just Gaby and her—no Dana, no cameras, nothing.

Gaby had called the apartment this morning, asking to speak to Jane, and Scarlett had explained to her that Jane no longer lived there. (After all, it *had* been over two weeks since Jane moved out. Hadn't Gaby gotten the memo?) Gaby had pressed for details, and Scarlett must have sounded depressed or something, because the next thing she knew, Gaby was saying that she would come over after work so the two of them could get ready for the party together. And Scarlett had, inexplicably, agreed.

Now the two of them were hanging out in Scarlett's room, their faces covered with some sort of overpriced, smelly paste that Gaby had described as a pomegranate-lemongrass mask. Gaby had also painted both girls' toenails metallic white. The whole experience was a bit girlie for Scarlett's taste. Still, it was nice having company. Even if the company *was* Gaby.

Scarlett hadn't been hanging out with too many people lately. She'd gone out with her trainer Deb and Deb's friends a couple of times, and also Chelsea, the super-smart girl from her French novels seminar. She hadn't spoken to Jane at all. She hadn't spoken to Liam, either—not since before that awful night at Teddy's nearly two weeks ago. She had seen him at several shoots—two at USC, and one at a charity fashion show Dana had forced her to attend (Jane had been absent)—but he had steadfastly ignored her on all three occasions. Not that she blamed him. It hadn't even occurred to her to try to reach out to him, to explain, apologize. She had figured it was way too late.

Gaby walked over to Scarlett's closet and began rooting through it. "So, that sucks about Jane moving out," she murmured. "You guys are totally gonna make up, though."

"Yeah? How do you know?"

"Aren't you best friends from when you were, like, babies? Best friends are forever. That's why they're called BFFs."

"Well, then, where's *your* BFF, Madison?" Scarlett asked.

"No, no. Madison isn't my BFF. She's my BFFN. Or she *was*, anyway. She's too busy to hang out with me lately."

"BFFN?"

"Yeah. Best friend for now." Gaby shrugged.

Scarlett laughed. She had to admit that was funny. "Yeah, well, my BFF is pretty pissed off at me."

"Why?"

"I don't know." Scarlett sat down on her bed and hugged a pillow to her chest. "Well, I do know. Madison may be your friend or BFFN or whatever. But I think Madison's not a very good friend to Jane. I tried to tell Jane that, but she wouldn't believe me."

For a moment, Scarlett contemplated telling Gaby

about the pictures. But maybe Gaby would think she was crazy, too. Especially since Gaby liked Madison. The whole thing *did* sound pretty convoluted. *Yeah, so Madison somehow got hold of those photos of Jane hooking up with Braden. She tried to convince Jesse to sell them to* Gossip, *but he said no. So she sold them to* Gossip *herself, and lied to Jane, saying that Jesse did it, or that maybe I did it. . . .*

Gaby was staring at her. Scarlett took a deep breath. "And then there's Jesse. I tried to tell Jane that he's a drunk, no-good man-whore. But she wouldn't believe that, either. And now she's mad at me because she thinks I'm being way too negative about Madison and Jesse."

Gaby held up a black silk top and scrutinized it. "You know what?" she said. "If Madison isn't a good friend to Jane, she'll figure it out. And if Jesse isn't a good boyfriend, she'll figure that out, too. It's hard to tell people who they should hang out with and who they shouldn't hang out with, especially if they're not ready to hear that. You have to let your friends make their own mistakes sometimes. You can't protect them from everything, or else they'll never learn. Ya know what I mean?"

Scarlett stared at Gaby. This was the most profound sentiment she had ever heard the girl utter. "Yeah, I know what you mean."

"And when Jane figures this stuff out, she'll be back," Gaby went on. "'Cause BFF, right?"

"BFF. Right."

"So who's the guy?"

Scarlett frowned. "Uh . . . what guy?"

"The guy. You're seeing somebody, right? I can always tell. I've got a fifth sense about stuff like that."

"Oh."

"'Fess up. Are you in L-U-V?" Gaby wriggled her eyebrows suggestively.

"No!" Scarlett felt her face grow hot. "I mean, I *was* dating a guy. But we're not dating anymore."

"Lame. Why not?"

Scarlett hugged the pillow more tightly to her chest. "Because I blew it with him. When Jane moved out, I was really, really upset. He tried to be there for me and stuff, because he's such a nice guy, but I didn't want his sympathy, so I just pushed him away. Actually, I didn't just push him away. I was an asshole to him."

"So why don't you tell him you're sorry?" Gaby suggested.

"Uh . . . because he probably never wants to speak to me again?"

"How do you know? Do you have a fifth sense, too?"

Scarlett sighed. "No. And I think that's *sixth* sense."

"No, I don't see dead people. It's different. Anyway, look, if you like him, and he likes you, just tell him you're sorry. Give him a chance. If he's such a nice guy, he'll probably forgive you, right?"

Scarlett considered Gaby's words. When did the girl get to be so smart? Or had she been this way all along, and was just hiding it beneath a veneer of complete and total ditziness?

Gaby bent down and pulled out a couple of cardboard boxes from the floor of the closet. She brushed off a layer of dust bunnies. "What're these?"

"What? Oh. Jane gets all these designer clothes for free. Sometimes she gives them to me. But I don't wear that stuff."

"Are you *crazy*?" Gaby started ripping open the boxes. She looked like a little girl on Christmas morning. "Oooh! I love this beaded top! Can I borrow it? Please, please?"

"Uh, sure. You can have it."

"Really?" Gaby extracted a short black skirt from another box. "Oooh, this would be perfect on you! With your black silk top! You're gonna look hot!" She shimmied her shoulders.

"Hmm. No, thanks."

"*Yes*, thanks! You're wearing it! No arguments!"

Later, as Gaby worked on Scarlett's makeup (Scarlett couldn't stand makeup, and rarely let anyone apply it to her except for Jane, although Gaby seemed pretty good at it), Scarlett's thoughts drifted to Liam. What if Gaby was right? Maybe Scarlett should give him another chance.

Or rather, ask *him* to give *her* another chance.

Trevor stepped up to the mike. "Ladies and gentlemen, can I have your attention?"

Scarlett sipped her drink and glanced around the large, packed patio. PopTV had rented out a luxurious Malibu beach house—more like a beach mansion—for the season finale party. The backyard was lit with dozens of tiki torches. Scarlett loved the sound of the waves crashing against the dark shore.

She couldn't help but compare this party to the premiere party at Area back in October, a little over three months ago. Tonight's event seemed bigger, nicer, louder, and *way* more crowded. There was even a red carpet out front, with press. Scarlett had spent nearly thirty minutes posing for photographers and talking to reporters. Answering the same questions over and over. "Are Jane and Jesse back together?" "How are things between you and Jane?" "Will you and Madison ever bury the hatchet?" All answered with the same well-rehearsed response: "You'll have to watch and see." (Cue cheesy smile.) It made sense that the finale was a bigger deal than the premiere, since *L.A. Candy* was becoming more and more popular. Not that she cared.

Scarlett's gaze flitted around the crowd, searching for Liam. He would be here tonight—wouldn't he? She spotted several other PopTV crew members. But there was no sign of Liam. She tried to bite back her disappointment.

"Thank you all for being here tonight," Trevor went on. "For those of you who haven't seen the season finale yet, we all worked really hard on it, and it turned out amazing." Cheers erupted, and people clinked glasses. Trevor looked very pleased with himself.

Unlike with the season premiere party, they weren't showing the season finale to the guests tonight. Scarlett had heard from one of the producers that the episode was called "Decisions, Decisions," and featured Jane deciding to move out. It ended with a cliffhanger, at Beso, about Jane and Jesse's relationship—would he forgive her for cheating on him with he-who-shall-not-be-named, blah, blah, blah? Apparently, it was supposed to be a surprise when they *did* get back together, so Jane and Jesse weren't allowed to confirm their relationship to the press . . . even though they were constantly being photographed together, kissing and holding hands. Or having a big fight. *Yeah, they were really fooling people.*

Scarlett sneaked a glance at Jane, who was sitting across the table between Madison and Jesse. The two girls had exchanged polite hellos earlier, but not much more than that, which was so sad. Jane looked . . . stressed, probably because Jesse was downing vodka tonics like they were water. He kept slurring his words and sniping at Jane about stupid stuff, like why did they have to be at this lame party (Scarlett was sympathetic, but still . . .), and whose attention was she trying to attract with her revealing dress? (Jane's neckline showed about a millimeter of cleavage and was *hardly* revealing.)

Also seated at their table were Gaby, Hannah, Jane's new agent, R.J. (who seemed smart in a wise-dad kind of way), and her new publicist, Samantha (who pretty much hadn't stopped talking since the party started—the woman had an insane amount of energy). Hannah had been quiet tonight, nodding a lot but not saying much. From the few *L.A. Candy* episodes Scarlett had seen her on, her job seemed to be to play the part of one-girl cheering squad for Team Jesse. It was a little nauseating.

"And while I have you all here, I want to share some exciting news," Trevor went on, grinning coyly.

"Hey! Maybe they're canceling the show!" Scarlett joked. Everyone at the table stared at her. "I'm kidding! Seriously, people!"

"Yeah, Tina Fey, maybe you should quit *L.A. Candy* and go into comedy," Madison said, rolling her overly made-up eyes.

Scarlett fake-smiled at her. But even fake-smiling was an effort, because really all Scarlett wanted to do was to throw her drink in stupid Madison's face.

Trevor raised his champagne glass in the air. "So . . . I'm pleased to announce that *L.A. Candy* has been picked up for another season. We'll be back with not ten, but *twenty* brand-new episodes!"

Everyone began applauding loudly. The DJ started playing the song from the opening credits.

"OMG!" Gaby cried out. "This is amazing! We need more champagne!" She waved at a passing waiter.

"This is soooo awesome," Madison agreed. Scarlett could practically see the dollar signs flashing in her eyes.

The girls were paid two thousand dollars per episode—or that was what she and Jane were paid, anyway, so she assumed Madison and Gaby were paid that as well—so twenty episodes was a lot of money. Or would they be paid even more for next season? Scarlett wasn't exactly sure how these things worked. "The press is here tonight, right? Trevor's probably gonna want us to talk to them," Madison went on.

Hannah didn't say anything, instead fumbling with her clutch and extracting a lip gloss. Scarlett wondered what was up with her.

R.J. leaned over and whispered something in Jane's ear. Jane smiled excitedly and nodded.

Jesse put his arm around Jane, not-so-subtly pulling her away from R.J. "Yeah, so I guess this means I have to keep wearing those fucking microphones every time I take you out," he complained.

Jane's smile disappeared.

You sorry little piece of shit, Scarlett wanted to say to Jesse, but stopped herself. Jane was no doubt already embarrassed enough by Jesse's behavior. Scarlett didn't want to add to Jane's troubles by getting into a fight with her boyfriend in front of everyone. Even though she would love nothing more than to smash her fist into his very photogenic jaw.

"Honey, why don't you and I take a walk? There are some people I want to introduce you to," Sam said pleasantly to Jesse, rising to her feet.

Jesse gave Sam a smarmy look. "Yeah? Sure, why not?"

Sam grabbed Jesse's elbow—he wasn't exactly steady on his feet—and led him away, turning briefly to wink at Jane. Scarlett wasn't sure where Sam was taking him, but she hoped it involved car service and a one-way trip *somewhere*, anywhere but here.

As she watched Sam and Jesse go, Scarlett spotted a familiar figure walking up to the bar. It was Liam, greeting one of the other camera guys. He had come to the party, after all! He looked so handsome, dressed in a black suit (she had never seen him in a suit) and a charcoal shirt with a skinny black tie. She felt her heart race.

Go talk to him, she told herself, remembering what Gaby had said. *Stop being such an idiot.*

But what would she say to him? *Um, I'm really sorry I've been ignoring you and acting like a bitch. And I'm really sorry I hooked up with that guy while you were filming, even though I didn't hook up with him, because I bailed on him as soon as we were outside. So are we cool now? Can we go back to the way things were?*

Yeah, right, Scarlett thought. *Like he's gonna listen to you after what you did.*

She glanced up and caught Gaby looking at her. She gave Scarlett a huge, friendly smile and a thumbs-up sign. *Huh?* Was she encouraging her to go talk to Liam? But she didn't know Scarlett was dating Liam. Did she? That "fifth"-sense thing of hers was creepy. Or maybe she was just excited about the show getting picked up for another season.

"Excuse me," Scarlett said to no one in particular, standing up.

Then she headed toward Liam.

32

JANE WHO?

Madison felt like a million dollars as she headed into the house in search of a bathroom. (There were restrooms outside, but she didn't do lines.) Trevor had just announced a second season with twice as many episodes. Jesse was self-destructing before everyone's eyes, which meant that the demise of the Jane-Jesse love-fest wasn't far behind. With Jesse out of the picture, that left soooo much airtime to fill with the adventures of Jane and Madison . . . or even better, the adventures of just Madison, dating, going to the gym, maybe even going back to school. Or finding some fabulous new job that would look good for the cameras. The possibilities were endless.

Her arrangement with Veronica was looking up, too. Madison had been faithfully emailing the *Gossip* editor details of Jane's sorry love life: Jane's intimate postfight-at-Teddy's lunch with Braden, Jesse's not-very-happy reaction when he found out about it. The story had made the cover last week (much to Jane's dismay—maybe her publicist wasn't such a hotshot after all?).

And tonight, as soon as Madison got home, she would send Veronica another email about Jesse's continuing descent from clean and soberish to drunk and ugly. How many drinks did he put away tonight? Five or six? If it hadn't been for the stupid publicist intervening, that number might have climbed to double digits.

And in exchange, Veronica would have no choice but to give her a huge, prominently placed piece. And someday maybe even a cover.

"Um, excuse me, could we get a picture?" someone called out. Madison turned to see two young girls, maybe thirteen, standing around the all-white living room. They pulled a couple of matching pink cell phones out of their matching Kate Spade clutches.

"Sure." Madison stopped, fluffed her hair, and plastered on a smile.

The two girls snapped away, giggling. "Thank you so much!" one of them cried out.

"We love you!" the other one added.

Madison waved as she walked away, still smiling. Gone were the days when Jane was the only one fans noticed in public. Things had obviously changed in a few short months. And they would continue to change, as Madison's face and name became more and more prominent, and Jane's faded into obscurity. Someday, people would be begging Madison for her autograph and picture, and they would be saying, "Jane who?" with blank, puzzled expressions.

Madison had just spotted the guest bathroom when she noticed a guy and a girl making out in a doorway down the hall. *Jeez, go to a hotel,* she thought, although maybe she was just pissed because she hadn't seen Derek in a while. If he didn't get back from his annoying business trip soon, she would just have to call one of her other boyfriends.

It was the long, wavy black hair that made her look again. Madison stifled her surprise. The girl was Scarlett. And the guy was—Madison definitely recognized him—one of the PopTV cameramen! The one with the bandanna, Liam.

Madison slipped into the bathroom before Scarlett or Liam saw her. (Although they seemed way too busy to see much of anything.) This was almost too good to be true. PopTV had strict rules about the crew dating the talent.

Oh, Scarlett, Madison thought, smiling. *I'm gonna make your life so miserable.*

This night had just gone from great to amazing.

33

THE TRUTH, THE WHOLE TRUTH, AND NOTHING BUT THE TRUTH

"I've lined up interviews for you with *Talk* and *Life and Style*," Sam said. "And I'll probably have *Gossip* and *Star* for you by the end of the day. Everybody wants to talk to you about the show getting picked up for a second season. It's all good!"

It was Tuesday night, and Sam had dropped by the apartment to update her on the latest developments. Madison was at a spinning class with Gaby, so it was just Jane and Sam and Tucker, who was busily gnawing away at his new bone.

Jane twirled a lock of her hair. "*Gossip*? Do I really have to talk to them?"

"Yeah. I know you hate them for publishing those pictures of you and Braden. And for the crap they've been printing about you and Jesse lately. But the only way to make them write nice things about you in the future is to be nice to them. I know it sucks, but that's just how it works in this business, sweetie."

"Ugh."

"I know, I know. Don't worry; I'll come with you for the interview. If the reporter goes off topic and tries to ambush you with personal questions, I'll take care of it so you don't have to be the bitch."

"Oh, really?"

"Yeah. That's what I'm here for: to be the bad guy so you never have to. I'm basically a bitch for hire."

Jane had to laugh. It was so nice to finally feel a little in control of the media circus that surrounded her. D was right—Sam was a miracle worker.

And her agent, R.J., was a miracle worker, too. He was in the process of negotiating a new contract for Jane for season two, which he promised would be way better than her package for season one. *If* there was a season two . . . for Jane. She still had mixed feelings about continuing with the show. Which was more important to her—having a private life or a fabulous life? She didn't have the answer yet. And the clock was ticking. In the meantime, her only remaining filming obligation was the Valentine's Day party at the Tropicana, which was coming up in less than two weeks. The party would be featured in one of the early season-two episodes.

After the Tropicana party, Jane and the other girls would have three weeks off, and then filming would begin again, with season-two episodes to start airing in the spring.

Jane picked up her mug of herbal tea and took a sip. She had started drinking a special chamomile, valerian, and something-else blend from the health food store every night, to try to destress. She had been having a hard time sleeping lately. "Soooo. You think people have forgotten about those pictures of me and Braden? And what about the stuff about me and Jesse?"

"I know, I know. We've gotta keep the public's attention focused on the good stuff, like the show getting picked up for another season and your wonderful career and your wonderful new apartment and—oh, yeah, your wonderful new dog! I think there's some kind of celebrity dog event coming up, to raise money for spay-neuter outreach." Sam pulled her BlackBerry out of her oversize Louis Vuitton bag and began punching keys.

Tucker had been living with Jane and Madison for a little over a week now, and Jane had gotten into the habit of buying him a new treat or two almost daily. There were bones and stuffed animals and balls scattered all over the living room floor.

"You're the best," Jane said to Sam, meaning it.

Sam glanced up. "Just doing my job. Speaking of which . . . we gotta talk about your boyfriend. Honey, what exactly is going on between you two?"

"What do you mean?"

"I mean, just how bad has the drinking gotten? And have you heard anything about a girl named Amber?"

Jane stared at her. "How do you know about Amber?"

"Small town, and it's part of my job to know these things."

Jane looked away. Why did Sam have to bring this up? She had already gone over this stuff with Jesse, and she was tired of discussing it. In fact, the subject was downright painful.

Shuddering, she reached for a soft white throw to wrap around her shoulders. She felt like crap. She hoped she wasn't coming down with something.

"Jane, honey." Sam's voice was gentle. "You've gotta tell me the truth. Otherwise, I can't help you."

"What do you mean, help me?" Jane demanded, a little surprised at the harsh tone in her own voice. "Why do I need help?"

"I mean, when reporters call me for a comment because they claim Jesse's been seen with some other girl, or he's passed out on the floor at Bar Marmont, or the two of you are having a knock-down-drag-out fight about Braden, I've gotta know what to say to them. My job is to protect you. And you have to remember that in this relationship with Jesse, you're guilty by association. So when Jesse does bad things, it makes *you* look bad, too. I know you don't want to hear that, but it's the truth."

"Sam, what do you want me to tell you?" Jane blurted out. "I love him." She paused. "There isn't anything I can do about that. He's not perfect, but I love him."

"I get it," Sam said sympathetically. "Love sucks, doesn't it?"

"You're preaching to the choir." Jane smiled bitterly.

"I had this girlfriend once. I thought she was the one. For our six-month anniversary, I bought her this gorgeous necklace. One day I noticed it was gone. I asked her where it was, and she told me her apartment was robbed. Turns out she sold the necklace to buy coke. I had no clue she even did drugs."

"That's awful!"

"Yeah. You never know about people, right?"

"Yeah, but this whole thing is not Jesse's fault. It's *my* fault. He was so sweet to me before I cheated on him, and before Braden came back to L.A., and—"

"Honey, you're not responsible for Jesse's behavior," Sam interrupted. "I've been in the business for a while, and I've run in some of the same circles as Jesse. This is just how he is. He was like this before you ever came along. You're in no way responsible for his behavior." Sam added, "That being said, I need you to tell me what that behavior is. The truth, the whole truth, and nothing but the truth. Otherwise, I can't do my job."

Jane took another sip of her tea. The truth was, things had gotten steadily worse with Jesse in the past couple weeks since the *Alt* party at Teddy's. He was drunk more often than not. She had gotten several middle-of-the-night calls from Quentin, asking her to come and pick up Jesse at Les Deux or Apple or one of the other clubs

Quentin promoted. Fortunately, Jesse thought of Quentin as a friend and liked hanging out at his clubs. Otherwise, who would take away his car keys, hide him from reporters, and send out an SOS to Jane? D was sometimes at the scene when Jesse had one of his "incidents" and was always ready with a sympathetic hug for Jane and a knowing look that said, *Why on earth are you with this guy, baby cakes?*

As for Amber . . . Jane had asked Jesse point-blank about her, and he had somehow managed to turn it around to make it all about her and Braden. "Yeah, well, are you telling me I can't have a drink with a friend?" he had snapped. "Because you're allowed to go out with your friends, aren't you? I mean, you had lunch with your *friend* Braden. So why can't I have a drink with my *friend* Amber? You're a fucking hypocrite, you know that?" After that, it had been impossible for Jane to argue with him.

He never used to talk to her like that. And the more he drank, the angrier he got. But it had gotten to the point where she was too tired to fight back, to have the same argument over and over again. So she let him say those awful and hurtful things to her, knowing that he would beg for her forgiveness in the morning and promise never to act that way again. Which was a promise he always kept—until his next drink.

Still, she loved him, and in between the drinking, they were happy.

But something definitely had to change. And Jane

couldn't bear another publicity scandal like the one she'd survived. Barely.

"Okay," she said finally. "How long do you have?"

Sam grinned. "For you, honey, I've got all night."

Jane started talking.

34

LUCKY SKIRT

Scarlett hummed to herself as she dug through her closet, looking for the black miniskirt from the season finale party. Ever since that night, when she and Liam had made up, she had thought of that skirt as her lucky skirt. She wanted to wear it tonight, because Liam was taking her out to his favorite dumpling restaurant in Chinatown. He claimed he had even learned a few phrases in Mandarin, so he could converse with the waiters in their native tongue and show up Scarlett, for once.

Life is good, Scarlett thought. She and Liam were together again. He had accepted her apology at the season finale party, and they had seen each other almost every night since then. It was hard for even her to believe, but for the first time in her life, she was in a relationship. Not a casual hookup . . . not a one-night stand . . . but an actual relationship. And it wasn't half-bad. In fact, it was pretty amazing.

Even school was going well. She was enjoying her

classes, especially her literature seminars, and she was writing an awesome paper on *Madame Bovary* by Gustave Flaubert that would surely win her the Pulitzer prize for brilliant school papers (if such a thing existed).

Now all she had to do was patch things up with Jane. Then things could return to normal.

She got dressed, even applying some violet eyeliner and shimmery lip gloss that Gaby had picked up for her at Sephora. (The girl was smart about clothes and makeup; Scarlett would give her that.) She glanced at the clock: 7:15. Hmm, Liam was late. Maybe it was just Friday-evening traffic?

Seven twenty, 7:25. Finally, the doorbell rang.

"Coming!" Scarlett yelled, slipping on a pair of cute black wedges that she had found in one of Jane's freebie boxes.

A moment later, she opened the front door, wondering if Liam would tease her about her outfit. Or would he just tell her how hot she looked and take her in his arms, as he had done at the Malibu beach house?

"Hey—" Scarlett began. And stopped when she saw the expression on Liam's face. "What's wrong?"

Liam thrust a rumpled-up magazine at her. "This just came out today."

Scarlett stepped back to let him into the apartment. He walked in right past her. She stared down at the magazine he had handed her. It was *Gossip*. The cover had a photo of that blond actress, Anna Payne, wearing a really unflattering bikini and devouring a doughnut. The cover line read, ANNA'S SHOCKING WEIGHT GAIN!

Scarlett frowned, confused. "I don't get it."

"Turn to page sixteen." Liam's voice was steely with anger.

"What is it? It's not some lame picture of me with that guy at the *Alt* party, is it? Because I told you, I didn't go home with him, and—"

"Just turn to page sixteen."

"Okay, okay. Oh . . . my . . . *God*!"

There on page sixteen was a photo of her and Liam walking hand in hand along Venice Beach. The bold letters above the photo read, *L.A. CANDY* STAR HOOKS UP WITH CAMERAMAN!

"No way!" Scarlett cried out. "We were so careful! How did they—"

"Obviously, we weren't careful enough," Liam interrupted. "Did you tell anyone about us?"

Scarlett's thoughts flashed to Gaby. But she hadn't mentioned Liam's name to her. "No. Why, did you?"

"No. I mean, my friends met you at the New Year's Eve party. But none of them know we've been going out since then. And none of them would be sick enough to tip off the press."

"How do you know someone tipped off the press? It could've been some random photographer who saw us, right? We were on Venice Beach day before yesterday."

"Yeah, except that the article quotes some 'source close

to the pair.' You got any friends like that?"

Startled, Scarlett scanned the article. Liam was right. The reporter quoted someone saying that Scarlett and Liam were "making out" at the *L.A. Candy* season finale party on Monday night and had left the Malibu beach house together afterward.

What the hell? Scarlett racked her brain for who could have seen her and Liam kissing there. They had taken great pains to find a secluded spot inside the house. *What* source? Could it have been Gaby, after all?

"What are we gonna do?" Scarlett groaned.

"What do you mean, what are we gonna do? If you're talking about my job, it's too late. I got the call this afternoon from Trevor Lord himself. I'm off the crew."

"He fired you?"

"Yeah, he fired me."

"Oh, no! I'm so sorry." Scarlett reached over to hug him. He pulled back, clearly not in the mood for a hug.

Scarlett folded her arms across her chest, feeling dumb because she obviously didn't know what he needed or wanted from her right now. "Maybe he'll fire me next. I broke his stupid rule, too," she muttered.

"You? He's not gonna fire you. You're good for ratings, now that you and Jane aren't speaking to each other."

"Great. Why is it that what's good for ratings and what's good for me are totally opposite? Seems a little backward."

"Yeah, you're right about that." Liam leaned against

the wall and rubbed his eyes.

"I guess you probably lost your appetite for Chinese dumplings, huh?" she said.

"Yeah. Sorry."

"No worries. We can stay in if you want. You wanna order in?"

"Can I take a rain check? I think I just wanna go home and chill."

"Um, okay. But you're not mad at me about this, are you?"

"No, Scarlett. I'm not mad at you. I'm just mad. I just got fired, and *I* don't get paid to go clubbing and shopping for some stupid show, so *I* have to figure out what the hell I'm gonna do."

"Hey. I get that you're angry, but you can't put this on me. And until today, you worked on that 'stupid show.'"

"Look, I'm sorry. I'm just upset, and I need to be alone. I'll call you tomorrow." Liam opened the door and started to head out. He stopped, though, and kissed Scarlett on the cheek. "I'm not mad at you," he said again.

"'Kay. Whatever," Scarlett said coolly.

Closing the door after him, Scarlett caught her reflection in the hallway mirror. So much for her lucky skirt.

35

PLEASE DON'T GO

Jane glanced at the clock on the DVD player: 3:22 a.m. Below, the TV was paused on an image from the *L.A. Candy* season finale, in which she and Jesse were staring at each other across a table at Beso. That was the night—was it really only a month ago?—when they had made up, after all the awfulness. She wasn't sure why she was watching this episode tonight. She remembered how awesome it felt to believe the bad stuff was behind them. But that feeling hadn't lasted long. She was trying to understand how everything had gone so horribly wrong between them. Again.

As if analyzing Trevor's beautifully lit, carefully edited scene could help her understand the complex, dark reality of her and Jesse's relationship.

Where the hell is he? she wondered, checking her phone again. No missed calls. No messages. Jesse had promised to come over to the apartment after he stopped by Hyde for a drink with some friends. He should have been here hours ago. Jane knew the clubs closed at 2 a.m. The neon blue numbers flickered: 3:23 a.m.

Madison was out; she had said something about a hot date. So it was just Jane and Tucker, who was curled up on the rug in front of the TV, his paws tucked around his new stuffed bunny. (Jane needed to relax on buying doggy toys.)

Jane picked up her phone again. Reluctantly, she started dialing. It rang once, twice. . . .

"Hello?"

"Hey, it's Jane. I'm so sorry to call you so late. I'm just—"

"I've got him, Jane," Quentin said before she could finish. "I was just about to call you."

Jane rubbed her forehead. She wasn't sure whether to be relieved or really, really pissed off at Jesse. In any case, she was grateful to Quentin, whom she had come to regard as a good friend. Not a good friend she actually hung out with, but a good friend who looked out for her by looking out for her boyfriend whenever he was . . . well, in need of assistance. "Thank you. Where are you guys? Do I need to come pick him up?" She was in her sweats, but it would take her only a minute to change.

"I brought him home to my house," Quentin replied. "Long story. He's fine. Why don't you go to sleep, love, and I'll drive him to your place in the morning? It's too late to come over here."

"I should come get him," Jane insisted.

"Jane, it's late. Go to bed. I'll have him call you when he wakes up."

Jane hesitated. "Okay. Quentin, thank you so much. I'm sorry if he was trouble tonight."

"No trouble at all . . . well, no more than usual. Just let him sleep it off, and you can talk to him in the morning."

"Okay, thanks."

Jane hung up. These phone calls between her and Quentin had increased in frequency in the past couple of weeks. And the incidents were getting uglier. Just a few nights ago, Quentin had called Jane because Jesse had fallen down the stairs and cut his face while smoking outside of Teddy's. Jane still had blood on the backseat of her car, where he had passed out on the way home.

Jane leaned forward on the couch and put her head in her hands. What was she going to do? She was so unhappy. When Jesse was sober, he was the sweetest guy in the world. Just yesterday, he had surprised her with a beautiful silver charm bracelet. She glanced at it now, at the single heart-shaped charm engraved with the words, JESSE + JANE 4EVER. But when he was drunk, he was downright cruel. She was constantly on edge, wondering which Jesse would walk through the door: sober Jesse or not-sober Jesse?

Jane hadn't gone out in public with him since the season finale party last Monday. She wasn't sure if she ever wanted to go out in public with him again. She didn't want to risk being out in the world with not-sober Jesse, especially because of the fights. The paparazzi were always following her now. She couldn't keep sneaking him out the back doors of clubs or covering up for him forever. At this rate, not even Sam the miracle-worker publicist could keep the truth from leaking out.

At least Sam knew the whole story now. So did Hannah, whom Jane talked to late at night on the phone sometimes about Jesse. Ever since Hannah's confession, their friendship had become much more real. She wished she could talk to Braden, but she wasn't sure where things stood with them, and she didn't want to complicate the situation any more right now. She hadn't spoken to him since that night he drove her home, although he *had* texted her a couple of times, just to make sure she was okay.

As for Scar . . . she *wished* she could talk to Scar the most. They used to share everything. But they had barely said two words to each other since Jane moved out. With everything that was going on, she really missed her old friend.

"God, how did my life become such a mess?" Jane moaned to Tucker. He gazed at her with his big brown eyes and thumped his tail. At least *he* was sympathetic.

She must have fallen asleep on the couch, because the clock on the DVD player read 4:02 when she heard someone rattling the front doorknob. Tucker bounded to the door and began barking.

"Madison?" Jane called out groggily. "Did you forget your keys?"

Bang, bang, bang. "Jane! Open up!"

Jane shot up. It was Jesse! What the hell was he doing here? He was supposed to be at Quentin's, sleeping. Had he talked Quentin into driving him over, after all?

She jumped to her feet and rushed to the door, opening it quickly while trying to restrain Tucker, whose barking had probably woken up the entire building by now.

Jesse was standing there, his shirt untucked. He reeked of vodka and cigarettes. "Shit, what took you so long?" he snapped.

"I thought you were staying at Quentin's."

Jesse just sneered at her, then stumbled into the apartment and over to the couch. He lay down with his shoes still on and closed his eyes. Tucker followed him and licked his hand, whimpering. Jesse pushed him away.

Jane sighed. This was getting so old. She went over to the couch and slipped off Jesse's shoes. Then she emptied his pockets. Going through the first pocket, she pulled out a pack of cigarettes, a lighter, his cell phone, and a cocktail napkin with *Hot Cheryl 310-555-1089* written across it. She shook her head and crumpled up the napkin. Then she reached into his other pocket and pulled out a black Montblanc money clip and a set of keys.

They weren't his keys.

"What are you doing?" Jesse stared at her with his

half-opened, bloodshot eyes as she tried to make out the initials on the key chain.

"Jesse, whose keys are these?"

"They're mine."

"No, Jesse, these aren't yours. They're BMW keys. Whose BMW?"

"How the fuck should I know?" Jesse rolled over, turning his back to her.

"Jesse! How . . . did . . . you . . . get . . . these . . . keys?" When he was this wasted, she had to speak to him slowly and patiently, as if she were speaking to a child.

"God!" Jesse burst out. "You're so annoying! They're Quentin's! I took 'em while he was sleeping! Now leave me alone!"

"You drove Quentin's car here?" Jane asked him quietly. The thought of him driving to her apartment in his state was terrifying. He could have gotten killed. Worse yet, he could have killed someone else.

Jesse sat up and glared at her. "Ahhh, fuck this," he muttered. He stood up, grabbed the keys out of her hand, and staggered toward the front door.

"Jesse, where are you going?"

Jesse kept walking, completely unaware that he had no shoes on. He started to open the front door. Jane ran over and quickly closed it, then positioned herself between the door and Jesse.

"Jesse, give me the keys. You can't drive right now. You're too drunk," she said firmly.

"Move!" Jesse said as he reached again for the doorknob.

Jane pushed his hand away and twisted the dead bolt shut. "Jesse, let's just go to bed, okay? You need your sleep," she pleaded.

"I don't want to sleep with you. You're too fucking annoying. Move!"

"No!" Jane pressed her back against the door. Her heart was racing a mile a minute. She couldn't let him leave. He could barely stand up straight, let alone steer a vehicle.

"God damn it, Jane!" His eyes blazed at her with pure, cold hatred.

"Please don't go," Jane begged, and realized that she was crying. She was afraid of him—she was always afraid of him when he got like this—but she was even more afraid to let him back outside, behind the wheel of a car.

"God damn it!" Jesse grabbed her shoulders and pulled her away from the door. He was so strong, much stronger than she was. Tucker nipped at his heels, barking, agitated by the commotion.

Sobbing, Jane threw herself at the door again. "Please, Jesse, please just stay here. You don't have to sleep with me. I'll sleep in Madison's room. Please, I'm sorry." She knew she was rambling almost incoherently; she could barely understand herself, she was crying so hard. But she had to stop him.

"*Move!*" Jesse shouted. Jane dug in, pressing her back against the door with as much force as she could. At which point Jesse grabbed her shoulders again and shoved her, hard. She landed on the floor, pain shooting up her side. She was so stunned that she could barely breathe.

Jesse didn't even look backward as he walked out, slamming the door behind him.

36

I DON'T KNOW WHAT I'D DO WITHOUT YOU

Madison yawned as she fumbled through her pink-and-gold Prada clutch for her keys. It was almost 5 a.m., and she couldn't wait to get inside and slip out of her spaghetti-strap pink dress and into bed.

It had been a long night, but totally worth it. Derek had managed to get away for a few hours on the pretext of entertaining some big-shot clients from Tokyo who liked to party late. They'd gotten a suite at the Beverly Hills Hotel, a bottle of champagne, and an amazing room-service spread. It had almost made up for the fight they'd had on the phone last week about Jane's mutt, who had already destroyed two of his favorite chairs (not to mention several pairs of Madison's favorite shoes). Of course, Madison would love nothing more than to see the animal go back to the pound. But she couldn't make Jane get rid of him. Not yet. It was all working. She'd already noticed more Madison time on the season finale, which she knew would mean more Madison in season two once they started airing episodes about Jane in her new apartment. Which meant that Madison still needed to keep her happy.

Granted, Madison needed to keep Derek happy, too, so she could continue to benefit from his generosity and his unlimited line of credit (not to mention his fabulous condo in Cabo). Otherwise, where would she live? Of course, there were always other Dereks out there. She knew, because he wasn't her first. And he wouldn't be her last.

The only low point in the otherwise perfect evening had been a mysterious text message Madison had received at the hotel, while Derek was in the shower. Someone with a private number had written: YOU CAN'T FOOL PEOPLE FOREVER. YOU'RE RUNNING OUT OF TIME.

WTF? It had to be a prank, although it did remind of her of the text she'd gotten during her and Jane's spa outing: I'VE BEEN WATCHING YOU ON TV AND I KNOW WHO YOU REALLY ARE. Obviously, there were a lot of sick people out there with way too much time on their hands.

She reassured herself once again that no one could possibly know. Still, it was eerie. She forced her thoughts to return to happier things, like the pair of pink sapphire studs Derek had given her tonight as an early Valentine's Day present. Pink diamonds would have been better, but she shouldn't complain.

Madison opened the door quietly, so as not to wake

Jane or Tucker. She stopped when she saw Jane lying on the couch.

Jane stirred. "Madison?"

Madison walked over to the couch and sat down next to her. Jane was curled up in a fetal position, her face streaked with tears. "Are you okay? What happened?" she said.

"I'm fine," Jane said, not particularly convincingly.

"You're *not* okay. What happened?"

"Jesse. He—" Jane began crying. "He was so drunk, and I tried to keep him from driving home, but he wouldn't listen, and—"

"Did you guys have a fight? What happened? Sweetie, calm down; I can't understand you when you're crying."

But Jane wouldn't stop crying. Madison wrapped her arms around her. Jane only cried harder, so Madison held her tighter.

"Oww." Jane touched her side.

"What's wrong? What hurts?"

"Nothing."

Madison frowned. "Come on, sweetie. Let's get you into bed."

Madison helped Jane to her feet and led her slowly to her bedroom. She knew that Jane and Jesse had been fighting a lot lately. She could hear their muffled arguments through the wall. But she had never seen Jane this upset.

Jane lay down on her bed and drew the covers up to her chin. The dog jumped up and curled up at her feet, looking subdued. He seemed to know something wasn't right.

"Can I get you anything?" Madison asked.

"Yeah, my phone. I think it's on the coffee table."

"Who're you gonna call? It's, like, five a.m."

"I just need to send a text. Please, Madison? It's important. Before I change my mind."

"Okay, okay."

Madison hurried to the living room and retrieved the phone, which she found on the floor next to a pair of black men's loafers. (*WTF?*) She noticed that the TV was on Pause, fixed on an image of Jesse and Jane at Beso. (*Again, WTF?*) She turned off the TV and brought the phone back to Jane.

Jane took it from her and began typing. "I should've done this a long time ago," she whispered to herself.

"Done what, sweetie?"

Jane held up the screen for Madison. The message read:

JESSE: WE'RE DONE. I MEAN IT THIS TIME. I NEVER WANT 2 SEE U OR SPEAK 2 U AGAIN.

"Good for you," Madison said, hugging her. And she was surprised to find that she meant it, and not just because she had been angling to break Jane and Jesse up for ages, but because Jane didn't deserve to be treated like this. Madison wanted to take Jane's place on the show, sure. But she didn't want to see Jane's spirit crushed by a drunk train wreck like Jesse.

She'd seen too many women go through crap like that. Including her own mother.

Jane hit Send, then sank back wearily against the pillows. "I'm so tired," she mumbled. "Madison, will you stay with me? I don't wanna be alone right now."

"Of course, sweetie." Madison slipped off her gold Miu Miu sandals and got into bed beside Jane.

"Thank you," Jane whispered.

"For what?"

"For being such a good friend. I don't know what I'd do without you."

Madison took a deep breath, trying to figure out how to respond. *You're welcome? You're a good friend, too? Sorry about trying to destroy your TV career and image—it's nothing personal?*

But she didn't have to worry about it, because Jane had fallen asleep. Madison closed her eyes, trying to sleep, too. But her mind was too busy and confused. So much was happening so fast; she felt overwhelmed.

The dog made a sighing sound. Madison smiled slightly, wondering how they must look: her, Jane, and the animal, all snuggled in Jane's bed, the first faint light of the Los Angeles sunrise shining through the curtains.

"So what do you have for me?" Veronica Bliss asked pleasantly. She'd been a lot nicer to Madison since she gave her the info about Scarlett and her camera guy. "When someone gets fired," she'd said after the story ran, "you know it was a good tip. Keep the good tips coming, Madison."

Madison shifted in her chair. The *Gossip* editor was sitting at her desk, sifting through piles of what looked like scandalous photographs of a familiar-looking brunette. That underwear model? That actress who played the little sister in *Animal Magnetism*? Madison felt sorry for her, whoever she was.

"Don't feel sorry for her," Veronica said, as if reading her mind. "She leaked these herself. Her career needed a boost. So." She folded her hands and stared at Madison expectantly. "What's going on with Jane Roberts these days?"

Madison hesitated. There was so much she could say, especially after last night. Jane had filled her in on the rest of the details this morning, over a late breakfast. But she couldn't get the image of Jane out of her head, nestled against her shoulder and whispering, "Thank you for being such a good friend. I don't know what I'd do without you."

Shit! She was going soft. Which she could hardly afford to do, now that she had this beneficial arrangement going with Veronica. Veronica had even come through, publishing a full-page piece about Madison's predictions for season two in last week's issue (the same issue that blew the cover off Scarlett's little romance). Madison deserved to be the star of *L.A. Candy*. And she was almost there. She could practically taste it.

Which meant that Jane had to go. There couldn't be *two* stars on the show. Besides, Jane didn't even appreciate what she had.

"Well?" Veronica's eyes flashed impatiently at her.

Madison looked away. "Yeah. So I think Jane and Jesse broke up last night."

"You *think* they broke up?"

"They did. They broke up."

"Where? When? Was there another girl involved? Or another guy? Is Braden back in the picture? I need details."

"I . . . don't have any details yet. I'm working on it."

"Well, get on it! I'm going to clear the cover for this week's issue. Deadline's end of business tomorrow. Can I count on you?"

"Yes."

"Good. Tomorrow, five p.m. I'll be expecting an update."

As Madison walked out of Veronica's office, she noticed her assistant staring at her. That little dude was so weird. But she was too preoccupied to stop and ask him what the hell his problem was. She had her *own* problem—namely, what was she going to tell Veronica tomorrow at 5 p.m.?

37

LOVE IS CRAZY

Jane scanned the patio of the Tropicana Bar, nervously going through her mental checklist of to-dos. Rose petals in the pool. Check. Red cushions on the chairs. Check. Vintage coolers filled with cans of Crazy Girl's latest energy drink, Psycho Remix. Check. The step-and-repeat with the Crazy Girl logo. Check. Crazy Girl gift bags. Check. Naomi was organizing them on a table by the entrance. DJ equipment. Check. DJ . . . *Uh-oh!* Where was the DJ?

Jane twisted her earpiece into her right ear, and she plugged the long cord that attached to the earpiece into a walkie-talkie. The extra hardware didn't exactly coordinate with her high-waisted black skirt and red silk blouse, but Fiona had dictated that they be mandatory accessories for the entire night, so that Jane and Hannah could be in touch at all times. Jane was also wearing her mike pack for the PopTV cameras (there were four of them tonight), creating an unfortunate lump underneath her fitted skirt.

She hadn't been able to attach it to her bra because the back of her top dipped too low.

Jane switched on the radio. "Hannah? Are you there? We've got a problem."

"What's wrong?" Hannah's voice boomed back. Jane cringed at the volume and twisted a knob on her headset to lower it.

"Where are you right now?" Jane asked her.

"I'm at the door. People are starting to arrive, and there was a mix-up with the guest list."

"Mix-up? What mix-up?" Jane demanded.

"Don't worry about it. Gaby's here with me, and she's on the phone straightening it out with her boss at Ruby Slipper. So what's going on?"

"Where's the DJ?"

"He's not here yet?"

"I haven't seen him. Has anyone talked to him?"

"Not that I know of. I have his number and . . . Listen, Isaac is here; I'll put him on it."

Isaac was one of the interns at Fiona Chen Events. "Okay, perfect. Will you have him call right now, and let me know if he gets ahold of him?"

"Yup. We're on it."

"Great. Thanks."

"Hey, Jane? One more thing. There's a girl here who says she's a friend of yours. She's not on the list, though. Her name's, uh, Fabiana? She's got three—no, four other girls with her." In the background, Jane heard laughter and someone screaming, "Hey, homegirl!"

"Fabiana? I don't know anyone named Fabiana."

"Didn't think so, thanks."

Jane clicked off and was about to see about the hors d'oeuvres when someone tapped her on the shoulder. It was Madison, looking stunning and barely PG in a magenta minidress that was nearly see-through. "Ohmigod, does your mother know you're wearing that?" Jane said, hugging her.

Madison grinned. "I guess I'm gonna be grounded, huh?"

"Yeah, no TV for a week." Jane laughed.

"Place looks amazing. You guys did a great job."

"Thanks. I don't know. There was a problem with the guest list, and we can't find the DJ, and—"

Madison squeezed her arm. "Don't stress. It's gonna be an awesome night."

"Yeah. It's just that it's my first big assignment for Fiona, ya know? And I've been kinda distracted lately . . ."

A waitress came by, carrying a tray of frosty-looking pink Cosmos. She was wearing the uniform Jane had come up with for all the waitresses: a red halter top and a pair of short shorts with the words CRAZY GIRL spelled across the derriere. "Care for a cocktail?" she offered.

Madison plucked a glass off the tray. "Absolutely."

Jane declined. She had to stay focused. "Did you like the invites?" she asked Madison. "Gaby helped come up with the theme, 'Love Is Crazy.' She's super-creative."

"Yeah, well, love *is* crazy." Madison took a sip of her Cosmo. "Speaking of . . . He isn't coming tonight, is he?"

Jane didn't even have to ask who Madison was talking about. "Don't know. He was on the guest list. We sent the invites out a while ago."

"Well, if he shows his sorry face, send him my way. I'll take care of him," Madison told her.

"Thanks."

Jane hadn't seen or spoken to Jesse since that horrible night last weekend. He had filled up her voice mailbox with messages, apologizing and telling her that he loved her . . . but she had ignored them all, and eventually started deleting them without even listening to them. This morning, she had received three dozen red roses from him, sent over from one of the most exclusive florists in L.A. Did he seriously think that flowers would make up for the way he treated her? She had given them to the elderly woman who lived on the floor below.

"Hey, isn't that Jared Walsh at the bar?" Madison said, peering across the pool. "I think I'll go see what he thinks of my dress."

"Uh, Madison? I think he's married."

"Yeah, I don't think that really matters with him. Wish me luck."

Jane laughed.

By nine o'clock, the party was getting crowded. The DJ had finally arrived—his car had broken down on the

Santa Monica Freeway—and was spinning a perfectly pitched mix of old and new love songs. Jane was stressed and running around—there were so many details to attend to (like making sure the in-house photographer was getting enough product-placement shots without bothering any of the guests), and a couple of fires to put out (they had seated two starlets-slash-BFFs at the same table, but it turned out they weren't speaking this week). And yet she was exhilarated, too, because everyone seemed to be having a good time, and Fiona had actually come up to Jane and said, "Things appear to be in order." Which, for Fiona, was a glowing compliment.

Jane spotted lots of familiar faces in the crowd, including R.J., Sam, and Quentin (who had shot her a sympathetic smile). Scar had arrived earlier with several girls Jane didn't recognize—maybe students from USC? Jane had been meaning to talk to her since the *Gossip* article about her and one of the camera guys broke last week. Jane had no idea that Scar was dating anyone, much less Liam, who seemed like a nice guy and was definitely cute. The thing was, Scar didn't date. Of course, knowing *Gossip*, the story had been twisted to make it *appear* as though Scar and Liam were in a relationship, when it was probably just a casual fling.

Or maybe Scar had changed her ways and failed to clue Jane in. It wasn't like they were confiding in each other these days. As frustrated as Jane had been dealing with Scar's negative attitude, she couldn't help but miss her. Madison was a great friend, but she could never be her *best* friend, not like Scar was.

"Jane."

Jane froze at the sound of the familiar voice behind her. He *had* come to the party, after all.

He kissed the back of her neck. "Did you get the flowers I sent?"

Jane flinched and turned around. Jesse looked stylish in his black Armani suit, white tailored shirt, and skinny red tie. He also looked intoxicated. Jane wasn't surprised. She knew the signs so well: the tired, unfocused eyes . . . the slurred speech . . . the flushed cheeks. Not to mention the stupid smirk on his face and the not-so-subtle scent of whiskey and . . . God, did she smell pot, too? *Nice, Jesse,* she thought in disgust.

She saw that he wasn't wearing a mike pack. He must have slipped in past Dana and also Trevor, who had made a point to be at the party tonight. They weren't exactly happy with her decision to break up with him via text . . . in the middle of the night . . . off-camera. Trevor said that he understood that she was upset, but they were going to have to "come up with something" later. Jane wasn't entirely sure what he meant by that, but she had agreed, just to shut him up.

Jane scanned the crowd, looking for Trevor and Dana. She figured they would track Jesse down momentarily in order to mike him. Although she didn't know if any of the footage would even be usable, because the finished episodes never showed Jesse trashed. After all, he was supposed to be the perfect guy who every teenage girl dreamed of being with.

"I'm working right now, Jesse." Jane turned to go.

Jesse grabbed her arm. Jane wrenched it away. "I said, I'm *working*," she repeated angrily.

"Whassa matter? Ya don't love me anymore?" He wobbled on his feet, clutching at the air and then at the back of a woman's chair. The woman spun around and glared at him.

Why did I ever think I could change him? Jane wondered. Her friends had been right about him. It pained her to admit this, and at the same time, she felt so free. Like she no longer had to continue her lonely, dysfunctional dance with him. Love *was* crazy. But it was supposed to be mostly good-crazy, not bad-crazy.

Jane was finished with her conversation with Jesse—for good. She fake-smiled at him and walked away. She heard him yell out her name, followed by a loud crash and the sound of something breaking. "Please get someone to clean that up," she called out to a passing waitress, without even looking back.

"Jane! Pssst, Miss Jane!"

Oh, God, what now? Jane glanced around and saw Diego waving to her from behind a nearby palm tree. Was he . . . hiding? "Hey, D!" Jane went up to him and gave him a big hug. It was nice to see a friendly face, especially after her encounter with Jesse. "How's it going? Did you just get here? Why are you hiding?"

"I'm hiding 'cause— Ohmigod, love your Loubs! Are they new?"

"Yeah, thanks. So what's going on?"

D pulled Jane behind the palm tree. "I can't let her see me," he whispered.

"Who?"

D pointed at Jane's mike pack, gesturing that they should speak in low volumes so as not to get picked up. Jane nodded to indicate that she understood. She leaned in closer and started to rub her thumb back and forth across the top of the mike. It was a trick she and Madison had figured out recently. That way, all the mike would pick up was a loud fuzzy sound.

"Who are you hiding from?" Jane whispered.

"The person who gave those pictures of you to Veronica," D whispered back.

Jane gaped at him. "What are you talking about?" she stammered.

D reached into the pocket of his leopard-print smoking jacket and extracted several pieces of paper, folded in quarters. "I'm so sorry, sweetie. I found these emails on Veronica's computer, like, an hour ago. I started digging around when I saw her in Veronica's office today."

"Her?" Jane took the printouts from him—reluctantly, because she wasn't sure she even wanted to read them. She had convinced herself a long time ago that the pictures had been taken by some anonymous tabloid photographer. She couldn't imagine—then or now—that anyone she knew might have been involved.

"I know it's hard, honey," D said softly. "But don't you wanna know the truth?"

No! Jane thought.

On the other hand, maybe it was time she stopped brushing things under the rug. She had faced the truth about Jesse. She should face the truth about this, too.

She took a deep breath, then unfolded the printouts one by one. And began reading.

TO: VERONICA BLISS
FROM: MADISON PARKER
SUBJECT: WTF???

You promised me that if I got you pictures of Jane, you would publish an article about me. You call the tiny mentions of the grooming habits of "Jane Roberts's friend and confidante" an article about me???? WE HAD A DEAL.

Madison? Jane clamped her hand over her mouth to keep from screaming. There was no way. This had to be a joke. D was making this up. *Someone* was making this up. Madison was one of her best friends, and she would never do something like this to Jane. In fact, Madison was the one who had gotten her through the whole ordeal, after the story broke.

D squeezed her hand. "I know. You can't believe it,

right? I couldn't either, at first. Keep reading."

She did.

TO: MADISON PARKER
FROM: VERONICA BLISS
SUBJECT: RE: WTF???

That was your article. If you want another one, you need to get me more info ASAP. What is Jane up to? Is she dating anyone new?

TO: VERONICA BLISS
FROM: MADISON PARKER
SUBJECT: RE: RE: WTF???

Nothing new on Jane at the moment. She's back at work and she's not seeing anyone as far as I know.

TO: MADISON PARKER
FROM: VERONICA BLISS
SUBJECT: RE: RE: RE: WTF???

FYI, "Nothing new," "back at work," and "not seeing anyone" isn't news. You can't get something for nothing.

There was another email, too, dated back in December, in which Madison had emailed her Cabo address to Veronica, adding, "Your guy should be able to find us on the beach, or else on the balcony of our condo." Jane's thoughts flashed to the photographer who had ambushed them on her last day. So *that* was how he had tracked them down. It all made sense now.

There were other, more recent emails about her and Jesse—and Braden, too. And there was one dated just four days ago, in which Madison informed Veronica that she couldn't get her the details she needed, after all. The details about what? But it didn't matter.

Jane had read enough.

38

BFFC

Madison pressed the button for the penthouse as she stepped into the elevator and wearily slipped off her Manolo stilettos. She was in a bad mood, mostly because it was Valentine's Day and she was going home alone. The problem, of course, was wives. Derek had taken his to Palm Springs for the weekend. And Jared Walsh's had turned up at the Tropicana just seconds after Madison had talked him into slipping away for a nightcap. Talk about missed opportunities—a photo of Madison and him sneaking out of the Tropicana's back entrance would have done wonders for her career. Then again, people weren't always fond of "the other woman." There were better ways to get publicity.

Madison told herself that she had a dozen other numbers she could call tonight, if all she wanted was a warm body. But it wasn't. For the first time in a long time, she wanted something more. Not a Derek or a Jared Walsh, but a guy who might have sent her roses for Valentine's Day and taken her out to dinner at Koi and told her how crazy he was about her.

God, what was happening to her? Something was definitely wrong. Just days ago, she had blown it with Veronica and failed to give her the dirt she wanted on Jane and Jesse's breakup. And now she was fantasizing about . . . what, giving up on her extremely lucrative love life, so she could have a real boyfriend like other girls? Romance was overrated.

Madison was not like other girls. She used to be, before the surgeries and before Hollywood—but no longer. She had worked hard to get where she was, and she couldn't stop now. She had to shake this funk she was in before she made more costly mistakes, like letting Veronica down. And all for what? So she could protect Jane? Jane was her BFFN, or more accurately, her BFFC (best friend for cameras)—not her real BFF. Madison didn't have real BFFs any more than she had real BFs. She knew that the only person she could truly count on was herself. She had had enough disappointment in her life to know that other people always let you down.

The elevator stopped. The doors opened, and Jane walked in—with her blue rolling suitcase in one hand, her goldfish bowl in the other, and the dog at her heels, his leash dragging on the ground.

"Ohmigod! Where are you going so late?" Madison said, surprised. Tucker sniffed at her dangling Manolos.

"I'm calling the movers first thing tomorrow," Jane informed her in an ice-cold voice. "They'll get the rest of my stuff, and my furniture, too."

"*Movers?* What are you talking about?"

Jane pressed 1. "I saw the emails, Madison."

"Emails? What emails?"

"The emails between you and Veronica Bliss. About the pictures and everything else."

It took every ounce of willpower for Madison to maintain her composure at that moment. Inside, she wanted to scream and lose it and kill someone. How the hell had Jane gotten hold of those emails? *Damn it. God damn it!* On the outside, however, she managed to tilt her head and smile a little, as if she were befuddled and maybe even a tiny bit amused.

"Veronica Bliss? You mean that really bitchy woman who works for *Life and Style*?"

Jane rolled her eyes. "Please. I have copies right here."

"Jane, I don't know what you're talking about. Copies of *what*?"

Jane reached into her bag and pulled out a wrinkled wad of papers. She thrust them at Madison, her face rigid with anger.

Madison scanned the papers quickly. Her heart skipped a beat.

Jane really *did* have the emails.

Someone had sold Madison out.

"This is soooo weird," Madison said, trying to keep

her voice steady. "Ya know what, someone stole my BlackBerry, like, right before Christmas. I think whoever it was sent out a bunch of emails under my name. I got complaints from some of my other friends about this, too. People are sick."

"Madison, please."

"I'm serious! I told Trevor about it, 'cause he got us the BlackBerrys, remember? He said he was looking into it, and—"

"Let me know how much I owe you for rent and utilities."

The elevator stopped at the first floor, and the doors opened. Jane got out, somehow managing to juggle the suitcase and the goldfish and the dog.

"Jane!" Madison called out. *"Jane!"*

The doors closed, leaving Madison alone. She stood there, trying to breathe, trying to figure out how her perfect plan had spun so horribly out of control.

How was she gonna fix this?

39

COSMIC SHIFT

Scarlett heard her phone ringing in her purse as she pulled into the parking garage. She frowned in irritation; it was probably Dana, wanting God knew what. The woman was impossible. Earlier tonight, at the Crazy Girl Valentine's Day party, she kept texting Scarlett, asking her to go say hello to Jane. Why did she even bother? Why would Scarlett want to embarrass herself by going up to Jane with everyone watching, when Scarlett knew perfectly well that Jane didn't want to talk to her?

Dana had also bugged Scarlett about Gaby, since she had (correctly) picked up that Scarlett was giving Gaby the cold shoulder. The truth was, Scarlett had concluded that Gaby had to be the one who had sold out her and Liam to *Gossip*. It was the only explanation. The question was, why? Madison was a ruthlessly conniving bitch. But Gaby was . . . *Gaby*. What could have been her motive? Scarlett had to admit that the realization kind of hurt—actually, *really* hurt—since she had grown to think of Gaby as a friend.

Fortunately, Scarlett had brought Chelsea from school; her trainer, Deb; and a couple of Deb's friends to the party. At least she'd had some people to hang out with. They'd even agreed to sign releases and wear mikes, although they'd complained (good-naturedly) about them.

Scarlett wondered how much more of this show she could take. Trevor hadn't spoken to her yet about her contract for the second season. Maybe he was planning to fire her, after all, either because of Liam, or because of her general inability to "play well with others." That was just who she was. And if Trevor and Dana and the rest of them couldn't deal with it . . . well, that was their problem. Scarlett had done nothing to hide who she really was when she met them. Maybe getting fired would be a blessing in disguise.

Her cell continued to ring. Why wasn't the call going to voice mail? Annoyed, Scarlett glanced at the screen.

It was Liam.

Scarlett quickly pressed Talk. "Hello?"

"Hey, it's me."

"Hey!"

They hadn't spoken in over a week, since the day the *Gossip* story broke. Liam hadn't called or texted, and she had decided to give him some space. After a few days, though, that space had seemed more like a void. Not knowing how to deal with it, she had thrown herself into her schoolwork, spending most of her nights at the library. She had written a fascinating twenty-page paper on Petrarchan sonnets (only ten pages were required), researched the entire history of the British monarchy, and learned how to conjugate compound tenses in French.

She had also finished rereading *Wuthering Heights*, which had unfortunately made her think of Liam even more. In the novel, the heroine, Catherine, and the decidedly unconventional Heathcliff were passionately in love, but Catherine was afraid of that passion and had ended up with a more conventional guy instead. It was like Scarlett's worst nightmare.

"Is this a bad time?" Liam asked her.

"Not at all. Just got home from the Valentine's Day party at the Roosevelt."

"Oh, yeah, the party-by-the-pool scene. How was it?"

"The usual. Actually, better than the usual. Jane did a great job. Uh, and Gaby, too." Scarlett hadn't told Liam yet about her suspicion that Gaby was the source.

"Sorry I missed it."

"You would've liked it. So what's up?" Scarlett got out of the car and started walking toward the elevators. She wondered why he was calling her now, after such a long silence.

"Yeah, so I'm in bed with the flu or something."

"Oh! Sorry to hear that." His voice *did* sound a little raspy.

"No, it's okay. I was only telling you that to explain."

"Explain what?"

"Explain why I haven't come by to talk to you in person."

"Talk to me . . . about what?"

"I've been doing a lot of thinking." Liam hesitated. "About us."

Oh.

"I know that our relationship is complicated," he went on.

"Yeah, kinda."

"I'm a pretty private person. And despite the fact that you are on a reality show, I think you are, too. But we don't have any privacy anymore."

"I'm sorry about that. And I'm sorry about your job." Scarlett figured apologies were futile at this point—she was totally about to get dumped. But she *was* sorry and she wanted him to believe that.

"Me too. But you know what? I don't care. I don't care how complicated this is. I don't care if we have to deal with photographers. I don't care if our pictures are in all the magazines. I really like you and I want to be with you. Like, all the time."

Scarlett practically dropped the phone.

A few months ago, hearing those words from a guy would have made her abruptly change the subject . . . or run . . . or both. Now, hearing them from Liam, all she wanted to do was get back in her car, drive to his apartment, and throw her arms around him.

But instead, she settled for the next-best thing. "I really like you, too," she confessed. "A lot."

"You . . . do?"

"Yeah."

"I'm so glad to hear that."

"You are?"

"Yeah."

Scarlett started laughing, because the two of them sounded so cute and dumb at the same time, like something out of a Trevor Lord–produced love scene. Except that this love scene wasn't produced. It was real, it was right now, and it was happening in the most un–*L.A. Candy* setting possible—she in a parking garage, Liam sick at home—and there wasn't a single camera or microphone to document the moment.

Liam started laughing, too. And then the laughter turned into a massive coughing fit.

"Oh, God! You sound awful. You want me to come over with some chicken soup or something?" Scarlett offered.

Liam cleared his throat. "That's really sweet, but I don't want you to catch whatever this is. Maybe if I'm feeling a little better tomorrow?"

"Okay."

"Wow, so you know how to make chicken soup?"

"Yeah, with the can opener and everything."

Liam chuckled. "So I'll call you tomorrow, okay?"

"'Kay. Feel better."

Scarlett smiled and leaned against the elevator door, listening to the pounding of her heart, just letting the incredible cosmic shift that had just occurred in her universe settle in.

Forget like. She was pretty sure she was in love.

Scarlett didn't know what to make of the barking coming from inside the apartment. She just stood outside her door, confused. Obviously, she was hearing things. She didn't have a dog. So why would there be a dog in her apartment? Liam didn't have a dog, either—or a key to her apartment, and besides, as of five minutes ago, he was at home, sick in bed with the flu. Maybe it was the neighbors' dog?

She clutched her cell in one hand as she unlocked the door with the other, poised to call 911, just in case. She pushed the door open a crack and cautiously peered in.

Yup. It was definitely a dog. It was medium-size, with a long nose and big ears and soft-looking beige-and-brown fur. It was cute. It pushed its nose up to the crack of the door and started sniffing her.

How had it gotten into her apartment?

"Um . . . good doggy?" Scarlett took a couple of baby steps into the front hall and reached out a tentative hand.

"You're home!"

Scarlett let out a scream. There was a *person* in her apartment, too.

She saw a familiar face peeking out from the living room.

Jane? What was *she* doing here? Scarlett was even more surprised to see her than the random dog, who was now licking her hand.

Jane was dressed in her blue jammies and holding a steaming mug of something that smelled like old, rotten leaves. "Hey! I'm sorry if I scared you," she apologized.

"It's fine. Um, how did you get in?"

"I still have a key. Sorry. I kept meaning to give it back."

"It's okay." The dog was now sniffing at Scarlett's shoes. "Who's this?"

"His name's Tucker. I adopted him from the shelter. Cute, huh?"

"Yeah, he's beautiful."

Scarlett bent down to pet Tucker, who panted and wagged his tail in response. She had about a million questions to ask Jane, and at the same time, she was at a complete loss for words. She was feeling so many emotions jumbled together: happiness, surprise, curiosity, confusion. Jane was the last person she had expected to see tonight, under these circumstances.

"So." Jane sat down on the cream carpet, cross-legged,

and stroked Tucker's fur. She took a sip of her funky-smelling tea. "I came here to apologize."

"Apologize?"

"Yeah. Because you were right about Madison."

Scarlett stared at her in disbelief. She had been waiting forever to hear those words. "How'd you . . . What made you change your mind?"

"D told me tonight that she was the one behind the pictures. He found a bunch of emails between her and Veronica, on Veronica's computer."

"Seriously?"

"Yeah. They were pretty awful."

"Ohmigod. I'm so sorry, Jane."

"*You're* sorry? I'm the one who should be sorry. I should have believed you from the beginning." Jane smiled bitterly. "She was soooo sweet to me, you know? In Mexico and after we got back. She acted like she was my big sister or something. She was acting the whole time. Just so she could find out personal stuff about me to tell Veronica."

"Why?"

"So Veronica would publish pieces about her."

"What a *bitch*!"

"Yeah."

"Are you okay?"

"Yeah. I'll get over it. I just feel so dumb. I should have listened to you."

"Don't feel dumb!" Scarlett told her.

Jane took a deep breath. "There were emails about you, too. And Liam."

"Oh." *Guess I owe Gaby an apology, too,* Scarlett thought. She had obviously been wrong, suspecting her. "I was way too pushy with you about Madison—and Jesse, too. I wouldn't have listened to me, either. I should have just let you figure this stuff out yourself."

"Well . . . I guess I did."

"Yeah, I guess you did."

Scarlett got down on the floor, next to Jane. They sat there for a while, just petting Tucker and not speaking, as though they were letting the emotional dust of all their drama settle. There had been so much drama these past few months: Madison . . . the show . . . reporters . . . Jesse . . . Braden . . . Liam. And most of all, their fourteen-year-old friendship almost coming to an end.

Scarlett wanted to tell Jane all about Liam. She also wanted to ask her if the rumor was true that she and Jesse had broken up. But there would be plenty of time for catching up later.

"So I'm guessing you need a place to live?" Scarlett said. "Because I've been looking for a roommate, and if I remember correctly, you're pretty good roommate material. Except when you leave the coffeemaker on every morning . . . or eat all my leftover lo mein . . . or shrink my favorite navy V-neck in the dryer."

Jane cracked up. "Ha, ha. I get it: I'm an awful roommate. But, Scar, I think I'm the best you can do."

Scarlett laughed and gave a little shrug. "You're probably right."

"What about Tucker? Can he live with us, too?"

"Sure. He and I are besties now. See?" Scarlett leaned toward him, and he started licking her face.

Jane giggled. "Yeah, well, just hide your shoes, because he likes to snack on them."

"I'll remember that."

"Hey, Scar? I'm glad you asked me to move back in, because I kinda already did."

"What?"

"Well, Penny's back in her old spot. And Tucker already took a nap on your bed. I think that's gonna be his new favorite place to sleep. You don't mind, do you?"

Scarlett smiled. Not only did she not mind . . . she was happier than she had been in forever. She had Liam back. She had Jane back. And eventually, she would figure out what to do about season two. Her problems with Trevor and the rest of it seemed insignificant now. Everything was falling into place.

Tonight was definitely a night of cosmic shifts.

40

SEASON TWO

Trevor leaned back in his chair, staring at the sparkling stretch of L.A. night sky outside his office window. He never got tired of this view. He loved watching dreary downtown Los Angeles, with its smoggy sky and dirty streets, transform into something so beautiful.

Funny that the same view could look so different at two separate moments. But it was something Trevor could understand. It was what he did. He captured moments. And like this view, he knew that the best ones were worth waiting for.

He'd been gazing at this view at the exact moment he had come up with the idea for *L.A. Candy* last June. There was something about it—its glamour, its energy, its sense of endless possibilities—that had spoken to him, and that had inspired him to create an entire show following the lives of ordinary girls against the backdrop of this extraordinary city.

He thought about that moment, and about everything that had happened since then. Starting with the first shoot in September, he had wanted to maintain an "invisible hand" approach to production. After all, it *was* reality TV, and he had wanted to keep it real. It hadn't always worked with his other shows, but he wanted this one to be different.

But he hadn't counted on all the ways in which things could go out of control—out of *his* control. Jane and Braden. Scarlett and Liam. And Jesse's nosedive into a vodka bottle. Sure, Jesse had always been a drunk. But his descent this time had been unprecedented.

And now . . . Jane had gotten herself a "team" and had a lot more demands, namely no future scenes with Jesse or Madison. In fact, he was still negotiating her damned season two contract with her damned agent. Trevor rubbed his eyes wearily. *God.* Why was this happening? A Jane-and-Jesse breakup scene would be great for ratings. Unfortunately, it had happened off-camera. And their subsequent encounter at the Tropicana party was worthless, because Jesse had been both very, very wasted and not miked. Trevor made a note to look over the footage once more. He might be able to salvage something with the help of a few voice-overs in the studio. He knew he could get Jesse to agree to that. The guy loved getting airtime almost as much as he loved getting trashed. The fact that Jesse was becoming more and more difficult to edit into the charming boyfriend that young female viewers pined after couldn't be ignored. Trevor knew he couldn't fight this particular reality for much longer.

Or he might even try to convince Jane to film a breakup scene with Jesse, despite what she (or rather, her pain-in-the-ass "team") had conveyed to him. She might be open to it, after she'd had a few days to cool off. The Jane-Jesse story line deserved closure. Their millions of fans deserved closure. That was how he would pitch it to her, anyway—privately, over lunch at the Polo Lounge, away from her annoying hired guns.

Jane and Madison's fight would have been a ratings spike, too, except for the *Gossip* angle, since in the world of *L.A. Candy* tabloids didn't exist. He had already come up with some great ideas for season two. Maybe he could work this twist in somehow. A feud between Jane and her former BFF and roommate, Madison. *Hmm.* He could make it seem like Jane found out that Madison had been the one who told Jesse that she had cheated on him. It might not have been the reality, but in a way it was true. Of course, Jane would refuse to be in the same place as Madison for some time, so an encounter would have to be arranged. Or at least a phone call.

At least Scarlett and Jane had made up. Despite his frustration with Scarlett, she could work well as Jane's newly restored BFF and roommate. And the scenes would be a lot easier to edit than Scarlett-and-Gaby scenes. Besides, now Jane had someone to talk to about her feud with Madison. Scarlett didn't have anything nice to say about Madison, and that would fan the flames perfectly.

As for Gaby and Hannah . . . well, Gaby could go on being the comic relief, as always. And Hannah had proved surprisingly popular with focus groups. But she hadn't turned out to be as malleable as he had hoped. Maybe he would give her a love interest of her own? That might be a smart move. Trevor smiled to himself. All of a sudden, he had a good feeling about all of this. In fact, if he played it right, season two just might be bigger and better than season one.

He booted up his laptop and began typing some notes.

SEASON 2. EPISODE 1.

41

A FAN LETTER

Madison moved around the living room, jabbing the weird white cleaning contraption around the floor. How did this stupid thing work, anyway? She was pissed. The cleaning lady had called in sick. She would have to talk to Derek about replacing his unreliable help—again. In the meantime, the place was a mess, and Derek was coming over later, so it was up to Madison to try to straighten it up.

Something squeaked, startling her. She reached down and picked up a rubber bunny from the floor. God, how annoying was that? She kept finding the mutt's toys all over the apartment, under furniture and behind plants. Jane should have been more thorough when she moved out.

Madison flung the rubber bunny into a nearby wastebasket, swearing. She wasn't sure why she was in such a foul mood. So the apartment was a pit. Big deal. So Jane wasn't talking to her. She would come around eventually.

Generally speaking, Madison's life was good. No, it was better than good. It was great. Things had actually been looking up since the nightmarish Valentine's Day aftermath two weeks ago (soon after which Veronica had fired her joke of an assistant, Diego, for snooping around on her computer—served him right). Madison had seen a lot of Derek lately, because his wife and their brat were in New Jersey visiting with her parents. Better still, Madison had been getting lots of press, with pieces in *Life & Style* and *Star* as well as *Gossip*. The one in *Life & Style* had been an entire page on "Madison's Rules for Dating," with photos of her with various good-looking, well-dressed, well-behaved men she had on hand to escort her to parties as necessary (and with cheesy speculations as to whether some of them might be more than "just friends").

Best of all, Trevor had invited her to lunch yesterday, just the two of them at the Ivy (Anna Payne was at the very next table, picking at a few lettuce leaves, no doubt to reverse the damage done by that hideous *Gossip* cover), to talk about how he wanted to give her more airtime in season two, and sharing some ideas he had about that. It was a dream come true. Being the star of the show was what she had been working so hard for and sacrificed so much to achieve. Granted, Trevor hadn't exactly used the word "star." But she was sure that was what he meant. And even if he wasn't thinking along those lines now . . . well, he would, after he saw what she had to offer. On-screen, that was.

Madison stepped on another squeaky object. A doggy bone. She picked it up and flung it at the wastebasket—and missed. Sighing, she bent down to retrieve it, and spotted a pile of mail on the Oriental rug. *Oh, yeah*. She'd brought it in yesterday, put it on the floor so she could flop down on the couch to watch TV, and forgotten all about it.

She picked it up now and sifted through the contents. Bill. Something for Jane. (She tossed that in the wastebasket, not missing this time.) Bill. A couple of magazines. Bill. A brown manila envelope.

Curious, she turned the brown envelope over in her hand. It had been hand-addressed to her, but had no return address. It had a postmark from New York, New York, and four stamps with hearts on it.

Probably a fan letter, Madison thought, checking out the hearts. She ripped it open, being careful not to damage her new set of acrylic nails.

There was a photograph inside, along with a folded-up letter. The photo was a school picture of a teenage girl. She had long, dark brown hair with bangs that hung unevenly over thick tortoiseshell glasses, and pale skin pockmarked with acne. Her cheap navy dress with the white polyester collar did little to mask a slight weight problem.

Madison's hand shook violently as she put the picture down on the coffee table, then reached for the letter.

It was simple, straightforward, and to the point, printed on plain computer paper in a nondescript font:

I'VE BEEN WATCHING YOU ON TV, AND I KNOW WHO YOU REALLY ARE. IF YOU WANT PEOPLE TO KEEP THINKING YOUR NAME IS MADISON PARKER, IT'S GOING TO COST YOU. THERE ARE PLENTY MORE PHOTOS WHERE THIS CAME FROM. THEY WILL BE SOLD TO THE HIGHEST BIDDER. I'M GIVING YOU THE OPPORTUNITY TO MAKE THE FIRST BID.

P.S. YOU WEREN'T SO CUTE WHEN YOU WERE FIFTEEN, WERE YOU?

42

A BREAK FROM BOYS

Jane stretched across the chaise longue and stared up at the cloudless blue sky. It was an unusually warm day for March, and she had the pool at the apartment complex all to herself. Scarlett was supposed to meet her shortly so they could enjoy an afternoon together of doing nothing, with no cameras. It was going to be perfect.

Jane pulled down the straps of her black bikini and applied sunscreen to her shoulders. She had started going to the gym with Scar a couple of weeks ago, and she could feel new muscles already—and some really *achy* muscles, too, because their trainer, a cheerful tyrant named Deb, had made them do about a hundred push-ups yesterday. They were easy for Scar, but Jane had struggled.

Still, Jane was so proud of herself for trying to get back in shape. It was all part of her new philosophy. Now that Jesse was out of her life, and (mostly) out of her system, she was going to focus on herself and only herself. She wanted to get healthy, physically and emotionally; she also wanted to work extra-hard at her job so she could advance her career. She planned to have a meeting tomorrow with Fiona to ask for advice on what she could be doing to become better at her job. Evening classes? Extra assignments? Jane was open to anything and everything. She was becoming a new-and-improved Jane Roberts.

For the foreseeable future, Jane planned on a daily routine of working, going to the gym, taking care of Tucker and Penny, and enjoying her friends—most of all Scar. Their friendship was stronger than ever, after what they had been through these last few months. And Scar seemed happier now that she had a boyfriend. Jane never thought she would see the day when her BFF was in love. But it really suited her, especially when the guy was someone as great as Liam.

Trevor hadn't said a word to Scarlett about dating Liam, and in fact he had thanked her for her hard work on season one and offered her a raise for season two. Scarlett had thought long and hard about it and decided to stay on the show, despite her reservations. The money had been a big factor. She'd decided to use it to pay for her college tuition herself, so she could be less dependent on her parents. She'd asked Trevor to stop editing her so much, and he had given her some sort of assurance. Which hopefully meant something? So for the moment, Scarlett would continue with *L.A. Candy*.

Jane had decided to stay on the show as well. R.J. had

negotiated a really lucrative contract for her. (Jane didn't have the heart to tell Scarlett that *her* raise was even bigger than Scarlett's raise. *Note to self: Talk Scarlett into getting an agent.*) And her press image had turned around, too, thanks to Sam the miracle worker. (*Note to self: Talk Scarlett into getting a publicist.*) Both R.J. and Sam had convinced Jane that being the star of a top-rated reality show was a huge opportunity, and could only help her career as an event planner. So . . . Jane had said yes to season two. In fact, she was actually excited about the new season. And she couldn't wait to see the episode about the Valentine's Day party—her first big event.

Shooting was scheduled to resume any day now. Jane had told Trevor that she didn't want any scenes with Madison, and he said he understood. Although he reminded her that she had signed up to have her life followed, and this—her rift with Madison—was happening in her life. But then she reminded him that Madison was no longer in her life—her real life. No matter—she would walk off the set if Madison ever showed her face. Jane hadn't seen her since Valentine's Day, and as far as she was concerned, she never wanted to see her again. Ever.

The one question mark in her life was Braden. She wasn't sure what to do about him. She missed him a lot—she had talked to him a couple of times since she'd broken up with Jesse, but she hadn't seen him—and she thought about him probably more than she should. But she didn't want to be the kind of girl who went bouncing from one guy to another: Caleb, then Jesse, then Braden, then Jesse again. The truth was that she needed a break from boys for a while. A *long* break. She wasn't sure she could handle being "just friends" with Braden, either. It was too complicated with him.

She spotted Scar walking past a row of cabanas, toward the pool. She was wearing a lime green cover-up over her bikini and carrying a large beach tote.

"Hey! What took you so long?" Jane called out, waving.

And then Jane hesitated, because she saw that Scar wasn't alone. Liam was right behind her. Jane frowned. Why was he here? It was supposed to be a girls' day, just the two of them. Like when they were younger, and they would build forts in the Robertses' backyard out of old sheets and clothespins and put up a sign that said, NO BOYS ALLOWED. Why did Scar bring him? He was a boy and clearly forbidden, according to the rules.

As Scar and Liam approached Jane, he removed his baseball cap—and Jane realized with a start that it wasn't Liam, after all.

"Caleb?" Jane gasped. She practically fell off her chair.

Caleb smiled and waved. Scarlett sat down on the chaise longue next to Jane's. "I found him in the lobby," she explained, hooking a thumb at Caleb. "He came by to say hi to us. I mean, you."

"Hey! I came by to see both of you," Caleb protested. He sat down on the other side of Jane. "Hi, Janie." He leaned over and kissed her on the cheek.

"Hi, Caleb." Jane took off her shades and stared at him, dumbfounded. "Why . . . I mean . . . what are you doing here?"

"It's my day off," Caleb replied.

"Your day off from . . . what?"

"My volunteer job. I'm doing construction for the L.A. chapter of Habitat Builders. I worked for them in New Orleans last summer."

Jane was so confused. She knew all about Habitat Builders—they were a really cool group that built houses for people who couldn't afford their own homes—and about Caleb's stint with them in New Orleans. But this was the middle of the school year.

"Wait—aren't you supposed to be at Yale?"

"He dropped out." Scar reached over and grabbed Jane's sunscreen, then started smoothing it onto her legs. "Can you believe it? My parents would murder me if I dropped out of Yale."

"I didn't drop out, nerd. I took a leave of absence," Caleb corrected her. "I left in January when the semester started. My brother and I backpacked around South America for a while. I moved here and started with Habitat Builders, like, a week ago."

"You took a leave of absence? Why?" Jane asked him.

"It's just for a semester or two. Yale's great, but my time in New Orleans last summer really changed the way I see things, ya know? School's always gonna be there, but

I feel like now is the time I want to experience things."

"That's awesome," Jane told him. Her mind was still reeling at the sight of her ex, here, sitting two feet away—after she hadn't seen him for almost a year. He hadn't changed a bit, with his curly brown hair, chocolate brown eyes, dimples, and swimmer's bod. (He was on the swimming team in high school, and Jane went to all his meets when they were dating—and even before they were dating, because she'd had a huge crush on him.)

"Soooo. How long are you in town for?" Jane asked him.

"At least for a few months, maybe longer. I'm crashing with my friend Naveen—remember him?"

Jane shot a look at Scar, who turned away and started rifling through her beach tote as though she were looking for something really, really important. Scar and Naveen had hooked up in high school, and even though Scar would never admit it, Jane had always suspected that she'd liked him as more than a casual fling.

"That's cool. Tell him we said hi," Jane said to Caleb. "You should come by for dinner sometime. Scar's a great cook."

"Yeah, I'm a genius with the microwave," Scar joked.

Caleb laughed. "Thanks, that would be nice. I don't know a lot of people in L.A. yet. And I really wanna catch up with you."

Jane blinked in surprise. This last comment was directed at her. Not her *and* Scar. Just her.

"Ohmigod, Liam's calling," Scar said suddenly. "'Scuse me, I gotta take this." She jumped up from her chair and walked away, pressing her phone to her ear.

Jane knew Scar wasn't taking a call from Liam; she just wanted an excuse to leave Jane and Caleb alone (even though Jane knew Scar had never forgiven him for breaking up with Jane). Which was crazy, because Jane didn't *want* to be alone with Caleb. Especially not when he was peeling off his T-shirt and reaching for Jane's sunscreen (she tried not to think of all the times she used to curl up against his bare chest on the beach). Especially not when she had just made a promise to herself to take a long break from boys.

Jane looked away and told herself that she would be able to keep that promise, no problem.

Wouldn't she?

ACKNOWLEDGMENTS

To my family and friends, Mom, Dad, Breanna, Brandon, Lo, Maura, Jillian, Britton, Natania, and Kyle, for all of your support. I am so lucky to have you all in my life.

To Max Stubblefield, who has stuck with me since the beginning and helped me to achieve so much.

To Nicole Perez for always making me shine.

To Kristin Puttkamer for everything you do. My life would fall apart without you.

To PJ Shapiro for always looking out for my best interests.

To Dave Del Sesto for helping me to keep my life together.

To Adam Divello, Tony DiSanto, Liz Gateley, and everyone at MTV, without whom this book would not be possible.

To HarperCollins for giving me this opportunity, and specifically Zareen Jaffery and Farrin Jacobs for guiding me through the world of publishing.

To Matthew Elblonk who helped in obtaining this opportunity for me and assisted in making my dream come true.

To Nancy Ohlin, my collaborator, for helping me every step of the way while I navigated the writing process and for making it such an enjoyable trip.

GOSSIP

YOUR #1 SOURCE FOR ALL THE HOLLYWOOD DIRT THAT'S FIT TO SLING

One little lie always leads to another...but what happens when nobody tells the truth? Sweet Jane is learning that the price of fame can be more than she is willing to pay.

Use your phone to take a picture of the code below to find out if there is anybody Jane can trust or if her celebrity has cost her too much.

- With your phone download the 2D bar code reader software at **http://lacandy.mobi/reader**
- Take a photo of the code using your phone's camera.
- Be the first to know about the sweet trouble that lies ahead for Jane and the cast of *L.A. Candy*.

L.A. is all about the sweet life.

TEXT **CONRAD** TO **READIT** FOR MORE GOSSIP!

U.S. residents only
Message and Data Rates May Apply

www.harperteen.com

HARPER
An Imprint of HarperCollins*Publishers*